More raves for THE KILLING . . .

"Superb storytelling with fully rounded characters in San Francisco and its Tenderloin area . . . as a longshoreman tries to cope with a dope-addict sister, and his own adopted daughter who has been raped by the sister's live-in man. The author's skill is such that he has been compared to Nelson Algren. Understandable."
—*Chicago Tribune Book World*

"The novel is tough, gritty, violent and packed with a spare dialogue that may remind some readers of the Boston novels of George V. Higgins."
—William Hogan, *World of Books*

The Killing

Lawrence Swaim

A TOM DOHERTY ASSOCIATES BOOK

PINNACLE BOOKS　　　　　　**NEW YORK**

This is a work of fiction. All the characters and events portrayed in this book are fictional, and any resemblance to real people or incidents is purely coincidental.

THE KILLING

A Pinnacle/Tor Book, published in association with Tom Doherty Associates. Reprinted by special arrangement with Holt, Rinehart and Winston.

First printing, July 1981

ISBN: 0-523-48004-0

Cover photography by Brian Leng

Printed in the United States of America

PINNACLE BOOKS, INC.
1430 Broadway
New York, New York 10018

You have heard it said, you shall love your neighbor, and hate your enemy; but I say to you, love your enemies . . .

— NEW TESTAMENT

I say that the soldier of Christ kills in safety and dies in greater safety. He profits himself when he dies and he profits Christ when he kills . . . Truly when he kills a criminal, he commits not homicide, but as I would call it, malicide.

— BERNARD OF CLAIRVAUX

THE KILLING

PART ONE

The Rape

Sunday

The traveler had only stopped for a moment. The park seemed incredibly green for summer in Nevada. It was in a small town about six miles off the interstate highway. The traveler had spotted it while cruising around looking for cheap gasoline, and when he saw the small pond in the middle and the geese standing near it, he immediately parked his car and fell facedown into the cool grass.

He lay there for five minutes before he heard the noise. It was the sound of a man and woman involved in a violent game that had gotten physical in a public place. There was crying and the sound of an open hand hitting a face. He looked up. They were about a hundred feet away from him, right next to the pond and its geese. The man was Black, the woman very white, blue-eyed with red hair.

"You ain't *got* no soul," she was saying in a tense Southern accent. "Ain't got no class neither. And you *sure* ain't got no cool. You ain't even got a mind left to think with!"

"You want me to walk? Bitch? In a moment I'll walk right up your backside!"

He was hitting her with his open hand. The geese were terrified and ran to the opposite side of the pond.

In a moment he would close his hand. The traveler got up and went to the nearest public telephone, which was near a Tasty-Cone stand. There were a few quiet families in the park. They stared at the couple with the intensity of religious devotees at an esoteric but necessarily private ceremony. The traveler knew from experience how crowds operate in such a situation. Nobody would call the police because everyone would hope somebody else had done it.

The number of the sheriff was featured prominently on the tattered front page of the directory. He dialed the number.

"I'd like to speak to the sheriff."

There was a pause. "This is the undersheriff. May I help you?"

"Let me speak to the sheriff."

The undersheriff sighed. In a moment the sheriff was on the line.

"Some pimp is beating up on his old lady in your park," the sheriff was told.

"Oh shit," the sheriff said. "That's not supposed to happen. Yeah—I'll be right down."

He was as good as his word. In two minutes he appeared at the park. As he stepped out of his car a strange thing happened. Exactly as the sheriff walked forward—and at exactly the same speed—the Black man who had abused his female companion began to walk away. By the time the sheriff had reached the woman, the Black man had disappeared into a Cadillac El Dorado parked at the far end of the park. The sheriff made no attempt to follow him, nor did he speak to the woman.

He stood looking at her silently, while everyone in the park watched him. At length the sheriff turned away and walked back toward his vehicle.

"You haven't heard the end of this, Penny!" he paused to shout back at her.

The traveler was relieved. He knew what might have happened if the sheriff had taken the woman away. The woman had already been beaten enough.

The traveler went back to his car and lit a Camel cigarette. He liked smoking, but it—like everything else—was making him tired. His car was a small oven. He sighed. It was not the sarcastic youthful sigh of the undersheriff with whom he had just spoken. Rather it was the full disgusted sigh of middle age. Fuck them. There were so many idiots in the world.

He drove back onto the interstate.

The traveler's name was Quinn Sutterfield Dunaway. He was forty-five years old and had come to Nevada to gamble. This he regarded as entertainment rather than a money-making opportunity. He generally gave himself two hundred dollars to lose over a weekend. He enjoyed losing, as long as he did so at his own pace. This time he had gambled day and night and still not lost it all.

That and the woman in the park struck him vaguely as a bad omen.

Quinn Dunaway had recognized the woman as being a prostitute he had chatted with in a bar the night before. When she had discovered he did not want sex she suddenly became talkative. The essence of her conversation was that now that she was working in Nevada, she no longer had to worry about getting pushed around by mindless pimps. Since she was talking rather than working he had believed her.

"Most of them are just cocaine hogs, anyway," she had said. "That's all they're good for, is snorting up your money. You work. They snort."

He had thought her unusually intelligent. For this reason the incident in the park was especially disturbing.

He drove on into the deepening purple evening, the hot wind beading the sweat on his face. It felt good, but did nothing to diminish his feeling of weariness. He drove past Reno, the tires of his little Chevy humming on the hot asphalt.

What had been the story with those two at the park? Had the pimp followed her to Nevada, figuring he might score off her one more time? If it was going to be straight strong-arm, why had he chosen a public place to do it? Or had they come out here together? He decided the last was most likely. That would explain her line. She put down pimps because it was her fantasy that someday she would cut one or all of them loose completely; but it was just a fantasy and had to be constantly reinforced by talking about it. And she could build a reputation for hating pimps. That would help her in Nevada, where pimps were supposed to be out of the picture. But of course he would never know the real story.

All day he had been repressing his desire for alcohol. At Truckee he gave up. He parked in front of an Old-West-style bar and went inside. Truckee was full of hippies; still, it was cooler here. He sucked happily at his bourbon and water. There were good-looking women in the bar, but he did not look at them. He was already thinking about his wife and daughter and how much he missed them. He had been married twenty years, and he and his wife had adopted an eight-year-old girl three years before.

The girl was now eleven and her name was Dawn.

He had a few doubles. Afterward, the miles between Truckee and Sacramento were over before he had time to think about them. The cool air started hitting him right after the Pinole turnoff. It got cooler as he got closer to the City. Driving on the Berkeley side, he saw the crisp white lights of San Francisco against the black sky across the Bay.

On the Bay Bridge the wind pushed his Chevy in short steady gusts. There was heavy traffic going his way on the top tier. When he came out of the tunnel on Treasure Island, the tall City lights hit him again. It was a lovely picture—the blue luminescence of Coit Tower; the finger-piers reaching like crooked hands into the bay; the slow, crawling ant-trail of lights that was California Street—but unreal. Even as it drew closer, San Francisco looked as perfect and distant as a postcard sent by one of the tourists who still, in early September, thronged its streets.

Hi ya!
Having a good time—wish you were here!
See ya!

San Francisco was full of bright people who understood each other too quickly. In addition, there were a number of people who were good at something, but not good enough for New York. It was not easy, living in a city like that. The only thing that made it acceptable to Quinn was that his occupation was extremely unfashionable. He was an officer in a union that organized longshoremen on the waterfront, and warehousemen farther inland. Consequently he did not have to be around too many disgusting people. Although he was one of the smartest people in town, his name would never appear in a newspaper unless there was a strike or he was violently killed.

He parked the Chevy on the street. They lived on one of the hills bordering Noe Valley in a house from which, on clear nights, you could see everything that moved on the Bay; but it had no garage.

There were lights on inside the house. That was strange. Usually Rozalyn would be in bed by this time.

He found her sitting at the kitchen table. She was smoking furiously and her eyes were red. "Quinn—?"

She jumped up as though fearing the intrusion of a stranger.

"What is it?"

She came to him and put her head against his chest. He reached around her and carefully put the Chinese vegetables he had brought her on top of the refrigerator. Something was wrong. She released him abruptly to inhale from her cigarette.

"It's Dawn." She closed her eyes and shook her head. "I can't believe it." She inhaled again. "Not now when everything was going so well—"

He grabbed her elbows. "What?"

"She's alive."

"Then what?"

She clenched her jaw and shook her head.

He backed away from her into the doorway. "Look!" He put up his hands to ward off any further embraces. "I can't help if I don't know what it is. Where is she?"

"Here! She's here!" Rozalyn pointed upstairs.

She was a fine, tall woman with gray hair and a Roman nose. At forty-four she was thin and high-strung. Her eyes were blue and slightly crossed. "She's *here*," she reassured him.

She was almost hysterical.

"Okay. Roz? Start at the beginning."

She inhaled and looked away. "She went to your sister's apartment."

"Grace's? What for?"

"I don't know." She passed her hand through her hair. "Grace wasn't there. The only person home was the man she used to live with."

"Andrew Deggan." A loser. His gut knotted. "Go on."

"He invited her in—" She looked up at him helplessly. "He raped her. The bastard raped her. He broke her arm, too."

He fought the feeling of unreality.

"What?"

"You heard me!" She marched to the kitchen table and put out her cigarette in four sharp, bludgeoning scrapes. "You wanted to know. Your sister's psychopathic boyfriend beat up your adopted daughter and raped her. An eleven-year-old child . . . "

"Is she awake?"

Rozalyn wiped her eyes. "No. And don't wake her up."

Quinn looked at his watch. It was past eleven.

"When did this happen?"

"Yesterday. I called every motel in Reno."

At the last moment he had decided to go to a place east

of Reno. He cursed.

"Did you report it?"

"Re*port* it?" She backed away from him. "Of course I reported it!" The nasal whine of her reply startled both of them. "They sent a woman to take a statement, then we all went to the hospital. The arm didn't seem to hurt her much at first. I was so furious at you for not being here. How was Nevada?"

"Don't make it worse." He saw she was sorry, and held up his hand. "Never mind. How is she?"

"Pretty good. She had bad dreams last night . . . "

He walked softly upstairs to Dawn's room and looked in. She was sleeping soundly. In the weak light he thought he saw something that outraged him. He opened the door wider to let in more light from the hall. He went to Dawn and looked carefully at her face. There was a large bruise on one side of her face, and a cast on her right arm. Both eyes were blackened. He retraced his steps, closing the door almost shut and going back downstairs.

"What now?" Rozalyn asked.

"I'll go talk to my sister. I won't be too long."

He poured himself a strong straight bourbon. The need for alcohol was hard on him now. While it warmed him he embraced his wife.

"Why us?" she asked in real grief.

This was a question she had asked before. They had had more than their share of bad luck. The answer that usually came to him was: *why not?* This phrase now tended to form itself in his mind in response to a variety of questions, many of them unrelated.

"I'll be right back," he told her. "It would help if we didn't lose our heads."

She nodded. It was her numb familiar nod of grief.

Quinn Dunaway's sister Grace lived in an apartment in the Mission District with her three-year-old son. He drove toward it slowly.

What was it about rape that made you feel so bad? Why did they feel such shame?

Their kind of bad breaks were always like that.

Good times, he thought, were mainly the absence of pain. Pain was always there waiting. His life had been going along so well he had even begun to control his drinking. It was Dawn who had been the special and unexpected kick in his life. Too good to last.

Many years before, he and Rozalyn had lost their first child in infancy. Crib death. The most guilt-ridden curse of death in the world—you would feel less guilt if you strangled the kid with your own hands. After that, there had been a child who was born an idiot. Four impossible years and the inevitable commitment to a state institution —and more guilt. After that they had wanted to adopt, but had been afraid. They had sweated and guilted and cried and talked about it; and then suddenly one day they had the courage, and began the process.

It had been a breeze. Dawn was dark and sensible, three-quarters Pit River Indian. She had a way of keeping her distance, but was perfectly happy to live with them. Pleasing her was not difficult. Life had become a bonanza of movies, ice cream parlors, parks, and beaches. Middle age had flowered. Dawn continued to have no complaints. It occurred to them perhaps their killer luck had gone.

But then he had left for two days and the good luck had run out.

He walked to his sister's place. It was on a quiet residential block with a few old homes. They were simple but kept up. Latino families mostly, working-class and working poor. At the end of the block there was an unexpected Victorian house with a yard and a single stooped tree. Each time Quinn saw this particular tree with its sloping downward profile, it reminded him of images he had seen on gravestones in Quaker graveyards. It was an Old World image—the Tree of Life.

He rang the doorbell. There were hesitant steps at the top of the stairway. An outside light went on. The door opened slowly and jerked to a stop. Grace stood looking over a chain at him, her gray eyes wide.

"Unlock the door."

When she had disengaged the chain, he opened the door and pushed past her. She swayed slightly; she seemed battered by invisible winds. He walked up the stairs and entered the living room. Here the air was heavy with stale tobacco and marijuana, body odor, and the ghostly funk of hard drugs. No housekeeping had been done for days. Probably she had not gone in to work last night. Blankets and a pillow lay on the couch. Her framed Kollwitz print glinted light from the kitchen; he saw dishes in the sink.

He hated this apartment. Death. He rarely entered it without imagining himself being interviewed by the police. *When did you last see your sister alive? Was she depressed?*

She had followed him slowly up the stairs. Now she stood staring at him.

"What are you taking?" he asked her gently.

Silent tears flowed from her eyes and nose. She continued to stare at him.

"Smack," she said.

The junkie look. A ghost haunting itself—haunting its own body. The intense shame but without a center, as though it had to be happening to someone else. Living in the third person.

"Are you shooting?"

She nodded.

"How often?"

She shook her head in bewilderment.

"Don't shake your head. How many times in the last twenty-four hours?"

"Three times since I took Dawn home yesterday."

Her three-year-old Martin was sleeping in her bed. Quinn stepped over softly and closed the bedroom door.

"Come over here," he commanded.

She came over and sat down slowly on the couch. There were a pair of Ben Davis jeans on the chair across from her. Quinn tossed them aside and sat down. He leaned forward his arms across his knees.

"Okay. Tell me what happened yesterday."

She spoke slowly, as if reciting a story she knew by heart.

"I've been going with Andy Deggan. Deggan—the ex-con I met at the halfway house run by the Quakers?" Although it was a question, she did not look up from her hands. "They had a reception. I went with Don Richards from the Post Office. Andy was nice at first and didn't rush anything. The bastard actually said he was going to marry me."

The tears thinned and the voice became a steady, introspective keen of resentment.

"Then he got violent a few times. I really wasn't bothered too much when he started popping. It seemed to calm him down. We bought a few bags from his friends. There were a couple of guys who had something on him—at least that's what they said. Yesterday he bought some parts for the Volvo and he was dropping reds and snorting coke. The reds were screwing him all up. You know? He was pissed at everything. I was supposed to make a run to Berkeley to score some scag to cook up with the coke so he could get mellowed out. When I got back—" She paused to remember. "When I got back Dawn was here alone, and there were bruises all over her face."

She pushed her matted hair back from her face. "I just couldn't believe it. Dawn has been coming over to visit me lately. It was nice having her visit."

Quinn leaned forward and took her left elbow and punched softly at the vein in the crook of her arm, the area junkies called "the ditch." He inspected the other arm the same way. There were tracks anyone could see but the veins were not hard yet. There was one abscess. She made no sound when he touched the inflamed tissue.

"Have you heard from him since?"

She shook her head.

"Did the cops come over here?"

"I let Roz call the cops. I had to come back here to—to stash something. After that they came."

She was thirty-three years old and looked several years older. The most disturbing thing about her appearance was that drugs made her oddly beautiful. Her hands and body were thin; with her high cheekbones and gray Dunaway eyes she looked like a nineteenth-century wraith of slow death by consumption. Maybe, Quinn thought, drugs were the modern equivalent. Fashionable, like consumption had been.

"Did you ever stop to think how much your suicidal tendencies hurt the rest of us?" He paused. "Do you? Do you think you can be a loser and not hurt the rest of us?"

He had not wanted to know about her for a long time, feeling she had the right to die in peace without sermons. Now he was surer than ever that she was dying; but the rape made it necessary that he intrude. It was a crime against his world. There was no way he could refrain from holding her responsible as an accessory.

He wished he had the freedom to hit her.

"You attract losers and you think it won't hurt everyone around you," he said. "You reward losers. You reward violence. Don't you think that affects the people around you?"

She looked at him dazedly. Her gray eyes were beautiful.

"I thought it was possible to take a chance and not involve anyone else," she said. "I haven't been shooting that much. It was just playing-around stuff. Codeine and Perks, not much smack until a couple of weeks ago. I'm not really strung out."

"Then you can quit."

If she scratched at her arm he would hit her.

"About Deggan . . . " he said. "Think hard. Do you have any idea where he went?"

She began to shake her head *no*, semi-hysterically. There were new tears. They were thicker and more harsh. The tears came at him through the heroin, a voice in the rain, begging understanding. It was dark; she just had to have some to keep going. Where, oh where, was that brotherly understanding?

He got up and sat beside her. He embraced her wearily and with anger.

"I didn't know he was like that!" she said. "Not Dawn . . . "

"I know, sweetie."

"I'm sorry, Quinn!"

He shrugged. "I know."

He had a double bourbon and water at the Latino bar at the end of the block. The middle-aged bartender served him with an exaggerated courtesy that was just short of insult.

"Buenas noches," Quinn said.

The bartender removed himself to the far end of the bar. His customers were Spanish-speaking. Quinn guessed most were illegals. San Francisco was full of them. They tended to sit close to the doors, ready to run. Anglos added to their anxiety. They had come to San Francisco to work.

Because people came to the City for different reasons, they gave it different names. A money town (how little they saw). An Irish town (a little truth there). A European capital in America (an evasion of reality). Although he had never discussed it even with his wife, Quinn had come to think of San Francisco as a beautiful place that was unfortunately also a capital of death.

> *Lo. Death had reared himself a throne*
> *In a strange city lying alone*
> *Far down within the dim West . . .*

Many people came to San Francisco to die. Grace had shown him that clearly. Some arrived before they were even conscious of the thing for which they came searching. Others came looking for an Athens, and found instead a too-familiar place of tensions, violence, trickery, and strident competition. It was not a good town in which to run out of money. Even its cool beauty could work against these pilgrims, enhancing their pain instead of distracting them from it, as they had imagined it would. These aspects of San Francisco were not easy for deranged people to accept. For many it was the last straw. A process of mental inversion took over. The suicides almost always jumped off the side of the Golden Gate Bridge facing the city lights—they were leaving, but they were also returning in triumph. One more voyage, back to the way it should have been. Back to Athens.

He stared at himself in the mirror behind the bar. His face was red and puffy around the nose, but still had the underlying hardness that caused people to trust him. Certainly his gray eyes were flatter than his sister's; there was nothing vague or ethereal about them. His smile was as hard and direct as his way of speaking. The red grog blossoms around his nose looked darker now.

No—you could never really see yourself in a barroom mirror. That was one reason these places were kept dark.

He finished his double.

He drove home slowly. He was almost there. The expression was *half drunk*. The way he felt now, he would have to get drunk to sleep and half drunk to work. Okay—Dawn's adoption had been a door opening all the way to all the hurts in the world. So what? They had had the three good years without trouble. Yet this was so typical of their previous bad luck. It was never anything easy. It was always something shameful and guilt-ridden and inexplicable; the one thing in the world that could hurt and bewilder them the most.

What they really feared was that this was the first of a series of disasters that could cause them to lose Dawn.

Rozalyn was waiting at the kitchen table. Quinn was somewhat relieved Dawn was still asleep.

"How long was Dawn at the hospital yesterday?" he asked.

"About two and a half hours. There was a doctor and a social worker. A team. They were pretty good. The woman cop didn't talk to her until later. She left her card with me."

"What kind of injuries were there?"

"Bruises and the fractured arm. The doctor said he took some stitches—" Her eyes fell and she made a vague downward motion. "Of course the main thing is the emotional trauma. What are we going to do?"

He reached for bourbon in the cabinet above the sink. "We'll let the police handle it. It's already a matter of record. On the other hand I'll have to make a big follow-through—dog their asses every step of the way to make sure they handle it right. I'll go in and see them tomorrow."

He sat down across from her with his drink. "Okay?"

She nodded without conviction. There was a long uneasy silence.

"How were things at Grace's?"

"Terrible. I . . . something's got to be done." His first responsbility was to Dawn—and Roz, of course. But Grace's poor little boy . . . "She's not fit to have the kid staying there alone with her."

He drank. When he set the glass down it clacked loudly. Rozalyn pull her hand over his.

"Watch it, honey."

He shook her hand off. "Did you say she had some bad dreams last night?"

"Some."

She was much calmer now. Maybe she had taken Valium. She was also just plain tired. She yawned groggily.

He was figuring strategy. "I don't want to wake her up. If she has any bad dreams tonight, we'll go in together. How's that?"

She nodded.

They would not take out their confusion and anxiety on each other too overtly, Quinn saw. That had happened before. Still—it was too bad they couldn't share and talk about the fear they both felt. But they were helpless at sharing anything having to do with a child's hurt. It terrified them and drove them apart. He sensed again what he had sensed many times—that the vulnerability of any child they called their own was also their own vulnerability.

Given the right circumstances, it could destroy them.

"Probably," he told her, "what's most important now is to keep calm."

2

Monday

Dawn poked moodily at her raisin bran. At last she looked up. "Do I have to go to school today?"

Quinn and Rozalyn sat across from her. "Of course not!" they exclaimed in unison.

Quinn sighed.

"Take it easy today," he said after a pause. "The doctor will let Roz know this afternoon when you should go back to school. Maybe tomorrow."

Dawn was disappointed. "Can't I stay home from school tomorrow too?"

"We'll see."

There had been no bad dreams that night. She walked with difficulty. Oddly, she had no trouble wiggling the fingers of her right hand, and even using the hand to pick things up. Apparently the fracture was the least serious kind.

"Did Roz tell you what happened?" she asked after she had finished, as Quinn stood at the sink washing dishes.

"Yes."

"Do you want me to tell you?"

He turned halfway. "Sure—but not until you're ready."

She frowned. Clearly she thought it necessary and proper to tell him something now.

He flapped his arms. "Okay," he said obligingly.

She had been waiting for the Muni bus on Mission and had decided to pay Grace a visit. Grace had not been there; her current boyfriend was. Quinn knew Andy Deggan as an ex-con from Oklahoma, whom he had once seen around the place when Grace was there. Dawn had accepted his invitation to step inside and wait for her. Deggan had been snorting coke and acting strange. He said abusive things and paced around, working himself into a rage. When she tried to leave he had raped her twice. The penetration was incomplete, but enough to cause her intense pain. He had threatened to kill her and struck her when she cried. His rage had increased. In the end he struck her repeatedly and broke her arm.

Finally he had left. Dawn had waited for Grace to come home.

"When I told Grace what happened, she just sat and looked at me," Dawn said. "Is she sick?"

Quinn started. "Very sick."

"Is she a drug addict?"

"Who told you so?"

"Roz said so."

He felt himself losing the thread of their conversation. Outrageous. Her story had infuriated him. Her blackened eyes and the large bruises on her face made his stomach sink. He wanted a drink but didn't want her to see him running to the bourbon so soon after her story.

"Drugs. She's had a problem with drugs for a long time. I think she's probably addicted now, or getting addicted. She might get better or she might get worse. It all depends on what she decides to do about it."

"They give themselves a shot?"

"Sometimes."

She wrinkled her small nut brown nose. "Yuck." She went back to her raisin bran.

Roz went into the front room. Quinn dawdled over his coffee in case Dawn wanted to say more. She said nothing. Instead she grimly extracted from her bowl raisins which she considered too old or in some way inedible, placing them in a milky row on a napkin.

He patted her hand. "Bye bye."

"Bye bye."

He walked the length of the hall without stopping at the door to the living room. He knew he ought to go in and kiss Rozalyn, but he sensed her somber mood and couldn't face her. But thinking about it was enough. Now he had to have a drink. Outside in his Chevy, he removed a bottle from beneath the seat and had a stiff belt.

Hidden bottles were the sure sign of alcoholism.

He knew the story by heart. Fuck it.

He drove to the Hall of Justice. He was wearing one of his older suits with a tie, and as he walked toward the Hall he took off the coat. Inside the Hall he put the coat back on and took off the tie. To hell with it. He didn't care how the clothes looked. He was in great shape. Although he was of average height, his open face and aggressive manner made him appear taller than he was.

The division he wanted was located in a drafty hall with rows of desks and people clacking away at typewriters. It resembled the city room of a metropolitan newspaper. There was a handsome marble-topped counter in front and partitioned spaces in back for offices. Quinn stood waiting at the counter. The man nearest him wore a small thirty-eight in a holster and sat at a desk typing.

In a moment the armed man got up and came slowly

toward him.

"Yes?"

Quinn glanced at the card Roz had given him.

"Inspector Wilson."

The armed man did not reply. He turned slowly and went to another desk. He came back presently with a well-dressed woman wearing tinted glasses. She was young and attractive, and was smiling intensely.

"Yes?"

"I'd like to speak to your boss."

She paused. "May I ask why?"

"You can ask. My name is Quinn Dunaway. My daughter was criminally assaulted the day before yesterday. You talked to her. I want to know what's being done about it, and I want to talk to someone in authority."

She gave in without a struggle, which aroused his suspicions. She was backing off much too quickly. "You'll want to talk to Inspector Monahan." She was actually walking backwards. "He's my . . . boss. I'll go and see —"

Without waiting for instructions Quinn walked around the counter and followed her. She was very edgy.

At the rear of the hall she darted in one of the offices, closing the door behind her. There were whispered voices, then silence. The door opened and a big man stepped out. He stood staring at Quinn as though he had been expecting him.

"Ralph Monahan!" he explained. He made no move to shake Quinn's hand. "Mr. Dunaway?"

Quinn nodded.

"Come on inside. You're not going to like this."

He turned and ambled slowly back into his office.

"You stay," he said in a threatening voice to Wilson. "I

want you to see just how bad police work can be." He
stopped to chortle insultingly at her. "Police Science,
huh?"

She shrugged but appeared intimidated.

Monahan had small square eyes and a harsh jowly face
the color of an oven-baked ham. Quinn judged him to be
in his fifties and about thirty pounds overweight. His
clothes were the uncoordinated pastel sportswear of the
kind sold at National Dollar Stores. He moved with the
slow but unmistakable hostility of a man who had long
ago reconciled himself to the worst in human nature and
rather enjoyed it.

Quinn sat down on a metal folding chair. The office
was small and quite bleak. Monahan slowly opened a
drawer, his fleshy eyebrows rising at an equally slow rate.
He took out a small vial of pills. He took one and drank
from a glass of water on his cluttered desk.

"I want you to understand, Mr. Dunaway, that the
district attorney's office has nothing to do with criminal
justice." He nodded sourly at Wilson, who sat in the
corner. *"They are complete jerk-offs.* Everything I'm
going to tell you has to do with that."

Quinn lit a cigarette without asking Monahan.

"Those people are political hacks."

"Get on with it."

"We're not indicting Andrew Deggan."

Quinn had not expected that. "Why not?"

Monahan sighed. "The DA's office has a policy. They
think kids make bad witnesses. The policy is that pedo-
philes — sex offenders whose victims are children — have to
offend twice in the city and county or they won't move on
it. Even if the guy has a history."

"My daughter can identify him."

"Defense lawyers can do weird things to a kid on a witness stand. Now, the DA ain't thinking of the child's potential emotional problems; obviously, he's thinking of winning cases. These cases are hard to win. In this situation there was no test for semen, and now it's too late. So it's her word against his. The guy has a history, believe me, but sometimes the defense lawyer can keep that out of court." He paused. "So what it all boils down to is that they're not going to move on this guy until he offends again. That way they have more than one witness—it looks better, chances are better that the defense attorney won't be able to shake the child's testimony."

"Why wasn't there a test for semen?"

"Incompetence. The first doctors who saw her didn't know there was penetration. The doctor who saw her afterward thought the first doctors had handled it."

"She has a broken arm—don't tell me that isn't physical evidence."

"It's not broken *enough.*" Monahan was shaking his head. "It's only a greenstick fracture. The defense would say she did it playing."

There was a silence during which Wilson cleared her throat.

"Here he is." Monahan handed him a single mug shot. Deggan was white and vaguely muscular in an unformed way. In the front view he appeared cross-eyed. "He's one of those merry little bastards who came running out of the Oklahoma hills thinking they were Pretty Boy Floyd or John Dillinger. Besides being a dumb Okie, he's a snitch, a sniveler, and a psychopath. Ask him why and he'll tell you he got kicked in the head by a mule, or didn't eat enough broccoli when he was a kid, or some such miserable shit. He's got all the answers. I guarantee you it's always someone else's fault. He's done it all—rape, manslaughter, burglary, and a lot of sex offenses against kids, a lot. He made himself into a big man at Q because of the manslaughter charge, but when the baby-raping business got around, they had to segregate him. He ended up at Atascadero. Deggan is a two-time loser, so the next time he does it all. He knows that. This last time the sneaky bastard waited until his parole was over before he did anything that even looked illegal, then he started all over again—heroin, second-story stuff, the works."

"Is this the first sex offense since he got out of prison the last time?"

"No. Now it gets worse. You may not believe this, but several other counties around the Bay Area have the same policy as the DA's office here. It's all politics. Deggan knows he can offend in these counties and get away with it, as long as he only offends once in each county, and as long as it's against a kid. He's already pulled this two other times that we know about, each time in a county where the same policy is in effect. He's cute. Cute."

"Once," Monahan continued after a pause, "he got into this group of ladies over in Berkeley. These were all *wealthy* ladies up in the Berkeley hills, very nice ladies— very . . . liberal." He said the word in such a way it was apparent it held a special significance for him. "Deggan was screwing the lady at the house where they held these meditation classes. One day the woman left one of the kids alone with him, and he raped her. Then he went around with one of his pals from Hayward and cleaned out several of the homes of the other ladies in this group. All the time he was hanging out with this woman he was looking for a shot at one of the kids, see, and he was casing the houses of the parents. There was no proof on the burglaries, and he only offended against one kid. The case really looked bad—then some psychiatrist said it'd be too much for the child to testify. They didn't touch him."

Quinn put out his cigarette in Monahan's ashtray. "Jesus Christ." He felt like beating Monahan up. "Do you think for one moment I'm going to sit still for this?"

Monahan turned to Wilson. "Okay. You can go."

Quinn stood to let her pass. She was happy to get away.

"I have to follow a policy," Monahan said after a pause, "but there are things that can be done." He stared moodily at the empty chair and smacked the desk with a flat red hand. "What about this sister of yours? No offense . . . but I understand Deggan was hustling her. Is that right?"

Quinn was still shaking his head. "Somebody's going to get his ass kicked."

Quinn's voice was as harsh and full-throated as a foghorn. He was known around town as a loud man. People liked that—there was a touch of Bogart in his voice. Few people could stand up to him.

"Take it easy."

He was also known as a scrapper, and was in fact an ex-boxer.

He sighed. "Okay. You said something could be done."

Throughout their brief interview Monahan had been sizing him up. Now he looked at him with something like approval. "Your sister has a habit. Right?"

Quinn shrugged. He was getting angrier. Still, he wanted to hear the man out.

Monahan leaned forward. "Look, he's just crazy enough to get in contact with your sister again. In fact I'd bet money on it."

Quinn nodded. "So?"

"Tell your sister to pump him for information. Find
out everything she can about what he's doing. Whatever
he's into, it's bound to be illegal. If we can't nail the
cocksucker one way, we'll have to nail him another. Find
out from her what he's up to, and tell me. If he's armed,
that's a felony. If he's got anything new to sell—it's
probably hot. But what's important . . . listen for anything that sounds like a drug sale. I'll feed it to the right
people and we'll scoop his ass up."

It was partly a hustle to get him out of his office, Quinn
thought. But in spite of himself he clung to it. He
couldn't bear the thought of doing nothing; that more
than anything could destroy him.

"Do you know where Deggan is?" Quinn asked.

Monahan's eyebrows rose slowly. "Never mind." He
paused. "Running, out of sight. But these scumbags
always turn up eventually at the same old places."

How much did Monahan know about Grace? About
Deggan? Enough to figure Deggan would call her sooner
or later—and that Grace would talk to him if he did.

Quinn sighed. "I buy it. But I could kill you for not
scooping him up now. That bastard is out on the
street—"

Monahan nodded sympathetically. After a moment he
asked in a low voice, "What's the story on your sister?"

"I'm handling that. If I help you—you help me."

Monahan put up a cautionary hand. "You're not
helping me. You're helping yourself—and some guy in
some other department."

"Tell them to stay away from her."

"I can't really do that."

Quinn made his voice harsher. "Tell them stay away or I kick their asses. Or somebody's ass."

The words came out like flat pieces of metal being stamped in a metal press. Each word had the clipped resonance of metal being broken cleanly. Monahan nodded and looked out the window; a moment passed. Quinn felt they had arrived at an honest understanding of each other, although the situation was much worse than he had thought it would be.

"Well—" They both stood up. Monahan took a card from his shirt pocket. "Call me."

Quinn let some of the anger he felt come through his eyes. The fat jowly man in front of him acknowledged it with a sigh and a short hand-wave.

"People just never want to know how bad other people can be." Monahan made a gesture of futility. "Maybe that's true of your sister. You'll forgive me for saying so."

"Oh, she knows, all right."

It wasn't any of Monahan's business anyway.

He persevered. "The Quaker halfway house where your sister met Deggan is nothing but a front for a heroin operation. Did you know that? And fencing. Everything you can imagine. The Quakers don't see it."

"Maybe the Quakers don't know what to look for."

"In the beginning." Monahan smiled sideways. He was sparring with him. "But then you tell them what's going on and they still don't want to see it."

"I've observed that." He would stay one move ahead of Monahan. "People like that can be very dangerous. And now I'm going to tell you something else. There are people all over this country—smart people, educated people—who look up to punks like Deggan and consider them heroes. To be a hero to those people, all you have to do is break the law."

Monahan nodded wonderingly. "It's true—ain't it?" They were moving slowly toward the door. Monahan nodded slowly and with great emphasis. "You're not a Quaker."

"I was raised a Quaker. What I *am* is none of your business."

Monahan sighed. A man of his age and ugliness did not have to apologize for religious insult. "Maybe your sister is."

"That's her business."

"The way I heard it, you were supposed to be a Communist once."

"People always get those stories wrong."

Quinn never discussed politics with people in law enforcement.

"Okay." Monahan nodded shortly. "I'm gonna pass this on to intelligence today. They're to keep track of anything on the street about Andy Deggan. He gets busted for anything. This is his third fall, remember, so he does *all* his time. You call me if you get any information. Right?" He stepped toward Quinn with one heavy red hand floating in front of him. "Look, I want to put the guy away as much as you do!"

He dropped his thick hand on Quinn's shoulder. Quinn gently removed it and squeezed it hard. The pressure was just great enough to cause pain. Monahan winced.

"No you don't," Quinn said. "Not nearly as much as I do."

The office of Quinn's union local was on a pier. His

secretary Mona was cross because he was late. She was an attractive middle-aged Black woman who designed and wore her own stunning garments. Several of the Black union members liked to hang around the office to bask in her beauty and shoot the breeze. Today she was alone.

"You might have called," she said as soon as he came in the door. "If we're gonna work together, we might as well work *together,* you know what I mean?"

Quinn went to one of his two file cabinets and opened the bottom drawer. From underneath some back issues of *Motor World* and the union newspaper he took out a fifth of bourbon. He poured himself a drink in a slippery glass from their little rest room. He felt like the male lead in a cliché-ridden movie about alcoholism. Alcoholism — what was it but the same thing over and over?

"I know exactly what you mean, Mona, but stay off my back anyway. If you can't, as far as I'm concerned you can go home now."

After the warmth of the bourbon his hands were still shaking.

Mona watched him closely. Finally she swiveled around in her swivel chair and picked up her bag. She opened it, scrutinized its contents carefully, zipped it up, and walked out the door. Mona was married to a white trade unionist who had been through the political wars with Quinn; this had allowed a certain intimacy to grow between them in the year or so she had worked for him, uncomplicated by any awkward sexual overtones. It was necessary that he apologize to her.

He jogged down the length of the pier. He passed several offices that looked like their designers wanted them to be boutiques. He caught up with her where the pier became a parking lot.

"Hold it, kid!" he ordered.

She stopped. He grabbed her arm and grinned.

"Hey—"

He put his arm around her shoulder. She was a good friend and she really was an exceptional secretary too.

"Cookie—look. I'm sorry. The sharks got holda me and I got trouble." He had a way of staring directly into a person's eyes that people found impressive. "I'd tell you about it, but you don't want to hear that stuff."

He let his face go serious and then put on a slow grin. He hugged her again and she thawed enough to smile.

"Lotta things got ahold of you, Quinn. I'm really starting to worry about you. Look at the way that bottle jump up every time you got a problem. You got a jones for that stuff. It's worse than you think."

He grinned and hugged her again. "I needed it."

"What'd I *say?*" She shrugged and nodded to show that the apology was accepted. "Well, if you need it, you better go back and finish it."

She leaned sideways and gave him a peck on the cheek. He smelled cologne from the little cotton ball she kept wedged in her bra. He released her, laughing. At the edge of the parking lot she turned and waved at him. He nodded good-bye.

Apology or no apology, she was taking off.

He walked back to his office slowly, locked the door, and sat down at his desk. In the next ten minutes he consumed one-third of the fifth of Bourbon Deluxe. It seemed to have no effect on his thought processes, which were clear and furious; the anxiety he had felt diminished somewhat.

He called an acquaintance who was a celebrated San Francisco lawyer and drunk. He asked a hypothetical question. Was it possible—hypothetically—for a citizen to legally compel the DA's office to take a case to court, when that office did not wish to do so?

"I would say hypothetically that you're out of luck," the acquaintance said. "Don't feel bad. It happens all the time. Those guys are pussy. I mean they're not exactly gamblers. If they could, they'd buy every jury they got in front of. What's up, Quinn?" The voice grew jovial. "You got something on somebody? Not the old man—?"

Quinn sighed. "Nothing like that." Like many San Francisco liberals, this man would not mind seeing a trade unionist get indicted. "Try to think of this call as some kind of privileged information."

He thanked the acquaintance and hung up. He forced himself to call his home number before taking another drink. Rozalyn answered.

"How's it going?"

"Okay! I mean, she's resting and watching TV. Real well—"

Her bad nerves came over the telephone and almost overwhelmed him.

"How do you think she's doing?"

Roz paused. "She thinks we're making too much of a fuss. The social worker said kids often say that. An experience like this leaves scars, but there's nothing the parents can really do until the trial. It's during the trial that the child really needs the support of the parents." She stopped to remember. "Until then, they say the parents should give the child a reasonable amount of attention, listen to her if she wants to talk about the experience, and stay fairly cool . . . "

He felt dread hooking into his solar plexus like a fist.

"There's not going to be any trial," he said before he

could think about it. "they're not even going to pick Deggan up."

"What the hell do you mean?" Her voice was suddenly and unreservedly hysterical.

He tried to explain. At one point he heard running feet and what he thought was Rozalyn closing the kitchen door. When she began to shout he poured himself another drink. He was oppressively aware of the extent to which their behavior was becoming predictable and hackneyed. They both wanted to do the right thing, but fear was swamping them. That made it difficult to think logically.

Rozalyn made him repeat several times the details of his conversation with Monahan.

"But I *told* her there would be a trial!" she said. "The goddamn social worker said to *prepare* her for it! I made a big deal out of it. I told her how they select juries, how the lawyers ask questions, what a courtroom looks like — the whole thing!"

"How did Dawn take to testifying at Deggan's trial?"

"She *loved* it! It was the one thing that kept us going until you got back from Nevada. The idea that this sick bastard would get put away, and that she could help put him away herself. She said she was looking forward to testifying at the trial."

Quinn sighed. There was little more to say.

"Are you drinking?" she asked after a pause.

It was unlike her to rag him about the drinking.

"I *always* drink."

That got him a laugh. "I mean are you drunk. More or less."

"Nobody cares out here. They don't even notice." There was another pause. "I'll be home earlier than usual. But now I have to get back to my drinking."

He could tell she was about to cry.

"Honey—it doesn't make any sense—"

"I love you," he said truthfully. "Tell Dawn hello and that I love her too."

He hung up.

He sat thinking of the conversation. He had told his wife nobody noticed on the waterfront if you drank. Untrue—untrue! That was one of the first things they noticed on the front, if the drinking had you by the short hairs. The word always got around about that. Of course, he would get away with it for a long time, because people liked him. He might even get away with it indefinitely. But that could be bad too, if he became a kind of pet of the union, a useless drunk the organization kept around because he was a nice guy. Colorful.

He shuddered. No—he had to be good for something.

His office was medium-sized, cooled by the Bay beneath the pier. He turned on the small floor heater that sat next to his desk. In addition to the two file cabinets, his office had two desks and chairs, and a large window through which he could look at the Bay. On the wall were framed letters from some people Quinn admired, and a United Farm Workers poster. Despite the thick carpet, the room had the pleasant dinginess he thought appropriate for a union office. On his desk was a small plaque that read LOVE YOUR ENEMIES—IT'LL DRIVE THE POOR BASTARDS FRUIT.

He sat listening to the crisp sound of the whitecaps hitting the pilings below. On windy days the pier swayed slightly with the big rollers. Today it was generally calm.

Monday was the day he usually did his correspondence. If nobody came in this afternoon, he could perhaps get some work done. He took a good look at his desk and saw that it was neater than usual on Monday. In a moment he saw why. In one corner lay several sealed letters with freshly typed addresses on them. Mona had evidently done them earlier that morning, probably signing his name as she sometimes did. To his left were all the letters that had been received that week, including some correspondence from an employer that he would have to go over carefully. On his right was another miscellany of older letters and circulars, a gang steward report, copies of injury statements, the longshore contract, a pile of stewards' manuals, a yellowing copy of the union newspaper, and a copy of the 1949 Pacific Coast Marine Safety Code. There was also a document advertising an event at which the president of his union would make one of his rare public appearances.

He couldn't concentrate. From now on it was going to take a lot of energy just to keep going.

He had himself another drink and put the bottle in a lower drawer in his desk.

He took a look at the remaining correspondence. His local was a relatively small one, but everyone wanted a piece of the action. Certain liberal and radical groups wanted union leaders on their letterheads or advisory councils. Naturally they always wanted people from *his* union, as if it didn't have enough problems. And why did they always come to this union? Because all the other unions in town were mainstream AFL-CIO outfits scared of their own shadows. Every Monday he would write careful answers to these groups, accepting certain invitations, declining most. As he got drunker his replies would become less careful. He and Mona had gotten some good laughs out of it.

It would take a lot of energy just to keep going.

He took another drink and unlocked the door. He took the bottle to the file cabinet and put it back in the bottom drawer.

When he came back to his desk, he realized he would get very little work done. Instead, for several minutes there was a steady stream of moisture into his eyes and nose, thick like his sister's junkie tears; tears of anger, frustration, and an overwhelming sense of guilt. His eyes traveled helplessly to the one thing he had been trying hard not to look at since coming into his office. It stood next to a picture of his wife on the corner of his desk. It was a framed photograph of an Indian child named Dawn, whom he had almost come to love and for whom he felt totally responsible. The photograph had been taken when she was nine. She stood next to a boat at Lake Berryessa smiling sadly. It had been a year after the adoption, and it was the first time he had been able to get the damn kid to smile for the camera.

PART TWO

Gaming

3

Monday Night—Tuesday— Wednesday Morning

That evening they watched their favorite TV programs. Dawn was very quiet and went to bed when they asked her to. Afterward they sat in the kitchen talking. How would they tell Dawn that the man who attacked her was still walking the streets—that there would be no trial?

Quinn thought perhaps she wouldn't care. "Maybe she's bored with the whole thing. Like you said before."

"But I *told* her there would be a goddamn trial." Sooner or later Roz always came back to this theme. "The police would pick him up. The bastard would pay for his crime."

She punctuated each point with a sharp nod.

"Very Hebraic," Quinn murmured.

Rozalyn had been raised by Jewish atheists. For business reasons her father had converted to High Church Episcopalianism. There had been jokes about people who read the Book of Common Prayer from right to left. She didn't like to talk about it.

"A kid needs to know there's some kind of right and wrong in the world," she was saying.

"*Very* Hebraic."

He did not intend it as a joke.

"Particularly when somebody has just done something very wrong to that kid," she continued.

"Particularly then."

"Is that Hebraic enough for you?" She was angry. "Is it?"

Her casual anti-Semitism went well with his dislike for some of his father's Quaker ideas, he thought. Not quite the same thing—but close.

"I couldn't agree with you more."

He was drinking bourbon and water while she drank coffee. They were both smoking like furnaces. In the past twenty-four hours they had gone through several packs of Camels. Every ashtray in the house was littered with crushed butts.

"Well—" she said. "I suppose getting up on a witness stand could be tough for a kid. But she liked the idea. I thought that was great. It showed courage. I thought you would approve."

He nodded. "You thought exactly right. I'm sick to death of parents who don't want their kids to testify in cases like this because they listen to some sick, greedy psychiatrist who says it'll put too much pressure on the kid. Fuck that. Right and wrong are hard things. You can't start early enough getting a kid to work on them."

"Now who's being Hebraic?"

"I told you I agreed with you." In fact he was stronger on it than she could ever be. "When you do something like this you have to pay for it. Otherwise it's all bullshit."

That seemed to break part of the tension she felt; she sighed.

"Also—I love you," he added.

They sat smoking and listening to Muzak-smooth KABL strings on the kitchen radio.

"Which puts us back on square one," she said presently. "Because there won't be any trial. I can't believe it."

"Neither of us wants to believe it."

It was decided he would skip work the next day to tell Dawn the bad news. He would mention it casually— there was always the chance she wouldn't be as angry about it as they were. It was automatically assumed by both of them that Quinn should be the one to tell her.

Dawn had two bad dreams that night. On both occasions when they heard her call out they rushed at breakneck speed into her bedroom to comfort her. They sat on her bed and told her stories. Once Quinn made hand-shadow animals on the fresh pink wallpaper. She stared at him as though he was mad. Still, she seemed amused and probably distracted from the bad dreams. Or so he thought.

He hoped she saw their clumsiness as endearing.

He and Roz were both up and around the next morning well before seven. As was their custom in the morning, they said little to each other. At eight there were slow steps on the stairs. Dawn stood awkwardly in the kitchen door watching them. At the sight of the bruised face Quinn felt the anger starting up again. He was glad there was bourbon in his coffee.

"Wake up . . . wake up . . . you sleepyhead!" Rozalyn sang.

Dawn started for the raisin bran near the sink. Quinn caught her and hugged her roughly. He was amazed—as he always was—at the thinness of her body. There was nothing but skin and bone and two small buds where her breasts would be; and her dark and (he thought) lovely face that could conceal so much. In its carefully balanced center were two large brown eyes that could stare for long moments without blinking. He noticed the swelling around them was subsiding.

Dawn wrinkled her nose and stuck her finger in his cup.

"I know," she said disgustedly.

He was all alarmed innocence. "Thash not true!"

"Shut up—"

"Ish only coffee!"

"You're crazy."

She giggled. She liked the kidding kind of attention. She punched him lightly and moved quickly away to pour her beloved raisin bran. The child had only average intelligence—or possibly below—but in the manner of kids who had been knocked around she was very smart about certain things, particularly those things she interpreted as having to do with her self-interest. One of the things she had apparently seen as being in her own interest was a refusal to tell either Quinn or Rozalyn anything about her life in the various establishments and foster homes in which she had resided prior to legal adoption. This decision Quinn deeply respected; in addition it had afforded him some private relief. He did not really want to know everything about her, even as she had not yet quite settled in as a full member of the family. It was her nature to be secretive. Still, that degree of secretiveness was odd for a child, any child.

"Got any homework to do today?"

She was attending one of the public schools and doing poorly academically.

"I never have homework."

"Right. They don't teach anything in school anymore. All you guys do is loaf."

"Then why do you keep asking?"

There were times when he had to look at her carefully to determine whether or not she was being sarcastic. She wasn't.

"I keep hoping they'll break down and teach you guys how to work."

She shook her head. "Gross."

Her two favorite words were *gross* and *yuck*. The latter she had picked up from Roz. As she grew older she would gradually pick up more expressions from them. The thought excited Quinn. It was like watching the most complex and mysterious living thing in the universe grow in front of you; and more than that you helped it grow, by giving it little bits and pieces of yourself. On the other hand she was a human being, not an exotic type of rose. You had to remember anything involving human beings could explode on you.

Quinn drained his bourbon-laced coffee. "Gotta talk to you. Roz's orders—"

He was sorry he had said that. It wasn't fair.

Rozalyn abruptly picked up his pack of Camels from the table and shook one out. When he lit it for her, her eyes glinted disapproval. *With all due respect,* he thought, *that's too goddamn bad.* This is father-to-daughter. Straight talk; straight shooting; straight from the hip—

But it wasn't Roz's fault he had to talk to Dawn—was it?

For the first time he realized how angry it made him that he, instead of his wife, always pulled the heavy duty.

But it was hard to imagine her doing it. They would have to talk about that.

Dawn ate her raisin bran grimly. Whatever was up, she didn't want to get involved until she had finished her breakfast. They decided to go to Stow Lake. He rented one of the paddlewheel boats that were powered by treadles. They paddled their way to the center of the lake, surrounded by ducks and a few other boats. They were separated by enough water to talk privately. Quinn told her what had happened in as much detail as he could without making anything up. When he had finished she sat thinking. The brown eyes turned inward, a study in concentration.

"They didn't put him in jail?"

He shook his head.

"And they won't have the trial?"

"Nope."

She wept. It had been a long time since he had seen anyone cry like this. It was a wail of outrage—or pure teeth-gritting anger. It was deeply personal, but there was also an echo of the tribal about it. It was the wail of the tribal woman who had been humiliated, a howl of shame. It contained within it an intransigent demand for action and revenge. He realized now why Dawn had expressed no curiosity about her attacker and his motives. To her, what was important was the pure wrongness of his act. Evil needed no explanation or analysis; it needed warriors to fight it.

She was even angrier than Rozalyn and himself.

He did not touch her. She stayed in her private place of incomprehension and fury for a long time. Quinn could feel other people in the boats around them looking.

He sat quietly without taking his eyes off her. When he

was sure she was finished he turned away to light a cigarette. When he turned back, she was wiping away the tears.

"You can go and kill him," she said.

In some part of his mind he had known she would say that.

"I want to help in every way I can—"

"Then why don't you go and kill him?" Her voice rose precipitously.

"Because I'd get caught and get put in jail myself. You and Roz wouldn't have anyone to earn money and it'd be harder on both of you."

She looked up at him scornfully. "Then I'll kill him when I grow up myself."

"We can't let one crazy bastard who's sick in the head ruin our lives."

She stared at a passing duck, assessing carefully what he had just said and what it could mean to her. The duck squawked loudly and stuck its head in the water several times. No one responded with bread or applause. It swam toward and another boat.

"No," she said. "I'll grow up and kill him."

It was said with childish stubbornness but ended with an unexpected whispered softness, which gave it a spooky tone of adult finality.

Watching her, he was aware of the extent to which he had come to feel similarly about crime. Compassion for the criminal? Another excuse to identify with the aggressor. Liberal bullshit from academic types who didn't know their asses from their elbows.

"I know I can," she muttered.

She wouldn't look at him directly.

"Okay. Get him. But don't forget something else." He

puffed on his cigarette in short comic puffs. When he was finished with it he threw it in the water. Thankfully, none of the ducks ate it. "You can talk to us about it anytime you want. We can be with you if you have any more bad dreams. Roz and I—" He could feel himself floundering badly. "We're doing the best job we know how," he finished lamely.

He had wanted to say they loved her. In fact they *would* love her, if so many other things didn't stand in their way. They would gladly sacrifice their lives to save her. What was that if it wasn't love? Guilt—that's what it was. *It was their fault this had happened.*

Of course that wasn't rational. But feelings rarely were.

He began to paddle back to shore. He was careful not to look at her face. She was the kind of kid who had been battered so much by life she wouldn't be able to acknowledge the lack of love (never mind love itself) for years; perhaps she never would. You could talk about love to such children, but it was stupid to expect them to acknowledge it or its absence as something real. That ought to be a break for Rozalyn and himself.

Unfortunately they were their own worst critics where Dawn was concerned.

They walked to the car in silence. When they were in it at last, she turned to him. She was looking slightly to one side of him.

"It isn't right," she said.

At least she was still talking to him.

"No, it isn't," he agreed.

She sat next to him in stony silence. At length he started the car, weighted down by a helplessness so palpable he could feel it pulling at his forearms. Steering the car was like lifting weights.

That afternoon Dawn hung out with a few of the kids on the block. Roz made much of it. "We should encourage her to go out. Help her get over her fear of the unknown."

"Unknown? Christ, she's lived on this block for three years."

"You know what I mean. Regain her sense of security."

He spent the afternoon working in the yard. He set the sprinklers up and spaded around the rosebushes on the north side of the house. He swept the garden patio. He weeded the small truck garden in the corner of the yard and got out the sackcloth he had been saving for the roses.

Their house was plain to a fault—three bedrooms with hardwood floors, copper plumbing, a garden patio, and a redwood fence—but somehow its very plainness had made it more of a refuge. Being around homeless men as a kid had taught him that owning a house made you a king. It had been the only big-money scrape of their lives. To keep the payments up, he had shipped out for a year after buying it. That had been heaven—lying in his bunk at sea, dreaming about coming home to a place of his own.

For his generation the American Dream had been owning your own home.

He was sweeping the patio a second time when he heard the back-porch window go up. "Where's Dawn?" he mimicked before Rozalyn could say anything. "Let her roam a little."

She leaned out and tapped the side of the house with

the nails of her cigarette hand. "You don't need me. Smartass."

"She'll be back. This is a safe neighborhood."

After a few seconds she withdrew from the window. A moment later he heard the whine of the Singer. She kept all her sewing things on the back porch.

"Let her roam," he muttered again to himself.

Of course the house had been invaded by death. Somehow he had never conceived that such a thing could happen to his children—as though his love were strong enough to protect them. His son Christopher, dead of crib death at six months. He would never forget the days and nights of horror that followed that. The house and the small world of the domestic had become monstrous overnight—the infant's blanket, his pacifier, the hideous little crib itself. They could not touch them. They had finally begged friends to take them away. And then Cynthia—born hopelessly retarded. The pain drawn out over years this time, as they finally admitted the defeat and let her go to the state institution. Long arguments about how often they should visit her, or whether they should visit her at all. Once more the home had become a prison. It was haunted with the ghosts of his two children. There had even been sounds they had heard—auditory hallucinations of course, but they had both heard them. Still, there was never any possibility of running away. Loyalty to Rozalyn and the long-standing need for a home worked together with his guilt and anger in some way to keep him here. At last he had come to terms with it—or at least thought he had.

But memories of his lost children pulled at him like a riptide.

Christopher. He had always wanted to name a son

that. He still liked the sound of it. He didn't have to worry about pain when he heard the name—he could literally feel no more pain about Christopher. Guilty? Who was guilty? He had finally accepted that he would never know.

Cynthia. Incredible hope, that time. Cynthia was going to wash away the pain of the crib death. Instead it was the same horror drawn out longer. During four years of trying unsuccessfully to take care of the child at home, the pain had become exquisite for them, and then gone beyond that to something he had no words for. After they put Cynthia in a state institution Roz had run away. In the middle of God only knew what kind of dark night, she had gotten herself a hysterectomy. Afterward she had crept home to him like a shell of something that had once been alive. Since then they had lived in each other's care like invalids with a special disease no one could understand fully but themselves.

He stopped sweeping and stood listening to the irregular murmur of the Singer on the back porch.

It all had to do with San Francisco. Hiding in the rhetoric of tolerance and cosmopolitanism, death was subtle here and frequently accompanied by aspects of comfort and beauty. It struck where you least expected— through the familiar and the everyday. The City had a way of making you more vulnerable even as you thought you were becoming stronger. They had retreated from the world, and death had penetrated here—here in their modest home where they had thought themselves most safe. They had been gut-shot and left to die on home ground.

And now Dawn—what about Dawn? All he could really know was that his life had become a struggle with certain shadows he called death.

He tossed his gloves in the toolbox just inside the basement door and sprinted up the back porch stairs. Rozalyn started slightly as he passed her on the porch. In the kitchen he poured himself a bourbon and water. Rozalyn stood in the kitchen door, smoking.

"The neighborhood rascals are standing around yakking it up about something," he told her. "Probably about the high prices of dope in grade school."

He knew without asking that she wanted a report on Dawn's activities.

"I wonder what she told them about the bruises on her face."

There was a painful twinge of guilt in his gut. "I have no way of knowing that."

"Are you going to work tomorrow?"

"Yes."

She put out her cigarette. "Why don't you start buying bourbon by the case? Seriously. If you're going to drink, you might as well drink good stuff." She prowled back and forth on the back porch, her arms folded stiffly across her breasts. "I'm sorry the talk at the park was so rough."

She was in an ecstasy of guilt. He had seen her like this before. Her adult life was given direction by her endlessly plotted conceptions of everybody's relative guilt or innocence. His Quaker background made him sympathetic, except that responsibility had always seem more important (at least theoretically) to him than guilt. He had often thought if she were a man she might feel the same.

She stopped pacing abruptly. "Christ, how could we not have known she was stopping at Grace's?"

"We *did* know," he said patiently. "Both of us. When we were teaching her how to use the Muni, we showed her where Grace lived and told her she could go there if she got lost."

Again and again they forced each other through the same conversational paces; a private liturgy.

"We should have known this would happen," she said.

"There was no way we could predict something like this."

"You shouldn't drink in front of Dawn. She'll know you're drinking because of what happened. She'll feel guilty."

"Dawn doesn't feel guilty about a damn thing. She's angry. And I say more power to her."

She paused breathlessly. "If you hadn't gone to Nevada, this never would have happened!"

He told her the same thought had been occurring to him and he didn't care to be reminded of it again.

"I'm sorry," she said without hesitation.

"And I'll tell you something else. I don't want this to become an obsession. I'm sick of talking about it."

She was already crying. "I can't talk about it to my friends."

He shook his head patiently. "Bullshit. If they're real friends, you'd be stupid not to talk to them about this. What about Marcie Loeb? She'll listen to anything if you let her talk about her divorce. Stop feeling ashamed!" He was aware of directing the words as much to himself as to Rozalyn. "Look—*we* haven't done anything wrong!"

They only felt as if they had.

That evening after dinner he went to see Grace. She admitted him after several loud knocks. She looked more ghostly and sicker than before. She sat on the couch in the living room, under a blanket. From time to time she shivered. Her son Martin crept forward through a clutter of toys to stare at them.

The child's father had been a very handsome Black man. Martin was a small and beautiful version of his father. Quinn bounced him on his knee for a few moments. The child was ecstatic with the attention.

"Is there a neighbor who could take him for a few moments while we talk?" he asked.

"I suppose it's not too late," she said dreamily. After a moment she added, "Although I don't see what a three-year-old is going to understand in an adult conversation." She found this quite funny.

"You never know."

He didn't want Martin to see them arguing.

Grace picked the child up and slowly disappeared down the stairs with him. Quinn was relieved. It was intensely painful to see a bright and good-looking kid like that stuck in such a rotten situation. So far he had not taken any major responsibility for the child's welfare, but now the situation was forcing his hand.

"Are you going to work at all anymore?" he asked her when she returned.

She sat down on the couch, pulling her blanket around her. "Not very much. When I do, it's more for Martin's sake than for mine." She giggled. "He loves it at the baby-sitter's."

He sat down on the easy chair facing her. Her eyes were as hard as his, but glassy, white and gray, with a pinhole at each center. They were the eyes of a frantic animal involved in a high-speed chase. On the other hand, her mouth was loose and almost slobbering, as though she were asleep. You could not read the expression at all unless you knew it was caused chemically. He did not know enough about drugs to read everything he saw, but he saw enough. She probably sat around dropping reds and drinking wine, waiting for her heart to stop, then mainlining stimulants. He thought he saw heroin, or perhaps Percodan or other painkillers. But most of all, tonight she was probably doing barbiturates, her favorite drug. Those and wine. The worst medicine.

"I'll make this short and sweet, Gracie. I wish you'd go to a clinic, but you probably won't, so I won't waste our time talking about it. I have two things to tell you. Tell. Not ask. So listen carefully."

The consciousness behind the lovely gray eyes was lucid, reasonable, and wished to engage in conversation, but was very far away and was having difficulty making the proper connections. He would have to speak slowly. He leaned forward toward her. She frowned in concentration.

"Sooner or later Andrew Deggan is going to call you. Find out where he's staying. Find out what he's doing."

She looked at him uncomprehendingly. "He's in jail."

He told her as much of the story as was necessary. He thought he saw a brief expression of fear pass over her face.

"Why do you want to find out about him?"

He hesitated. "It's been suggested that it might be possible to nail him on some unrelated charge."

She nodded wisely. In a moment her face became blank again.

"Okay," she said reasonably. "Is that all?"

"I have to do something about Martin. I can't leave him here alone with you, the way you are now."

"What are you going to do?"

"I'm open to suggestion. Maybe somebody besides me has some ideas on this situation. We'll have to work something out, even if it's a foster home." Did she have any friends who could stay with her for a few days? "Think about it—if you can."

She blinked and shrugged. She seemed surprised. At the same time, she was nodding in agreement. The drugs enabled her to accept anything.

Maybe the babysitter would take the child full-time. It would cost a fortune to hire someone to stay here around the clock.

He got up to go. "I think you know we're all ready to help you. If you want help."

Already she was sliding back into her glazed ice-world. Probably thinking of her next joyous rush. She waited patiently for him to leave. Waiting was her perfect Cinerama universe of lunar cools, explosions, and special effects.

He was heading for the stairs when he heard her call him. She was taking something out of her purse.

"Look," she said. "Quinn—"

She walked over and handed him something. It was a checkbook. It had a picture of the Golden Gate Bridge on it. Over it was a printed word—JUMP.

"Personalized checks," she said triumphantly. "An advertising gimmick. You can have any phrase or slogan printed on it that you want. That's what I wanted. Over the Golden Gate Bridge."

He shook her like a kindergarten teacher shaking a child who won't listen. He held her arms tightly enough to make bruises. He increased the pressure; he kept shaking. She apparently felt no pain.

"No—don't hustle me." In the male world of the waterfront, bluffs were called regularly and usually early in the game. "I'm warning you. That's kid stuff. I don't take that kind of silliness. No way."

She giggled. She seemed unable to understand why he should be angry. She was not angry at him.

"Dig," she said. "Hey. I know it's bad taste but . . . don't be so up*tight*."

He got home from Grace's at five minutes after nine. At forty-five minutes after he sat in the kitchen in his socks, drinking bourbon and water. He was looking at the lights of Alameda across the Bay. Roz and Dawn were in the front room. The TV was talking to them about a new kind of hamburger that was almost guaranteed to improve the quality of anyone's life. Hamburger Helper. It could change your life for the better.

When the hall telephone rang he rose wearily and trooped down the hall to get it.

"You know where the Celtic Palace is?" a male voice asked him. There were bar sounds in the background.

"Why should I?"

Stall for some time.

"Because you should come on down. We got something on Andy Deggan."

Quinn seethed. He disliked strangers calling up cold to set up a meeting at night. It was all wrong. But they had his number. If it had anything to do with Deggan, he had no choice.

"My partner's wearing a brown sports coat. We'll be together at the back."

"That's nice of you to identify your partner." Quinn's voice was threatening. "This better be good."

The caller hung up.

He went upstairs to his bedroom closet. After a moment's reflection he decided not to put on his pea jacket and boots. Instead he selected a hunting jacket and some old shoes. He put a scarf around his neck inside his shirt to keep out the damp night air. After another moment's reflection he decided not to take a knife. He had not owned a gun for five years.

He walked quickly downstairs and had a quick shot of bourbon in the kitchen. He walked halfway back, slowly, and stood in the doorway to the front room. Dawn lay asleep on the couch under Rozalyn's shawl. Roz sat in the Naugahyde recliner, knitting, the needles flashing in the silver light of the TV. The TV music swelled. There were sounds of automobiles chasing each other.

"Drive carefully." She went back to her knitting. "I believe you're already legally drunk."

After twenty years of marriage they had developed a good system of signals. If he appeared wearing his jacket, she would usually not ask where he was going, or why. He was not a criminal, but as a union officer he had been in odd situations. Sometimes it was better for her not to know.

"Go on," she said brightly.

"See you later."

He drove slowly down to Twenty-fourth Street, then toward Mission. The Celtic Palace was a cop hangout. In the beginning they had apparently come from the Mission station, one of the roughest in town. The bar had gradually attracted the rougher cops from all over the City. There were frequent fights and there had been rumors of shootings.

He cruised by twice. Easy, he thought. Slowly. He could see little of the interior except dark shapes and yellow-green jukebox lights. But he had no choice.

He was glad he hadn't brought a weapon. No way could you get in a shooting beef in there. You'd never make it out alive. Even if you did, you'd spend the rest of your life in prison.

He parked at the end of the alley behind the bar. He walked around the block, entering through the front door. He paused to let his eyes get used to the darkness. The place was about half full. There were beefy-looking men of all ages dressed in windbreakers and ill-matched sports ensembles. They all gave off the dangerous vibrations of men who were armed and drinking. In these vibrations there was something vaguely Irish, a whiff of the old Irish gun-love, warfare on the border. A peasant people afraid of sex, who had made the revolver, religion, and alcohol into a way of life. There were also the women who hung out at cop bars; rugged unattractive Catholic girls prowling for husbands and a few dissolute-looking types who looked like they might be gun freaks, the kind who would ask a cop to leave his gun on when they went to bed.

The young men had short hair and moustaches and quick eyes. Men who had handled M-16s and M-60s. He spotted two older men at a back table. They were middle-aged and their faces were red with drink. One of them had on a brown sports coat.

He was being watched closely by the males in the bar. He vaguely recognized a couple of the older cops. They were plainclothes inspectors he had met around town. He deliberately did not speak to them or acknowledge their presence. Instead he went to bar and ordered bourbon and water.

Whatever was happening, several people knew about it and were waiting to see how it turned out.

"Busy night?"

The bartender rolled his eyes; the gesture was too quick and too mannered to waste on a stranger. "Don't you just know the Friday crowd would come in on Tuesday?"

"What's your secret?"

The bartender averted his eyes. "You never know with people." His smile was strained. "You never know," he repeated in falsetto.

Quinn smiled politely. "Yeah—with people."

While the drink was being made the man wearing the brown sports coat came to the bar and stood beside him without looking at him.

"Ernie," the man said to the bartender. "Came in Friday morning, Frank was on, left my fucking smokes with him. He put 'em in one of those drawers behind the bar. Take a look, huh?"

It was an ancient hustle. The premise was that someone always left their cigarettes behind the bar. Quinn had seen variations on it all over the world when he had been shipping out, including once in Hong Kong, except then the desired substance had been opium instead of tobacco. He almost offered the man a cigarette, but thought better of it. Instead he lit one for himself.

"Cheers," he said.

When he had paid for his drink, he went straight to the back table and sat down next to the man's partner. The partner looked at him sadly. In due time the man in the brown sports coat came back to the table with two fresh drinks. He was also smoking a cigarette.

"Damn filter tips," he was saying.

He handed one of the drinks to the other man. This man wore a nylon windbreaker that looked like it had been manufactured especially for off-duty cops. Both men were in their late forties or early fifties. Both were moderately drunk.

The man in the windbreaker raised a magisterial finger. "Names," he said in a voice that contained a suppressed echo of drunken laughter, "aren't going to be too important here."

The three of them sat quietly as the country-music record ended and another one came on.

"We'll see about that," Quinn said in a low and threatening voice.

The man in the windbreaker leaned forward. "This conversation. It never happened. My partner—he's my witness."

"Come on. Everybody here is your witness."

They laughed. Quinn sat looking at them. He was very good at parleying with men. What he feared were ambushes. But this—face-to-face across the table—was where he excelled. The tracking and games were over and you were staring at each other man-to-man across a cleared space, and someone had to make a move. He felt not fear but exhilaration. When men put pressure on him a steel gray fire came into his eyes and his voice became harsh and almost charismatic. He was well-known as a former boxer and had brawled in public. He thought it important that other men be reasonably apprehensive of him.

"Take it easy, Dunaway," the man in the windbreaker said. He paused to drink. As he thought of what he was about to say he began to smile. It was a strange smile. "We heard all about your talk with old Monahan down at Juvie. Not too encouraging."

Quinn shook his head. "I talked to the guy yesterday morning, and now it's all over town. Am I crazy, or what? I can't believe this."

Quinn used his voice like a whip. He could see the others flinch slightly. They thought he was talking too loud. That was what he wanted them to think.

"All I can say is, Dunaway, for a guy who's supposed to have been a Communist once, you got quite a few friends around this town."

Quinn smiled and put his arm around the man's shoulders. He pulled him slowly but powerfully toward him. The man suddenly became tense. Quinn did not take his eyes off the man in the nylon windbreaker.

"That is an insult to my intelligence." The man's face was only inches away from his. He smiled. "Want to give me a kiss?"

The man's partner decided to interpret it as a joke. "Kiss and make up—"

"Don't play around with me," Quinn said.

He released the man and they all relaxed. Now neither of the two cops were looking at him directly.

"How would you like to kill Andy Deggan?" asked the man in the windbreaker.

For the first time Quinn was really angry. He stared at him.

"How would I like to get convicted of homicide?"

"Not in this town," the cop said quickly.

He was starting to get it.

"Okay—explain," he said.

"You waste the little fucker's ass. It never gets investigated. *We can guarantee that.* It'll just be another ex-con found dead in the Tenderloin."

"It sure as hell *could* get investigated. By the DA—he has his own people. He could connect me with Deggan, because of the attack on my kid. That's a matter—" He paused. "A matter of public record."

They both began to smile triumphantly and hugely. They glanced at each other gloatingly. Apparently they had him covered.

"There *ain't* no records," the man in the brown sports coat said. "They all get pulled and destroyed. There's no way the DA can connect you with Deggan. Even if he wanted to, which he wouldn't. It wouldn't even occur to him. Deggan gets whacked out—the DA won't even know about it."

Probably Monahan was in on it in some way. Or at least knew what was going on.

The two cops were staring at the table with undisguised pleasure. They were bestowing a profound gift, so wonderful it was embarrassing. The man in the nylon windbreaker looked up shyly at him.

"How about that?" he whispered.

Quinn felt the need to push. They assumed too much. "Identify yourself," he said to the man in the windbreaker.

It was a command. Both men seemed to expect it, however.

"I'm not going to fool around with you," he told them. "I could find out who are you but I want to make it easy for me. It just so happens I've had a very rough time these last two days. I'm telling you to identify yourself, or there's going to be big trouble right here in the Celtic Palace."

The man in the nylon windbreaker took out his ID. His name was Jones. He was an inspector in Homicide.

"How many people know about this?" Quinn demanded.

"Homicide knows. Intelligence knows. They know we're going to let someone put a hole in his head." He was slurring his words slightly. "They don't know who, though."

"But everybody in this bar knows."

"They just know there's a meeting happening. They don't what about."

"Do you always have backup when you meet?" He held up his hand. "I'm not criticizing—just curious."

"At night. We heard you were a rough boy. Unpredictable."

It was their first attempt at ingratiation.

Quinn ordered another bourbon at the bar, and came back to the table. People said crazy things in bars. It could be a setup; still, from the beginning he had sensed it wasn't. Anger and intense curiosity kept him alert. He sat staring at the two men. They had finished sizing him up, and were at ease in his presence.

"Now, here's where your insurance comes in, Dunaway," the inspector named Jones said. "You do it with his own piece. The timing is up to you. It looks like he got in an argument with another punk off the street, and the gun went off."

Jones pushed a key and a napkin across the table. An address and a telephone number had been typed on the napkin.

"Listen to me. He's in a goddamn Tenderloin hotel full

of junkies, perverts, guys that fence welfare checks, you name it. You call first, on the hall telephone. Get somebody to check the door, to make sure he's not there. You go in the apartment building next door on the right—all the way up the stairs to the roof. You step across the roof to the hotel where Deggan is staying, go down the stairs to number 611 on the sixth floor. Make sure nobody sees you. Put on rubber gloves and get in his room with the key. The smart cocksucker has a stolen gun under the second floorboard from the left wall in his closet, a cheap thirty-eight. Bring some standard-velocity thirty-eight ammo in case he doesn't keep it loaded. Get a pillow and wait for the little scumbag to come home. You shoot through the pillow, up close through the heart, and you don't even have to see where the slug goes in. Remember to keep the gloves on. Bring a ski mask, just in case he has a friend along with him. You go out the same way."

The man in the brown sports coat got up. "Gen'men. I think I'll buy some smokes and get it over with. I'm tired of bumming."

He looked at his partner. It was a cue for a joke, but Jones sat looking at Quinn. The other man shrugged and ambled away toward the cigarette machine.

"I'd like to know who made this decision," Quinn said. "At least on what level."

"Forget it. It's your decision now, Dunaway."

Quinn genuinely disliked the melodramatic, at least in his dealings with men. On the other hand, he sensed he would not get an answer to his question, and that it would be a mistake to push. He picked up the key and napkin and put them in his pocket. He could always throw them away later.

"You hate him so much, Jones—why don't *you* kill

him?"

"I would, if he raped my little girl. Does Deggan have you scared?"

"No."

"Okay. What we're giving you is an opportunity. Take it or leave it. We know all about what happened to your kid."

Jones's partner returned. He was smoking happily. There was a long silence while the three men drank. Quinn went to the bar and ordered a last bourbon and water.

When he came back Jones and the other man were talking as though he didn't exist. They had apparently both been sheriff's deputies when they were much younger. This seemed a source of mutual nostalgia and amusement.

"No way could you pass the fucking test now," Jones was telling his partner. "In the old days the test was fifty percent oral, fifty percent written. You know what they say about it now. Fifty percent oral, fifty percent anal!"

Jones's partner laughed until he wheezed.

"They're squirrels over there now. Only thing we did that was funny in the old days over there was make little holes in the end of the fucking slug, little tiny holes with a knife. It was completely different then."

Down memory lane.

"You know who uses dumdum bullets now, don't you? Canarsy, is who!"

"Look—you don't have to sweat it unless he shoots you, right?"

"That's what I'm worried about!"

There was another explosion of laughter, this time from both men. They continued to talk shop and reminisce. Quinn finished his drink and stood up.

"Thanks," he said.

He drove home slowly. He was letting that part of his mind that was still lucid sort it out. He had some strong gut feelings about the things he had just heard. He allowed these feelings to rise to the surface; his best decisions were always made when gut and brain faced each other off.

Motive. That was fairly simple. Cops like Jones and the others were pride-ridden creatures; men who lived with frustration but never conquered it. Their days were spent dealing with smartasses. This made them vengeful. They would like to see Andrew Deggan get whacked out because he was a punk they hadn't been able to nail, and they were sore about it. The smarter punks in the Tenderloin would get vibrations of a setup—something the police had a hand in—and it would scare the shit out of them. That all fit.

He could see himself doing something similar if he were a cop.

Cute, doing it with Deggan's gun. Very good. You got into Deggan's room, and if the thirty-eight wasn't there, you knew something was wrong and you could take off. But if you did it with his gun, silencing it with a pillow, it would be insanely easy. And it would look like another punk off the street, just like Jones had said. They were always finding bodies in the Tenderloin hotels.

Could he trust them?

Over the years Quinn had learned that law-enforcement types were more trustworthy in the short run than were progressive and enlightened types when offering unsolicited help, although they could be skilled practitioners of the double-cross if you got them in situations requiring long-term solutions they couldn't understand, or (worse yet) crossed them first. If a cop gave you something, he usually had a simple and immediate reason for doing so. He knew what he wanted. It was the liberal, college-educated types you had to watch out for when they came bearing gifts. They were too good at fooling themselves.

His gut instinct for what was real was extremely strong. All his life he had been following it.

He was absolutely sure Jones and the other cop were on the level.

He parked his car on the street outside his house. All the lights were out except for the light in the bedroom.

He came through the darkened hall without the light. In the kitchen he turned on the light and gave himself a stiff drink. He sat down at the table. He felt he was getting there. He had been drinking before the call, thinking he might go to bed early. Now he wanted to get more than half drunk to go to sleep. Soused—that was what he wanted to get tonight. He got up angrily and poured himself another, no water this time. Crazy. But yes—he had to do it to get to sleep.

To his left was the sink. There was something wrong with it. It was full of dishes and pots from the stove. This was his job, but he had let it go the last couple of days. Now it had piled up on him. He sighed and put on an apron. *Shit*. He took a drink straight from the bottle.

Shit. He was almost staggering. The fifth was almost empty.

At least a fifth a day. More like two, some days.

He did the pots first, saving the glasses and dishes until later. Every so often he stopped to drink. The only sound in the house was the lonely clinking of the glasses. By the time he was finished he was drunker than he had been for some time.

He had some difficulty in getting up the stairs.

He looked in on Dawn. She was sleeping soundly; her breathing was shallow. Rozalyn's light was out. As he had hoped, she had given up on him and gone to sleep while he was washing the dishes.

Urinating in the bathroom, he thought of guns. He had once owned a thirty-eight revolver, but had fired it in anger in a tense moment during a strike in a neighboring county. What looked like a small crowd of people had been running at him with bats and other implements of mayhem. He had shot a couple of them in the legs. Immediately the crybabies in this particular faction had gone around saying he should have fired warning shots. For legal reasons he had been forced to throw his thirty-eight in the Pacific during a fishing trip off the Farallons.

He folded his clothes as neatly as he could. He set his glass of bourbon on the dresser, next to his wallet and pocket change. He finished the drink and crept in beside Rozalyn. She was dead to the world.

He couldn't quite make it—he wasn't quite bombed enough. He crept downstairs and found the fifth. He finished it and opened a new one. He took two deep swallows. That would do it.

He made it back upstairs and into bed again.

He couldn't remember the dreams starting. The

feeling was terror from the beginning. At first it was a
show of lights—lights from the highway at the back of his
neck, crawling across the roof of his head like cars' lights
on a ceiling. He was having the shakes, disguised as a
dream. He was too drunk to wake up. There were still no
shapes, only the dark rushing force pushing in on the
edges of his mind. A few faintly recognizable images
whipped by. Gradually the uncompromising part of him
—the hard part—took over. The terror became partly
anger. He could see now what was going on.

Their house was under attack.

The walls were transparent. The callous, the sick, the
vicious, the pathologically maimed, the animals of empty
cunning who ran the world, the smaller creatures who
infested the cities with their confusion, lies, double-
dealing, and hate—all swam around the house, peering
in and droning away in hopeless monotony with their
futile, disgusting stories. They sought not money, time,
commitment, guilt, or even attention, but fresh lives.
They wanted to suck the Dunaways dry and leave them
dead. Around them swam the parasites—the lawyers and
psychiatrists and theologians who made their fat livings
explaining why these monsters had to exist. Soon they
would swim in through the insidious TV, the Nixon-tube
where daily they were being conditioned for this moment
—when the difference between right and wrong, clear
and obscure, fact and fiction, would come to an end. The
animals who swam around his house were singing
hosannas. They could see inside and they saw how
vulnerable they were. The stupid, violent creatures and
the clever ones, monstrous and tiny alike, all worked together in the same circus of destruction. They were
launching their final attack—

He did not think of the danger Dawn was in until he heard her cry out. He was up and out of the bed almost instantly, gritting his teeth against the pain of trying to make his body work enough to see and walk. He staggered down the hall and into her room, throwing open the door so the light from the hall could flood her room. She was twisting and crying out.

"Wake up! Wake *up*—"

His hands shook helplessly, and he was drenched with sweat. He shook Dawn with unintentional roughness. He felt her go limp when the bad dream left her. Rozalyn was right behind him.

"You're *hurting* her—"

He got up and went into the bathroom and sat trembling on the edge of the bathtub. He had the shakes before. "Do your worst," he muttered. In a moment he vomited. "That's better."

Still the dense force pushed in on him.

He heard Roz opening a folding chair from the hall closet. "I'll be right here if you need me," she was telling Dawn.

"I'm okay," Dawn complained weakly.

In a half-hour the twitching in his arms and legs stopped.

He dressed quickly and slipped his keys into his pocket. He went down to the car and fired it up. He had forgotten his watch. It had to be after midnight.

He drove down to Mission and across Market. When he reached the Tenderloin his stomach twitched. It was a slow night, but even so there were two or three streetwalkers on each corner. He drove down the street where the hotel would be. It was called the Regina Hotel.

He circled the block.

There were prostitutes and raunchy-looking drag queens on the corner. Outside the Regina Hotel, a crowd of junkies nodded and dealt stuff to each other in the shadows. They were about evenly divided between Black and white. He saw no one who looked like the picture of Deggan he had seen in Monahan's office.

He continued to circle the block.

A cop friend had once told him one-half of all ex-cons arrested in northern California gave Tenderloin addresses. But it was not just a place for criminals (although it was definitely that too). It was not just a place for sexual outlaws—transsexuals and S and M enthusiasts had nicer and more fashionable places to meet in the City. It was not just a place for insane people. Insane people lived everywhere. And it was not just a place for outsiders and outcasts.

It was for those to whom violence was everything. It was the free-fire zone of San Francisco.

No one wanted to know about it.

There were always such places. Germans did not want to know about the death camps—not because the majority of those Germans were bad, but because most of them were decent. What decent person wanted to believe in death camps? Good people did not dwell on the sordid.

At the red light on the corner he rolled down his window. There was action at the hotel next to the Regina. In a first-floor window stood a Black man dressed pimp-style, angrily throwing women's clothing onto the sidewalk. Each time he threw out a handful of garments, there was a pitiful wail from an unseen woman inside the hotel.

A pale, trembling junkie wearing wraparound sunglasses rushed out and started going through the clothes. The pimp was furious.

"Shoot you *all* in the head, boy—" The pimp left the window and reappeared with a pistol. "Tear yo *ass* you don't put them clothes down."

The junkie was almost weeping. "Ain'chu thrown 'em away?"

The pimp snorted. "Don't mean a damn thing to you, sucker."

Quinn drove on by. As he passed, the pimp left the window. In his rearview mirror he saw the junkie scamper back. Some of the hangers-on around the Regina Hotel were laughing. There was no sign of police.

This was it.

"Now thas *cold,*" someone on the street whooped.

The heart of the sickness.

The Tenderloin was hell and evil and the heart of pure death. But nobody believed in any of these anymore except death.

That was enough.

He was sitting on the edge of the bed when the light turned blue in the east. Roz was asleep beside him. He went into the bathroom and rinsed his hands and face with water. Although he had lain awake all night, he did not feel tired—beating the shakes had pumped him up.

That and thinking about Deggan.

As he shaved he stared somberly at the hard familiar face in the mirror. There was steam on the glass and he had not turned on the light. His face was the color of silver. Iron mouth and jaw. Not flint—no—it was iron.

Hard gray eyes like wet metal. The full brown hair with
the wiry gray at the sides. Around the neck, dark leathery
red from the days as a rank-and-file longshoreman.
Around the nose red and puffy, but you could see the iron
underneath.

He tried to remember the picture of Deggan he had
been shown in Monahan's office. It was necessary to
remember it correctly.

As he stroked off the last strip of shaving cream, he
turned on the bathroom light. Something was wrong with
his face. It was redder and puffier than he remembered
ever having seen it. The red veins tunneling away from
his nose had swollen, and there were creases of red in his
forehead. The nose had gone bulbous and the blue
arteries at the side of his head pulsed like snakes. Why
had he not seen this before? Perhaps because he was in
the habit of shaving with the light off in the morning, in
order not to wake Rozalyn up. Perhaps because he
normally saw himself in barroom mirrors where the darkness kept you from seeing the unpleasant. It was as
though his hard honest face had gone rotten in the night.

But who did he think he was kidding? You couldn't
drink as much as he had without it showing. Wounds of
alcohol—

It was time he fought back. How?

He saw with perfect clarity that taking care of Andrew
Deggan was in some way the key. A line had been crossed.

Shortly after 6:00 A.M. he called a bartender
acquaintance on the hall telephone. While the bell rang
on the other end he sipped coffee laced with bourbon. "A

hair of the dog—"

In the gray hallway the whisper echoed lightly.

"Orran?" he asked when the receiver was picked up.

There was a pause. "What is it?"

"A friend. I have to meet with you about a little thing."

"Mmmmmmm," the acquaintance said sleepily. "Yeah —I think I know what this is. I think there's something out on the street about this."

"That's unlikely. Especially since you don't know who I am."

"I know."

"Who?"

There was silence. Quinn was not surprised. The man was a pathological liar. You couldn't expect any kind of truth from such people unless you were in a position to ask fairly detailed questions while applying pain or terror.

"Don't say it on the telephone. I'm coming right over."

He drove across Market on Van Ness. He had just showered and felt surprisingly fresh and full of energy. The man he was going to see was the owner and morning bartender of a place on lower Nob Hill. This man was a naive adventurer who liked to think of his hangout as having mob connections. In reality it was an unlikely meeting place for the criminal fringe washed up from the Tenderloin, and aging neighborhood ladies on social security.

He was also in the extremely risky business of selling guns.

"Something on the street," Quinn muttered disgustedly.

In fact there *would* be something on the street if he made a buy from this man. There was an almost

Byzantine stupidity about the criminal fringe and the people in it. The most important aspect of this was their inability to keep their mouths shut. Snitching was their lifeblood.

But it had to be done. He needed a backup gun.

He parked and entered the bar. "Orran," he shouted.

Behind the bar was a small squirrelly man drinking coffee. He began to nod as soon as he saw Quinn. "Unh-hunh!" There were no other customers. "I knew it was you!"

Quinn seated himself. "Sure."

He bought the bartender a drink. They exchanged a few pleasantries.

"What are you in the market for?" the acquaintance asked.

He told him. He needed a gun that was of sufficiently high caliber. It couldn't be registered to him, and preferably would be stolen.

"I got lots of twenty-twos."

Quinn shook his head. "No Saturday night specials."

"You could rent one."

"*Rent* one?"

The bartender explained that in some large cities it was a common practice to rent guns out. When it had been used, it was returned.

"That's an insult to my intelligence."

"Don't ask me." The acquaintance shrugged. "That's what they do."

He bought the man another drink.

"Well—I have a pretty nice little thirty-two semi-automatic."

"*Semi*automatic—?"

"Automatic," the acquaintance said. "That's what

people call 'em. Of course it's really a semiautomatic. If it was really full auto, you wouldn't have to press the trigger but once." He launched into a lecture on popular misconceptions in the field of small arms. He was by any standards a gun nut. "Everybody calls 'em automatics anyway."

"Okay, okay, an automatic."

In the middle of talking price they were interrupted. Two chain-smoking old dolls with blue-rinse hair and tote bags took up seats at the far end of the bar. Quinn and the bartender continued in the storeroom. When their negotiations were concluded Quinn was surprised to find he had enough cash with him. He had expected it to cost several hundred dollars.

"You won't be sorry," the acquaintance said. "Even the other guy—it might be better this way. Who knows?"

The gun was stashed and waiting for him in the men's room.

When he came out the old ladies were gone. "One more!" he shouted. The bartender reached for his bottle. "One more for the road."

He sat listening to the acquaintance talk about his sorry life. A few minutes passed.

"What's Andy Deggan doing these days?" he asked as he got up to go.

"Turning out fags, I guess. I saw him at Jax."

Jax was a hangout for drag queens in the Tenderloin.

"Tell him I said hello."

Outside, the world seemed new. An orange-and-white sanitation truck was hosing down the street, and from the east came the chaste and pearly gray light in which San Francisco looked best. The air was clean. He walked past a fish-and-chips place and breathed in the warm smell of deep-fried fish. His body craved protein — it was starving on the empty sugar of alcohol. He bought an order of fish and took it to the car with him.

Before every fight you needed protein.

Of course Deggan would hear of this. It was foolish to have mentioned him by name. Yet on another level he was glad Deggan would know. It was good to think of Deggan running scared.

4

Wednesday

After buying the gun he went directly to his office.

He left the gun in the trunk of his car. For a few hours
he was so busy he forgot his problem. He was surprised at
the number of people who came by the office. He enjoyed
the contact with other men and had nothing to drink. All
morning, people came in.

"You'd think it was a hiring hall," he told Mona.

Actually the hiring hall was three blocks away. His job
was not dispatching but policing the longshore contract.
But people liked Quinn and did not always come with
grievances. When they came by just to talk, he exchanged
quips and rumors with them.

Mona was happy to see him reinvigorated. "Don't
mean a damn thing to me," she insisted. "I'm just your
jive secretary."

But he could see she was pleased. "Anything you say."

"Poor mouth!"

"Ratchet-mouth!"

"You are some kind of character," she said.

"It's an elective office." Several of the men in the office
laughed. "Seriously. We're all friends here. But would
people vote for me if I didn't make a lot of noise? Raise
hell?"

Mona shook her head. "That's cynical."

"Politics," someone suggested.

He shrugged. "Exactly."

What was he really but a waterfront character to them? To Mona? He pushed the question away. He was a good trade unionist and they were his members — Mona was his friend. He did his best.

"Jive turkey."

He didn't know himself how much was an act.

"You're the one got the turkey mouth." He imitated a turkey by wagging one hand underneath his chin. "Gobble-gobble-gobble . . ."

She giggled.

"Anything you say."

He went home for lunch.

Dawn was still home from school. In the living room she and Roz argued fitfully. Dawn wished to see a popular current film about a child possessed by demons. He sat in the kitchen eating a bacon and cheese sandwich.

"No, goddamn it!" Rozalyn was saying. "Every time that damn advertisement comes on TV . . . it's so *creepy.*"

It was her nature to argue with those she cared about. Her slightly crossed blue eyes would remain puzzled and distant but always gentle. Waiting for definitive answers. Quinn was used to it.

"*Jesus,*" she said.

She was waiting for a reply. This was a game at which both she and Dawn were skilled. Dawn would be staring at the floor, or at her hands. Sometimes she appeared to read her own palms.

"Besides . . . "

There was a pause.

" . . . after what's happened to you, I don't think you *need* that kind of movie."

Quinn sighed. It was faintly ridiculous. On one level she was right—on another it sounded like Dawn was to blame. It sounded like a pitch. A hustle.

Kids wanted to probe. To see the mysteries.

"Anyway, *I* don't need that kind of movie."

That was probably why Dawn wanted to see it. A child in control and scaring the bejesus out of the adults around her.

"Come on . . . " Roz was saying.

He couldn't stay out of it. He stood up. Now he too was waiting for Dawn's answer.

"All the kids are talking about it—" she said finally.

Rozalyn snorted. "Well, if that's the only reason . . . " There was the pop of her cigarette lighter. "Look—"

"Look—" Quinn said from the kitchen.

"All right, *you* talk to her!" Rozalyn appeared at the doorway.

He paused. "Of course we should have the final say about the films she sees. She's only eleven." He brushed past Roz into the front room. Dawn sat on the couch and stared at them good-humoredly. "I don't know anything about this film except that it's a horror film. On the other hand—if she really wants to see it I don't see how we can refuse outright . . . "

" . . . without seeming overprotective." Roz stood haughtily, awaiting a reply. She clutched her cigarette at waist level, like the reins of a horse. "Isn't that what you're saying?"

"Something like that. It's something that seems—" He wished he had bourbon to loosen the words. "Seems important to avoid at this stage of our lives."

Or even the appearance of it, he thought.

"*Seems* important—"

"What if she has bad dreams?"

"She *already* has bad dreams."

He glanced at Dawn. There was the faintest trace of a smile on the bruised face. He noticed that the bruises were subsiding.

"What if the dreams get worse?"

He shrugged. Despite evidence to the contrary, he had always found it difficult to imagine anything as artificial as a movie really harming a child.

"Okay." He turned to Dawn. "If you want to see a movie real bad and it gives you bad dreams, you have no one to blame but yourself."

Dawn stared at him. "Sure."

"This is ludicrous," Rozalyn murmured.

"Maybe the way I'm expressing it. Anyway—" What was ludicrous was their raising a child. Nothing came easy for them. "You're going to miss the bargain matinee if you don't hustle. Assuming you choose the enchanting world of Walt Disney."

Dawn groaned.

"That would certainly be cheaper," Roz said.

Apparently they had talked about it all morning. Dawn groaned again.

"Okay, let's get going," Rozalyn said briskly in her who's-the-parent-here voice. "We'll discuss it on the way!"

Quinn cleared his throat. "Maybe we'd better resolve it now."

"*You're* the one who said we're late."

He shrugged. They went upstairs to gather purse and coats. Dawn dawdled on the stairs. When Roz appeared, he noticed her cigarette hand was shaking slightly.

"Nice try," she said.

In her smile was not only fear but anger.

"What do you want me to do?"

"Lay down the law. Tell her flat-out she can't see it."

"It's just a movie. And she goes back to school tomorrow."

The old formless tension was building up between them. As usual it was not so much mutual antagonism as a bittersweet but explosive fear, which ended up making them angry as an effect of something deeper. He reached awkwardly into his pants pocket for the car keys. Dawn stood near the front door watching them.

"Just a movie?" Rozalyn crushed out her cigarette.

"We can't keep the real world out."

"You're telling me."

As he handed her the keys to the Chevy, she turned to go. Their hands collided jerkily. The keys fell to the floor. They exchanged glances and hesitated; when they stooped to retrieve the keys, they collided again. He finally picked them up and stuck them awkwardly in her purse.

By this time they were laughing.

"Thank you!"

"You guys . . . " Dawn said.

"Anytime!"

They both turned toward Dawn. The door was open and Dawn was walking toward the car. She turned and waved. They waved back.

"I just don't think it's suitable . . . " Rozalyn was

murmuring.

"Of course it isn't." He sighed. "If you let them get hurt too much, they hate you. If you overprotect them, they hate you too. They have to make their own mistakes. That's the only way they can grow. Let her see the damn film if she insists."

She appeared to be searching for words. "Live and learn?"

More like walking a minefield.

He gave her thumbs-up. "Live and learn."

He thought he knew the scene about to be played out. She and Dawn would slip into the long pauses that made up their basic fighting rhythm. As they approached downtown, the traffic would make her nervous. Dawn would insist, and she would give in to her.

"As long as they live," Roz murmured.

He didn't miss a beat. "Yeah. As long as they live."

Don Richards was in their address book. He knew Richards from labor and Democratic party functions around town. He sat at the kitchen table and dialed the number. He hoped it wouldn't take a long time to get hold of him. He wanted to get back to the office.

A male voice answered sleepily. Quinn apologized for waking him up.

"I worked last night," the voice said defensively. "Yeah . . . I was just getting up anyway."

"Don Richards?"

"Who's this?"

"Quinn Dunaway. We met a couple of times."

Quinn recounted the times and places.

"*Say* now." The voice became friendlier. "Grace Dunaway's brother. You're with the longshoremen. Yeah. I remember you."

"You worked with Grace in the postal union."

"Every day for the longest time." Richards's voice had the smooth country twang common among Black men of his generation. "Hold on—okay? Got to turn on the coffee thing." He pronounced *thing* as *thang*. "Know what I mean?"

"I know." Richards had been president of the postal union. He had met Grace at the post office, and at one time lived with her. "Take your time . . . ."

He wondered if Richards knew he knew about the living together.

"You heard I got dumped?" Richards asked when he came back to the phone.

"Yeah." He grunted in commiseration. "Still on the executive board?"

"*Oh* yeah. What about you? You still president of your local?"

"*Oh* yeah."

"Full salary?"

Quinn laughed. "Sure—for what it's worth."

Richards laughed. "Sounds like my union. But it was nice. President of the local for two years—then raise, man, right back on the fucking workroom floor where I started out!"

"Hard to take."

"I heard *that*."

There was a pause.

"This is about Grace," Quinn said finally.

There was another pause. "Ohh . . . " Richards said.

Normally Quinn hated the telephone. But this was an

emergency; he had to work fast. Also the subject matter was so personal it probably couldn't compromise him. That struck him as ironic.

"You and Grace worked together in the union."

"Still do. I see her at work every so often. Technically she's still an officer in the union."

"Except she hasn't been too active lately."

Richards sighed.

"In fact she hasn't even been in to work lately."

There was another pause. Quinn disliked stalling and was surprised to find himself doing it. "Listen—she's out of her mind. Seriously. This is the worst. I think she's already hooked on something hard, and she's threatening to kill herself."

"Tell me something I ain't already heard!"

Quinn heard the anger. "Well—these things are usually temporary. I'm not so sure this one will pass so easy. Anyway, I've got to get her little boy out of here." He paused. "I understand your mother babysits Martin."

He felt the apprehension flowing back at him.

"Yeah?"

"I think maybe your mother might take Martin full-time for a few weeks. Like a foster home. You know?" There was a long silence. "I'll pay whatever she thinks is reasonable."

"I'll talk to her about her."

"Think she'll go for it?"

Again a sigh. "She needs the money all right."

"Can she handle it?"

"She can handle damn near anything." Another pause. "Can't remember if we did that before. Seems to me like this is the first time this happened since Grace had Martin—"

The telephone made it hard to know anything for sure about the other person at that moment. You could not see him or touch him. Still he had heard enough in Richards's voice to gamble. Of course with the telephone, you understood people too quickly—too quickly.

What you heard was not always what you got.

"That woman is crazy when she's like this. I'm scared of her when she gets this way." Richards seemed to want judgment or forgiveness. "Aren't you?"

"Sure."

"I guess that makes monkeys out of both of us."

"I guess it does."

Their laughter was somewhat hollow.

Quinn cleared his throat. "I'd like you to take the child to your mother's house yourself."

There was a small explosion at the other end.

"Why the hell are you calling *me?*" Richards said with unmistakable bitterness. "She's got a new old man. Let *him* handle it."

"You mean Deggan? She dumped him."

Here all the cards went on the table. By now Quinn was giving himself good odds. Richards bitterness was the tip-off.

"So what?" Richards was demanding. "Why the fuck should I get involved? You think I'm simple? Or what?"

"You stayed with her before when the drugs were too much for her. You asked her to marry you."

It was a blues voice that came back at him.

"Oh, man . . . "

He had him.

"One thing," Richards said.

"Shoot."

"What happens if she really tries to kill herself?"

"I'll have her certified. A year in a state hospital might not cure her mind, but it sure as hell might change it."

Richards hesitated. "The state hospitals are rough."

"I can't afford anything else. Can you live with that?"

The hesitation was gone. "Okay."

"Okay. Good."

He drove back to the office.

He liked Richards. Most people of sensitivity got jammed when it came to doing anything real. As a result, they went around angry at themselves and the world. Grace was like that. He was sure Richards wasn't. He could take responsibility for something too.

He parked in the lot at the foot of the pier. He left the ticket on the dash where the attendant could see it.

The world was corrupt and amoral. If you wanted to act with fairness and a personal honor you had to negotiate — but also to intervene or retaliate when anyone tried to screw you. That included family as well as strangers. It included people who didn't know how much they were hurting you as well as those who did.

He ran into Mona. She slipped her arm through his.

"That was a short lunch," she said.

He felt a pang of thirst. "You mean a dry one?"

She shrugged. "Whatever."

"Whatever."

The hardest and most necessary lesson for a man of honor to learn was there is no practical limit to the number of people who will hurt you if you let them.

Don Richards hung up the telephone.

He was a medium-tall Black man with a smooth and rather somber face. Although he was in his fifties, the lack of wrinkles in his face made him look younger. His most striking feature was his dark eyes; they were large and had the steady, liquid quality of a born preacher. In fact his speaking style was humorous and somewhat tentative. He was aware of his own vulnerability, and the vulnerability of the people around him.

He went upstairs to practice his alto sax.

His practice room was bare with peeling green paint. Taped to one wall was an old newspaper photograph of Charlie Parker. He played favorite phrases and repeated them methodically for two hours. Toward the end he was sweating and pushing out short high bop phrases without a false note. The tension in his stomach had spread to his mouth and throat. He spat out the sharp notes cleanly, as if he were spitting small pieces of metal.

He stopped and looked at the picture of Parker. *Walking around in real life and they didn't know you.*

He sat in his kitchen and drank wine for two hours. He consumed one and a half quarts of red wine and smoked his pipe until his tongue throbbed with the bite of the cheap tobacco.

At 5:00 P.M. he could no longer wait.

He sighed and got his sheepskin coat. There was no sense in putting it off. He went outside and warmed up his new pickup. There was a brisk cold breeze blowing and there were heavy blue clouds and fog above. He was glad he had on his cowboy boots and the thick coat.

He drove toward the Mission District. He talked to

himself. *No way would that woman mess with my life this time! No way!* But how the hell could you know? The thought of seeing her again made him more fearful (and more excited) then he would have thought possible.

He parked his car and walked to her door.

When he pushed the button the doorbell rang upstairs. There was a lusty toddler's yell.

He smiled. That had to be Martin.

There was a long silence. Slowly there came the shuffle of feet moving down the stairs. He had heard this slow shuffle before. When Grace was not doing a lot of drugs her step was light and nervous. When she was ripped, she walked like a robot.

Like she was already dead—

Grace opened the door as far as the chain would allow. The light was gray from the fog, but even so she squinted. She was hunched over in a wrinkled blue robe. She swayed slightly.

"Grace?"

She squinted as though seeing him through binoculars.

"I was just driving by," he said without conviction.

Her mouth was opoen as though she were seeing a vision.

"Oh yeah," she said finally.

It had happened again. Once more the tall college-educated lady had transformed herself into a barely ambulatory piece of meat—a mindless rag doll. Her gray eyes peered out from a chalkwhite face. Her hair was so matted that for a wild moment Richards thought she was going bald.

"Grace?"

Quinn had been right. This was the worst.

"Hi," she said.

She was transfixed by him. Somewhere behind the gray eyes, fireworks went off in slow motion. In a few seconds she would remember who he was. In a few more seconds she would remember his name.

"Don—" she said.

The old Grace Dunaway feelings hit him. They poured up from his gut into his chest. Much of it was pure sex. It was happening partly because of—not in spite of—her terrible appearance. That struck him as indecent. There was something wrong with a man who got hot for a woman who was losing her mind.

"Don," she repeated triumphantly.

"Chrissake woman, I KNOW my own name!"

"Okay."

She would be reasonable, even if he wouldn't.

"Don't just be standin' there—lookin' simple!"

That came out sounding more downhome than he intended. He could whip into a street riff if he had to. Usually he didn't care for heavy sounding. He tried to make the feeling tone more lighthearted.

"Looka here! You gonna let me stand out here in the street? You might could go ahead on and open the door—" He was almost begging. "Raise, woman!"

She stared at the chain that prevented her from opening the door wider. She seemed to have difficulty in understanding why it was there. "Don't you know what bad news is?" she asked him finally.

"Let me in, Gracie."

"Why should I? You'll only get hurt. That's what I'm good for. Why did you come over here? To get hurt again?"

In fact Richards feared he was a freak for certain kinds of pain. He sighed. "Just open the door."

"Why? Seriously."

A personality defect—obvious to others but not to him.

"Because if you don't, I'll kick the motherfucker down."

She unlooked the chain. He had not forgotten that the main objective at this point was simply to get into her flat. Still, he had noticed a warning tone in her voice. This time was something special.

A junkie feast.

"Did Quinn talk to you?" she asked as she moved unsteadily ahead of him up the stairs.

"Yeah."

She stopped at the top of the stairs. She tittered. "I'm sure he did."

Richards was not surprised to find all the lights out in the flat. Once while living together, they had gone on a candle binge: Grace liked candles or complete darkness when she was this high. He turned on the kitchen and living room lights. Martin sat blinking at him from a small swamp of wet magazines near the bookcase.

He was naked. In one hand was a piece of bread.

"Terrific."

The child yelled happily.

Richards walked into the bedroom and went through the dresser drawers. There was nothing that wasn't dirty or too small. He selected a pair of rubber panties and returned to the living room. Grace sat on the sofa in a state of shock from the lights being turned on.

He hoisted Martin at arms' length. He was dripping urine.

"All weh—" Martin said sadly.

"Yeah—all wet."

He set the child down and pulled on the rubber panties

over his bare bottom. There seemed to be no diapers.

"I'm taking him over to Momma's house." He paused. "Did you hear me?"

Grace was still in shock from the lights.

"Jesus God!" he muttered.

Martin dropped the piece of bread and chewed a wet copy of *Psychology Today* instead.

"You mean Martin?" Grace asked finally.

"Who else?"

"Tonight?"

"Tonight."

She seemed somewhat relieved. She did not attempt to hide the relief from him.

He picked him up and sat down with him in the easy chair. The child now understood he was the center of attention. He balled his fist and cried. This did not bother Richards. Screaming kids were nothing new to him.

Besides, Martin was the most beautiful child he had ever seen.

"He's got his own potty in the bathroom. If he wants to stay dry, he can go in there and use it like he's supposed to."

"Yeah . . . but good *Lord* woman—round about this age, you got to point it out to 'em. He shouldn't be pissing all on the floor. Round about this age, they piss in bed maybe. Not all out on the floor." It seemed important to find fault with her. Wasn't he about to take her child away? "Every kid needs *some* kind of mother—"

His own mother used to say that.

"Don't lecture."

He sighed. "Where's his stuff?"

"Most of it's already over at Beverly's."

Beverly was Richards's mother.

"How'd you know Martin was going to stay at Momma's?"

"I didn't. The stuff just gradually accumulated over there."

"Jesus."

She laughed. It seemed directed at herself yet coming from a great distance. It made him feel weary. It was unfair she should be so free. With drugs, such people were no longer earthbound. They became too free. They became dangerous.

"You want to come with me?" he asked her.

"Sure."

It came easy to her.

He called his mother and set it up.

He gathered what remained of Martin's things and stuffed them in the laundry bag. He started up Grace's Volvo and checked out the engine. His pickup ate too much gas. There was no sense in wasting money on a humbug errand like this.

Before they left Grace washed her face carefully, like a child.

"How come?" he asked her.

"I want to look good for your mother."

"Good for her, but not for me."

She had always been oddly intimidated by Beverly.

"You're just a man."

They were quiet on the way over. His mother lived in a house that she owned right off Geneva; Martin had been there many times. Surprisingly, Grace carried him on her lap. He had stopped screaming and was looking at the passing lights.

Lord only knew what emotional scene would ensue.

"You can come over anytime and see him," he said. He tried to keep the anxiety he felt out of his voice. "Any old time—"

"It's okay."

"I just want you to know that."

"Re*lax*, goddamnit."

Beverly was happy to see them. She badly needed extra money and she liked Martin besides. There was no scene. Grace handed her the child under the porch light, and turned away without a word.

She paused halfway down the walk. "How've you been?"

Beverly gave the child a squeeze. "I'mo have a wing-*dang* time wit my baby here!"

"I hope it's no imposition."

Richards guffawed. "Impo*si*tion—"

His mother was in her seventies and little could surprise her. She stood holding Martin in the lighted doorway. "Seem to me like just about *ever*-thang happen at the last minute anyways." She waved to show it was all right. "Don't mean nothing. Go on, honey."

Richards felt cheated out of the emotional scene.

"Okay," he said uncertainly to his mother.

He was too old to work himself up for nothing.

"Okay," he said to Martin.

The child was staring at Grace. At the exact moment when she got in the car, he began to cry piteously. As they pulled out, Beverly was waving his hand for him. Grace did not wave back. In her kitchen she poured wine for two. He rolled two joints.

The grass was Mexican but pleasant. It lightened their mood. Yet it was only a few minutes until she became restless again. It was time for her to do something to her body once more.

She put white pills into a spoon and teased a drop of water from the faucet. "Whites?" he asked her.

Whites were street amphetamines.

"Whites."

She hunched over the spoon, staring at it. He poured more wine for himself. She rushed into the bathroom to shoot up. "Single-minded about it, ain't you?" he shouted after her.

Presently he heard deranged laughter from within.

"I only *got* one mind."

The bathroom door slammed shut. A strained silence ensued.

He felt her probe for paydirt. At the crook of his arm he felt the tooth of the needle bite through the skin and slide into the fat rope of vein. It was as though she probed for his veins and not her own. He shuddered.

She wandered out and poured herself more wine.

She was still restless. He had seen this before. She was having trouble making veins, or the stuff wasn't kicking in the way it ought to. She was coasting in neutral.

"I would like to know what the fuck is really going down here," Richards said. "And what the fuck led up to all this happy horseshit."

"You got it." She made a vague here-I-am gesture. "What you see is what you get—"

She was halfway across the kitchen when the delayed rush caught up with her. He saw the shutters in her eyes closing in slower time. She melted back to the good time where she had been before.

"Wow—" she said.

People who loved drugs often used that word. It was easy to say. Richards considered it a punk sound. It was a white imitation of the Black *oooowheee,* which whites could never get their mouths around and make it come out sounding fit to hear.

"Oh, wow—"

She drank her glass of wine and relit a joint. She did not even bother to sit down.

"Now hurry up and do some stums," he said bitterly.

Again she disappeared into the bathroom. "I will!" she yelled through the door. He heard running water. "Thank you doctor!"

He didn't know whether she meant him or the MDs who inexplicably kept giving her prescriptions for barbiturates. "Someday those turkeys'll get caught for writing scrips for you, woman."

"They'll do it for everybody."

"It ain't right."

"In this country, people have trouble getting to sleep."

He sighed. "Uppers and downers all at once . . . " There was silence from the bathroom. "It's a trick to keep your body from knowing how much it wants smack. You know that?"

There was more giddy laughter. "That's good!"

Grace became addicted to heroin very quickly.

She came out and leaned against the sink. She motioned for her drink. She did it so abruptly he handed it to her without thinking. He remained standing.

"Does her imperial fucking majesty want anything else?"

She had just taken barbiturates and was now drinking wine. She always did this. The only way you could stop her from doing it was to knock the glass out of her hand. She stood in front of him, smirking like a schoolgirl. She wore jeans and a tight-fitting peasant blouse. Her feet were bare, and the gray of her eyes matched her skin. She grinned insolently and gave him a feathery get-along wave of the hand.

"You may go, Donald—"

Look like a schoolgirl. Standin there actin the fool.

Yeah she does, he thought—*like a schoolgirl with some kind of rich parents!*

"What is this bullcorn?"

The thinness of her face pierced him like a thorn.

"Hot child!" she said.

He stepped forward and took her into her arms. He fully expected to be rejected. He rested his arms across the back of her narrow shoulders. There was a sex rush in his belly.

He felt her smile underneath his kiss.

"Don . . . " she murmured.

To his surprise she responded.

They stood without words in the deep silence of the kitchen. Behind the soft breasts he felt the heart jump and strain like a team of mad dogs. She looked straight into his eyes. Stoned and no regrets. Inviting him to crawl through the speeding pinholes of her pupils. Perhaps they *would* crawl into each other's eyes. Maybe that happened when two people kissed. You closed your eyes and . . .

It's a world a trouble.

"It's very complicated," she said in a whisper.

He kissed her again. Once more she responded. At the moment when their lips met it occurred to him that if she had turned her head away he might have been free of her for life. So close! At the same instant he knew why he wanted to have sex. Somewhere in his mind was the childish idea that if he made love to her with enough heart and madness, he could win her away from drugs.

That too wasn't going to happen.

I got a graveyard disposition and a tombstone mind.

Or could it? No—it couldn't.

Be one mothafucka don't mind dyin—

"Jesus God, woman!" he said with feeling.

She led him to the bed. He sat down feeling very excited. Slowly but without hesitation she knelt before him and laid her head in his lap. He was amazed at her coolness.

Shit oh shit, he thought.

"For crying out loud *relax*, Don, honey," she said. She pulled his shirt out and nuzzled his stomach.

"You turn me on." He started taking his clothes off. "And it's a crying shame."

She didn't ask why. She began to take off her clothes. When she was down to her panties, she turned on the dusty FM on top of her bookcase. Over it came the soft drugged bass of a white KJAZ announcer trying to sound Black. "Don't you know why it's a crying shame?" he asked.

She had a way of leaning forward and covering her face with her hands that meant *no*. A gesture from junior high school, lost these many years and suddenly revived.

"Just guess anyway," he suggested reasonably.

She walked past him to the other side of the bed and stood looking at him as though the bed were a football field and she was about to kick off. He got a good look at her. Her thin body was as desirable as ever. She cupped both breasts with her hands. The dark red nipples looked almost purple against the gray flesh.

"Come on over and let mama do you!" she screamed.

"That shit made you say anything. Everybody tryna sound hip, ain't they?"

"Miss Ann—callin you boy!"

"Slap you side the head!" he said weakly. There was no energy left in him for sounding. By now it was all sex.

It was a crying shame because when you were young, any woman could turn you on. Then you could pick and choose. Later on, it was only a few could do it. You couldn't pick them. They might not be nice or sane or safe. But you had to go with it because that was your only shot.

When you fell for them it was double trouble. You clung to them like the sex was life itself.

He could hear the sensible side of himself preaching and carrying on. It spoke in the rhythms of his mother's speech. Against it was the counterpoint of the man in him —and of loneliness of the body so strong it was also loneliness of everything else. It made the sex so sharp in its pleasure it was almost pain.

She knelt before him, kissing his body.

"Tell me how you love me," she said. "Tell me the ways . . . "

Come on baby don't you pout!

"Ahhhh . . . do that again," he said.

Be a bad motha hubba an a water trout!

"Go on," she murmured. She paused deliberately. "Come on now . . . you can wait . . . "

First she made him feel strong and then weak as a baby. It was like she was playing with him—

"Ahhh . . . " he murmured again.

Come on man—ain nothin bad about you but your breath!

She sat beside him on the bed and pulled him toward her. She had a crazy way of moving slowly with a maniacal amphetamine coldness, and then with something like mindless frenzy. Every time she changed up on him it made him hotter.

"Come on—"

Come on man the woman got you on a string—

"Don come on—" she shrieked.

Yeah and you know she has a thing for Black men. She's using you to get at something else—maybe somebody else—

He entered her slowly.

"Come on tell me," she whispered.

She teased and talked to him always when he was inside her. As far as he knew, she never had an orgasm herself. This made him even more lustful. In this Southern boyhood he had picked up the belief that white women of quality didn't enjoy sex. That made them even more special.

He moved. It was already ecstasy.

Miss Ann! Miss Ann! the sensible voice preached. *Miss Ann and the old man!*

"Tell me about it," she said from far away.

He was an old man. But she already knew that.

"Come on sweetie tell me!"

Ain't no fool like an old fool!

But now the sex in him bubbled up from his toes and hardened into pure pleasure between his legs.

Say what? Say fuck?

"Old man!" he shouted.

Throwin' that muscle like a ten-ton truck!

"Dying . . . " she said.

She gripped him tenderly.

*Ain got nothin but death and dope and she's fresh
outta dope!*

"My God!" he said.

He wished the liquid pleasure could make her well. Its
electricity would astonish her and turn her away from
drugs forever. They would have the secret together. They
would share its power. But as the sweet and powerful
orgasn ebbed he was aware—however pleasurably—that
he was feeling it alone.

He lay exhausted and happy beside her. He could tell
by her silence that something was coming. He relished the
moment of peace.

She reached into a tangle of clothes and got two cigarettes. She lit two and handed him one. He took a deep
drag; it was delicious. He could feel her heart popping
beside him like the points in a car that had run dry of oil.

"There are just three things I want you to do for me,"
she whispered in his ear, "and you can stay here with
me . . ."

"Ah shit—" he exploded.

It was a curse and a moan at the same time. The
cigarette blew out of his mouth.

"Just *listen,* goddamn you," she whispered.

He tried weakly to crawl away. The woman is crazy, he
thought desperately. Sure enough you got a real jones for
the dizzy broad. She *told* you she was bad news. What
could you do about it? Not a damn thing!

Cover your ass and run.

She grabbed him around the waist. "I want you to
shoot for me if I can't hit the veins," she began

reasonably.

She held him in an iron grip. He could not even get enough elbowroom to smack her. She was giggling. She was holding him in such a way that her head pressed against his ribs.

"Why don't we call over a fucking needle freak from the Haight!" he yelled. "Come to the fucking house and pop you for five bucks! Under the tongue! Between the motherfucking toes!" He paused to get his breath. "Don't you think I know that shit? I *done* that shit! I don't need it! Don't nobody need it!"

What had she done to him to make so weak?

"And I want you to make some connections over in Berkeley." Her voice was slightly muffled but unwavering. "Smack. You can have some."

Paying him no mind whatsoever.

"You seen worse," he murmured to himself. "So much fucking worse. This ain't nothing . . . "

"And I need some help with Quinn."

He lay completely beaten. After a moment he became aware of the need to get his head around something solid He had long had the superstitious dread that Grace could make him crazy. He needed contact with the world beyond to keep his sanity.

"Help with Quinn?" He raised himself weakly on one elbow. She still held him. "What the hell are you talking about?"

"There's a rumor going around. I don't know what it is yet. It's something about Quinn. I don't want him to get hurt."

"What do you want me to do?"

"I don't know yet. Stay with me."

He sensed immediately one part of it. Deggan had

found some way to work on her. Without knowing it, she would try to protect him. He was filled with fury at Deggan. That scumbag! He had been hip to that mangy dickhead's scuffle right from the start. Oddly, he felt no anger toward Grace. She had a way of going so far you just didn't care anymore.

"Well!" she said brightly. "Now! You go down to the store and get the candles. I'll put on the special dress. I'll be Miss Ann when you get back, and you can be . . . you know."

He moaned and turned away from her. Crazy people always wanted one more thing. It never stopped.

"It's *camp*," she explained. "It's a cliché, but we *know* it. That makes it okay."

She put a record on the record player. It was someone singing in a foreign language. The sound was distant and scratchy.

"What the hell is *that?*"

"Lotte Lenya. It's in German."

"Can you understand that stuff?"

"Oh, yes." She pirouetted merrily. "I studied it in college. That stuff—"

You had to admit the woman was interesting.

She sang with the second verse. " . . . liegt ein toter . . . "

Some kind of second childhood. For real.

" . . . *Mann am Strand* . . . "

But what a price.

Rozalyn watched TV in the living room. There was the sound of recorded laughter. In the hall Quinn called Grace's apartment. The receiver was picked up. There was silence at the other end.

"Hello?"

"Who is this?"

"Somebody's brother."

"Martin is okay," Richards said after a pause. "He's over at my mother's."

"Good. How is Grace?"

Richards sighed. "What can I say?"

"Are you staying with her?"

Another pause. "Probably."

Quinn thanked him and hung up. He decided to drive over and drop in cold. He needed to talk to Richards. If he mentioned it over the phone, Richards might put him off.

If Richards didn't know his style he soon would.

He walked down the hall and took a corduroy jacket out of the closet. He put it on and stood at the living room door. Roz looked up abruptly. She was still jumpy from the film that afternoon. The TV laugh track roared laughter. She jumped.

She saw he had his coat on. "I was counting on having you around tonight."

"I won't be long."

He drove to Grace's place. At first he thought her lights were off. When he parked and got out of his car he saw weak yellow light coming from somewhere. There was a candle burning in the window.

Candlelight.

When he rang, Richards answered the door. He wore nothing but pants and cowboy boots. He was smoking a cigarette, squinting in the smoke. Quinn thought he heard Grace's giggle in the background.

"Quinn?"

His voice was not unfriendly, but simply tired.

Quinn jerked his head toward the lights on Twenty-fourth Street. "Let me buy you a drink at the place down the street?"

Richards went back upstairs and said something to Grace. When he came back he had put on a shirt and jacket. He threw away his smoke.

"Remind me to buy more," he said.

They walked to the Latino bar on the corner. At the sight of an Anglo and a Black man, the customers and bartender looked uneasy. That's too damn bad, Quinn thought. The only other bar within walking distance was a redneck joint.

They ordered their drinks. Quinn had a double bourbon.

"Last time I saw you," Quinn said, "you were smoking a pipe."

"I smoke everything when I'm with her."

They drank.

"Don't know why you're taking the trouble on yourself."

Richards appeared mildly scandalized. "It's my problem."

"Still. You take a problem on yourself—you have a reason."

"Even if you *don't* have a reason," Richards speculated, "it's *still* your fault."

"Either way, you deserve what you get."

"I heard *that.*"

Richards seemed to relax. They would understand each other.

"Look—I think you staying with her is a big break for her."

Richards took a checkered tobacco pouch and pipe out of his shirt pocket. Quinn was glad to see this. Pipes were the playthings of human owls, people who used strategy.

"Let me tell you something about Grace—" Richards said. "Something I know about."

"You may not know as much about her as you think you do."

"I know a couple of things. She said some things tonight."

This was what Quinn had come for. His gut told him something would get said or in some way communicated to Richards; and he would have to have some idea of what it was.

"Okay," Quinn said. "Tell me something you know about Grace that I don't know. That I need to know."

"Deggan is working on her. She has a jones for the dude."

"A what?"

"A *jones*," Richards said patiently. "He has a hold on her. It's something like . . . well, like a pimp will whup the shit out of his old lady, yet she comes running back. It's like somebody could put a spell on you. Mess with your mind over a long distance. It's a mind game. Dude like Deggan will try to game her off on somebody else."

"How does he run the game?"

"At first he was calling her up and hanging up before she could say anything. She knew it was him. You know?"

Quinn nodded. The caller who hung up as soon as you picked up the receiver was taking the first step toward a death threat. It was an attempt to scare somebody with a minimum of effort. In the criminal world, such tactics were essential to the game plan.

"Is that all?"

"No, the last couple of days he's been calling her up and telling her things, telling her all kinds of trash. Some plot to snuff him that he heard about on the street. He says you're behind it."

"What's Grace say?"

"That she's afraid you'll get hurt. She wants me to talk you into keeping out of it."

"How do you read that?"

"That she's trying to protect you — but that she's trying to protect Deggan at the same time." Richards snorted. "That little maggot."

"Deggan calls up — he pumps her for information? About me?"

Richards nodded.

"And anything you tell her about me will get back to Deggan."

Another nod.

"Okay," Quinn said. "We run the same goddamn game on him. Anything she gets about Deggan's situation that she tells you — you let me know right away. Call me up at the office and we can meet somewhere. Okay?"

Richards nodded enthusiastically. "I haven't got a chance with that cocksucker around."

"What does that mean?"

"Just helping."

Quinn thought: *so he believes the rumor.* Fuck it. He stared into the dark bar mirror. Even in its considerable darkness, he could see the red flesh growing around his nose.

Ripeness was all.

"I could go back now and she could be laying there stone dead," Richards was murmuring angrily.

He bought cigarettes from the machine. They finished

their drinks and started back.

"Will you be going to work?" Quinn asked as they walked.

"Can't—not with her the way she is. I'll take a couple of weeks' sick leave."

They shook hands near Quinn's car.

"I'm not coming in," Quinn said. "Remember what I said."

"Yeah."

He had to turn his Chevy around in a driveway to get back on the through-street that would take him home. As he did so, he saw Grace standing in the window beside the candle. She was wearing a full-length dress or gown that appeared to have frills. It was outrageous—like a costume for some kind of amateur theatrical production. It made him furious. He knew she was standing there so he would see her. She waved gaily as he passed.

At home Dawn was having trouble getting to sleep. Roz prowled the kitchen and living room. Her arms were folded stiffly across her chest. He knew without asking what the trouble was. Even before the rape, Rozalyn had always felt bad when Dawn couldn't sleep.

"It's that goddamn movie."

"Take it easy," he told her. "Relax."

"Why should I?"

"She'll hear you marching around down here."

She lit a cigarette. She threw the cheap lighter down on the kitchen table. It made a loud cracking sound and skidded off. "If I relaxed the way you do, I'd be passed out drunk half the time!"

"Then walk around the block."

It was most unlike her to talk about his drinking. From the living room he could already hear her murmuring apologies. "Quinn, I'm sorry—"

He poured a drink. He wasn't quite ready to forgive her.

"Go on. Take a hike."

After finishing the drink he went upstairs. He took care to tiptoe in case she had already fallen asleep. He stood at the door of her room. He was mildly shocked to find her chewing bubble gum.

"I thought you were supposed to be suffering from insomnia."

"What's that?" She blew a bubble.

"That's when you can't get to sleep."

She popped the pink bubble and reinserted it in her mouth. "Yeah," she said noncommittally.

"Then you shouldn't be chewing that bubble gum."

She pointed at the newer and better bubble she was blowing. It prevented her from communicating with him.

He put out his hand palm-up and did a Looney Tunes sign-off. "Bleowp-bleowp-bleowp th-th-that's *all* folks!"

She popped the bubble and resignedly put the wad of gum in his hand. If he was cool, she was even cooler. She did not look at him directly.

"Now," he said. "About the movie . . . "

She wrinkled her nose.

"Yuck."

"Did it scare you?"

"It was gross." She frowned. "But neat."

She wasn't giving him enough clues.

"People go to scary movies because they like to be scared. If you don't like being scared, don't go to that kind of movie again."

She nodded. He thought he heard the creak of a stair. That would be Roz, listening to them. He smiled—how idiotic they must appear to Dawn. Still there must be something more he should say about the film.

"Well—" He stood up. "Try to get to sleep."

She shrugged to tell him it was all right.

"Bye," she said without looking at him.

He stood in the doorway looking at her. So frail. In the shadows, the bruises and blackened eyes were hardly noticeable.

He went downstairs to the kitchen. He threw the gum in the garbage and made himself another drink. He felt very tired. In the past he had used alcohol as a defense against fatigue, and it had worked; now it was failing him. He was drinking too much of it. Also Rozalyn was making him tired the way no one else could.

It came with love.

"I'm sorry what I said before," Roz called from the living room.

"Come on in the kitchen and have some coffee."

She came to the kitchen door. "Too close to bedtime."

It occurred to him that they had had no sex since the rape. When Rozalyn was tense it was no good for her. Even before that the alcohol had taken the edge off it for him too.

"Come on in and sit down anyway. Come on."

She sat down. Although she appeared calmer, she continued to chain-smoke.

"If you say 'I told you so' about the movie, I'll bust your jaw."

She extended her middle finger. "I told you so."

They laughed. That took some of the tension out of

them. Still, he could feel her hurting. It always affected him too, eventually—except he felt anger toward her as well as fear of the unknown.

"Tell me about it."

She narrowed her eyes and blew smoke. "There was this one scene—it really scared me." He smiled. He was glad she admitted her fear. "They had the lighting set up to make everything look strange. It was eerie. The camera came in slowly. There was no music. It looked just like an ordinary living room—but you could tell something was . . . *wrong.*"

He nodded. "Like right before the shakes . . . "

She could not know personally what the shakes felt like—or right before, either. But they had been married twenty years. You could often know what the other person was thinking, and know sometimes what they were feeling as well. Sometimes such intimacy worked for you —other times it worked against you. There was no doubt it could make you stronger. Also it could make you more vulnerable.

She took his hand. "Yes."

He looked down into his glass of bourbon and water. " . . . or maybe something like they say it feels right before an epilepsy attack—"

She squeezed his hand. "That too."

It came with love.

Richards lay beside Grace watching her sleep. On her face was the junkie peace of the dead. Her gaunt Adam's apple moved once or twice; her pale lips pursed as if she dreamt of drinking or kisses. She had a small stash of heroin and had shot it. He was almost sure she had done more barbiturates too. Her breathing was very shallow.

If she stopped breathing Richards intended to call the fire department, then give her artificial respiration. He had done this once before.

"Goddamnit," he murmured.

This time he would do it more slowly. Not because he wanted to see her die — it was just each time you did it you were a little less excited about it.

It became a habit.

Maybe I ought to keep a fucking respirator at the house, Richards thought. *Make the dizzy broad carry it on her back.*

They both lay on top of the covers. They were both naked. He lit a cigarette and lay propped up against a pillow, watching her. Her face was set in childish drooling open-mouthed sleep; the features themselves were deep into middle age. There was much gray in the hair, and the face was so white it looked dead. Dead — already dead — there was no other word for it. Yet there was that curious innocence. The sex was so pleasurable, so beautiful. You could know it was a hustle on one level, and love it on another. It had something to do with that odd innocence . . . that the woman really couldn't help herself.

And of course that she was white.

She had a jones for Black men herself. Not always — but often enough. A real bimbo. A Freedom Fucker. Jezebel. Ofay Chick. Yeah — fool for black meat!

He let the words carry him back to Harlem of the 1940s.

His mind had been blown when he first came up from the South. Every night the bop greats blew somewhere in Harlem. Besides the bop kingdom, he had invaded and become a peripheral member of a Communist Party publishing and theater front group. This circle was fairly interracial. White women! White women who were Jewish! White women sleeping with Black men! White women living in Harlem!

He had never really recovered from the electric shock of seeing a well-known musician enter the Cotton Club with a beautiful blonde on his arm. She had had blonde hair down to her waist—some kind of Scandinavian princess.

Forbidden fruit!

Afterward he was in and out of the army and had seen the bowling alley of Korea. He had married and seen his wife run off with his children and another man. He knew drugs and women and had left hard drugs far behind. He was reasonably content and somewhat surprised to be alive. Yet nothing could match those first few years when not only his world was new, but Harlem itself was a new world.

That was what Grace brought back—that taste of youth. Yet mingled in it was also the taste of death. She stood with her feet in two worlds; she had the power to bring him to the threshold of either or both. She was dangerous. She hurt others beside herself. Yet it was intoxicating beyond all drugs.

He kissed her forehead. Maybe he could stop her from hurting too many people this time around . . . .

Again he rambled back in time. He remembered a white woman he had known in 1943. Of course that was Harlem before the Muslims and other nationalist groups made a world of trouble for the whites. Actually he had always preferred an interracial scene. Richards believed the greatest mistake of Black jazzmen had been to chase away the whites. They had all the fucking *money* for shit sake! Now the white kids were spending all their money on rock.

And where was jazz now? Nowhere, baby!

He was glad Quinn hadn't asked him about getting dumped by his union. Actually, it had happened because he was seeing Grace. This was during a period when she was fairly sane. He had tried to keep it a secret, but it must have been fairly obvious because a clever opponent in union politics had started a rumor. By the time it went around the grapevine a couple of times it came down among the Black membership that he was a Tom. It had been a close election, but the rumor mill had been just enough to tip it.

Of course Grace never suspected.

Goddamn! Richards thought. Goddamn the Graces of the world—so smart about events ten thousand miles away, so blind to catastrophes affecting those closest to them! Goddamn also the old women who sat at the center of every Black grapevine, weaving their tales and lies and low-life gossip!

Were they not hustlers in the same scam?

He wondered if Quinn had heard the details of the election in his union. Probably—he was apparently on top of a lot of things around town. Quinn Dunaway had a big rep with San Francisco Blacks (including most of the civil rights heavies) because he was with the longshore-men.

It was easy to get a rep with Blacks if you were white. If you were Black, you couldn't do the first thing right as far as they were concerned.

He wished Grace would wake up so they could have sex again.

The telephone rang. He picked up the receiver without getting out of bed. "Uuh hunh?" he said.

There was an ominous silence.

"Eehhhh blood!"

Richards felt the skin along his spine stiffen like hackles. " . . . get back, Deggan!" he choked out.

Of course. He should have kept his mouth shut. He should have made Deggan say the first word.

"*Daawg*, man!"

A proficient white imitation of a Black voice. Signifying he knew to whom he was speaking.

Richards lost his cool.

"You come around here—sumpn bad happen a you!"

"Balls a shit—ain't you a jive motherfucker?"

"Got sumpn here for you!"

"You know how to use it?"

"Why don't you come on around and find out?"

Richards hung up.

He lit a fresh cigarette and sat on the edge of the bed, smoking. He glanced at Grace. She hadn't stirred once.

Depressing.

His sound had been very weak. That's why he had hung up. No matter how bad he was, you couldn't let yourself get capped in any way when you rapped to a white guy. If it came to that you had to sound fearsome.

Deggan had been in the joint, and had picked up on all that signifying and sounding horseshit.

Richards felt old and inadequate. That made him angrier than he would have thought possible.

Quinn Dunaway stood washing dishes in his kitchen. Rozalyn had already gone upstairs. He finished the drink he had been working on and began washing pots. He was not yet ready for the next drink. First he wanted to do his exercises.

When he had washed the last of the soapy water down the drain, he went upstairs to the basement. He turned on the lights. In this part of the basement were shelves on one side. On the other three he had put cheap insulated siding and painted it white. There was a punching bag in one corner and a tumbling mat. There were various weights: leg weights, wrist weights, barbells. On a nail hung a T-shirt and a jump rope.

He took off his shirt and put on the T-shirt.

On the far wall was a full-length mirror like those at the downtown gyms. In it he checked out his stomach. He would have to work on that tonight. Tonight was the night for freehand exercises—respiration and stamina, blood circulation, general fitness, the gut. He spent a lot of time on the gut. Other nights he worked muscle tissue in the legs and arms.

He did a hundred push-ups in sets of ten and fifteen. Each set of ten he did on his knuckles. There was no pain —he had huge calluses on the first two knuckles of either hand from twenty-eight years of doing this exercise. The nerves were dead.

He did one hundred and fifty sit-ups in sets of twenty-five. By now he was enjoying the sweat and bother of it. His hair was completely wet. After the push-ups he did stretching exercises to loosen the legs. He could touch the damp concrete easily with his palms without bending his legs. He did neck and stomach isometrics. He watched himself in the mirror as he pushed his stomach in and out. He did seventy-five push-ups with his legs bent and seventy-five leg stretches from chest to floor. He did a hundred fast body twists for the oblique muscles at either side of the stomach. If the obliques were developed, the hooks to the body couldn't hurt you. His obliques were lean and powerful as biceps.

He took off the T-shirt. His hairy upper body still had the V shape of his youth. He ran in place, watching his stomach. The gut jiggled ever so slightly. He practiced tightening it while he ran. Afterward he went down on the mat for the next stomach exercise—this one for the lower belly. He put on ten-pound ankle weights and held his legs six inches above the floor for a full minute. He was panting at the end of the minute. He did it once more for thirty seconds. At the end of the exercise he was feeling pure pain. During his boxing days he had been able to hold his weighted feet six inches off the floor for as long as four minutes. He had won bets with this skill. He thought he could still do two minutes if he had to—but he wouldn't want to bet on it.

He was feeling good. He was now ready for the last part. He stood in front of the mirror and took a deep breath. He slowly exhaled and concentrated on sucking his stomach inward as tightly as he could and then pushing his rib cage upward with great force. He counted slowly to ten and relaxed. The gut was hard as stone and marbled into a perfect network. Still, it required great concentration to make the separate muscles push upward at the same moment. At the end of a single set of ten most of the muscles in his body were pushing up. It was an aikido exercise he had learned in Hong Kong.

He didn't want to use the bag because he thought its muffled stutter might bother Rozalyn or Dawn. Instead he concluded by working out for ten minutes with the jump rope. He pushed himself hard. Regularly expose the heart to stress for short periods, and you ended up with a stronger heart. The heart was a muscle like any other.

When he had finished he went upstairs and poured himself straight bourbon. He weakened it with water and set it on the sideboard. He took down a bottle of desiccated beef liver and poured twenty grams in his blender. He added a teaspoon of edible bone meal and a gram of sodiuim ascorbate for the chill of the basement. He mixed it with water and drank it down. He could feel the protein jump into his bloodstream.

He sat at the table, drinking and watching the lights of Alameda.

The exercises were old friends. It was mind over matter. He rarely exercised less than five times a week, and when he did he pushed himself. It was very important. There were two places a man went soft — the gut and the face. If you let your gut hang out it was a sign you were getting old and lazy. Worse — it was a signal to younger men that they could start moving in on you. Of course, it was the same with the face.

Now that his face was going, it was more important than ever to keep the gut hard. With all the drinking his gut would have gone soft on him long ago without the exercises. It was essential to keep them up. For this reason one of his secret fears was of a long and debilitating illness or injury that would prevent him from working out. He would come out of that suddenly an old man. It was horrible to think of.

Forty-five was a dangerous age — particularly in union politics. You weren't old enough to be some kind of elder statesman or be stuck away in a research department somewhere. Yet you were vulnerable because you weren't as young or as quick as you once had been. Younger men sniffed him out when they saw the red flesh around the W. C. Fields nose, searching for weaknesses. They smelled death and defeat. The thrill of blood was on them. All during those ten critical years between forty-five and fifty-five, you had to be constantly on your guard. He had seen this in the lives of other men.

And people wondered why women lived longer.

He could feel his strength diminishing every day. It was only the discipline of twenty-eight years that kept him doing the exercises. They required a major concentration of stamina and effort. But they were necessary. All these years he had done them—thirty or forty intense minutes a day, perfectly geared to his body and its survival. Along with bourbon and his wife they held him together.

Now he was being challenged by the Enemy itself. He took his drink into the living room and passed out on the couch.

It was well after midnight when the telephone rang. As he plunged upward out of sleep, he knew immediately who it was and what it was for—he could almost hear it in the ringing itself. He made sure not to hurry. He walked barefooted to the hall telephone. His crotch was itchy, as it usually was when he fell asleep with his pants on. He stood scratching himself and staring at the telephone.

You couldn't pretend you didn't hear it.

He picked up the receiver. There were bar sounds or sounds of talking and laughing. He thought he heard soft breathing.

He waited.

Click.

The dial tone.

If Roz asked who it was he would say *wrong number*.

If Dawn asked he would say nothing.

He thought this because he was suddenly aware they were both awake. That surprised him. While he thought this the telephone rang again. He picked up the receiver.

Click.

The dial tone.

He left the receiver off the hook and lay on the couch staring at the ceiling. **The house was quiet.**

5

Thursday

Quinn woke at dawn.

He shaved and showered quickly. He dressed quietly so as not to awaken Rozalyn. He had a cup of coffee and bourbon in the kitchen, and took another with him in the car. As he left he heard Roz stirring.

The light was purple blue with red in the east. All along the Embarcadero the little cafés were open. There was very little breeze on the Bay and already a few gulls were wheeling at the end of the pier next to his office. When he got out of his car in the parking lot, he saw someone was out there fishing.

He sat at his desk drinking vodka. The office was dark and quite damp. The waves slapped softly at the pilings below. He turned on the floor heater and did some paperwork.

Fishing—that was a nice idea. How long had it been? Too damn long. He liked the Sacramento Delta. Rozalyn liked to fish too. Dawn didn't—she found the idea disgusting; so gradually they had stopped doing it. But it was relaxing. It had to do with the water—

No. Don't even think about running away.

First came the battle. At noon he locked the door and left.

He was meeting a friend who was in City government. They got together from time to time to exchange rumors and information and because they enjoyed each other's company. They usually met at an Embarcadero bar under the freeway. It was run-down and not readily visible from the street.

He angled across the parking lot. The day was bright and clear.

Today there was something special he wanted his friend to find out for him. It had to do with Deggan. He hunched his shoulder and spat.

His friend was already there. He was sitting at the bar, carrying on with Old Escobar the bartender. They were reading a Xerox copy of doggerel of the kind passed around by working-class males and politicians. "Here you go—pluralism in America!"

He handed it to Quinn.

> *Sunday morning is the best time to be on the freeways in California—*
> *The Catholics are in church*
> *The Protestants are still asleep*
> *The Jews are in Palm Springs*
> *The Italians are making wine*
> *The Indians are still on the reservation*
> *The Chinese are stuffing fortune cookies*
> *The Blacks are all in jail*
>
> *And the Mexicans can't get their cars started!*

Quinn handed it back to him. "You want a sandwich?"
The friend laughed. "In this place?" He drew his hand off the bar and shook it like he had been swimming in

garbage. "This place—you can't open the door without getting trampled by the bugs!"

As always Old Escobar said nothing.

"Well—you're a dirty old man. Aren't you?"

"Not that way."

The friend was a stocky exuberant Italian-American in his late forties. Like Quinn, he had patches of red in his face. This man had once worked out of the mayor's office. He had solicited Quinn's advice on some labor matters.

They helped each other.

"Nutted up!" his friend was saying. "Just you let them once get on the Big Tit—you can't talk to them. Anybody! Gimme gimme gimme. Talk about tunnel vision—"

From experience Quinn knew he spoke of City Hall.

"What else is new?"

Today the friend was unusually keyed up. He expressed this by outbursts of exuberance alternating with moody silences. Quinn had seen this before. "I didn't say it was new," the friend said. "I didn't even say it was wrong. I'm saying it's the wrong people making the money."

Quinn laughed. Old Escobar arrived with his drink.

"Sure you don't want a sandwich?"

The friend was suddenly sullen. "You heard me. Who wants a fucking disease?"

Quinn winked at the bartender. "Goddamn knife-thrower. It all depends on what kind of disease you want. You get one here—at least it's not the kind that makes your cock fall off."

They usually began their meetings with an exchange of insults.

"That kind of disease ain't prevalent in my circles," the

friend said after a long pause.

Quinn motioned for two sandwiches. "That's because you guys on the level of municipal government only use your dicks to piss with."

"You can kiss mine if you buy me a drink!"

"Whyn't you bend over and let me make a boy outta you, the way they do at City Hall?"

Several patrons laughed. There were no women present. The male patrons were used to the insults and enjoyed them. They were mainly retired seamen.

The friend stared at his drink. "Filthy old man! Dirty filthy old man." Laughter slowly filled every part of his face like a soft explosion. "Buy me a drink!"

Quinn lit a cigarette. "The knifethrower is outta money."

"I got more money than you got trouble."

"Well—money talks and bullshit walks. Ask old Escobar there."

"My good looks ain't good enough?"

"If good looks could get you a trip to the moon, you wouldn't ge ten feet off the ground." Quinn turned to the other patrons. "The poor bastard is down there at that City Hall zoo getting reamed every day by those uncouth bastards, and he thinks it's because of his good looks! It's a fringe benefit—haven't you figured that out yet?"

"Fuck you nimrod!"

"*Fuck* you? I ain't even kissed you yet!"

There was more appreciative laughter. Quinn bought his friend a drink and Old Escobar brought sandwiches. Now that the insult part of their meeting was over, they could get down to more substantive matters. They went to a booth at the back and spoke in low voices.

An old man in the booth next to them got up and went to the bar.

"Somebody at Hunter's Point is fucking up," Quinn said.

"Who?"

"Somebody we both know. A contractor. Somebody who thinks he's a contractor. He's not acting sensibly."

"Shit."

They discussed several things going on around town. They stayed away from names. Quinn was careful not to ask his friend too much. The friend did not currently possess the access he had once had—as a consequence he was necessarily more jealous of his remaining store of information.

There was a lull in the conversation. The friend raised his eyebrows.

"Something on your mind? On the phone you said there was something special . . . "

Quinn took a drink. Now was the time.

"Guy name of Jones," he said. "An inspector in Homicide. You know him?"

The friend paused. "I know *of* him."

Quinn was watching his friend's face. There was no reaction when he mentioned Jones's name. "What?"

"Kind of a big shot. Depends on who you talk to. What do you want to know? Specifically?"

"If he can be trusted completely. Has he ever pulled any kind of switch or hustle on anybody? Are there any stories of him ever doing anything like that?"

"I can check it out."

"I'd appreciate that."

"Okay if I call you at the office?"

Quinn nodded. "Just don't use names."

The friend put the Xerox copy of doggerel in his pocket. As he did so he glanced away. For a fraction of a second Quinn caught an unfamiliar expression going across his face. Or thought he did.

"These days . . . " the friend said. "You can't be too careful."

The friend was giving off vibrations he couldn't read.

"How's that?"

"Every which way."

"Does it have to do with Jones?"

The friend looked away again. "It's . . . " He obviously didn't want to talk. "I don't know. Something in passing. Anyway I'll find out what you want to know."

It had to do with fear. "You talking about me when you say be careful?" Quinn asked in a low voice.

"Everybody wants to be careful."

Quinn heard the warning. He shrugged. "What-a you got? I give-a you the Vaseline. You no give-a to Quinn!" The friend rattled the ice in his glass. "Don't worry. I won't pump you."

"That's good. You know how I feel about that. What's mine to give."

"I know. Real well. Anything I can do for you?"

The friend stood up. He was shrugging. He was starting to look philosophical. Whatever had bothered him before had passed.

"I was gonna say 'take care of yourself,' but what the fuck. I know it won't do any good. So I won't." He paused. "We're gonna talk together next time about I'm gonna need that favor come next month?"

"Just about anything," Quinn said. "Just about anytime."

They never asked each other for unreasonable favors.

The friend stood looking at his unfinished drink. He seized it suddenly and finished it with three quick swallows. He prodded Quinn's shoulder with two stiff fingers; his eyes watered from the ice he had swallowed.

"Thanks."

"Help each other."

"It's appreciated."

The friend buttoned the coat of his expensive suit. As he walked the length of the bar Old Escobar smiled and nodded. The friend laughed and thumped the bar once with his fist. At the door the friend turned and extended his middle finger.

Quinn waved.

A big kid. But unlike most City Hall hangers-on, he would rather tell you nothing than something false. Quinn thought that remarkable. Furthermore the man was loyal and close-mouthed about friends. The best thing about patronage was the loyalty it bred.

Maybe the good things always had to come as a by-product of something else. Most people were interested not in loyalty or truth, but in power and money.

And of course diversion.

Quinn set out for a mom-and-pop grocery three blocks away where he could buy fresh fruit. He was halfway there and enjoying himself in the sunshine when he became aware of a young man following him. He had quick intelligent eyes and long hair; he moved with the grace of someone in excellent physical shape. Quinn felt his adrenaline starting to pump. He was already quite angry and willing to take it out on anybody who crossed him. Also he hated people following him.

Too many people had followed him since the McCarthy days. Whenever possible he took it personally.

Nail the cocksuckers when they're out in the open.

He stopped dead in his tracks and turned around. The young guy was bearded and dressed in a coarse Mexican sarape, tie-dyed T-shirt, and flared purple pants. He stopped a few feet behind Quinn and stared at him steadily. Quinn saw he wore engineer boots of the kind favored by bikers. There was something subtly wrong with the way he was dressed—he was trying too hard. The result was a mixture of styles that looked counterfeit.

He stood a few feet back. Quinn took a step toward him.

"Come here."

The young man continued to eye him coolly. His biceps were well developed and suntanned dark brown. Tennis? Weekend basketball?

"Quinn Dunaway?"

Finally it was the quick days that made him some kind of cop.

"I'm gonna break your arm," Quinn said in a conversational voice.

The young man stepped back smoothly so Quinn could not get a grip on him. He hastened to pull out some ID. He had not taken his eyes off Quinn's face. "Thomasson. Narcotics."

He took a good look. "Thank you."

The ID was good.

"I have to talk to you," Thomasson said.

He couldn't be more than twenty-five or twenty-six. Quinn decided to push. It was necessary to see his reaction. He turned around and walked.

"Go fuck yourself. I don't borrow trouble."

Thomasson followed patiently at a three-foot distance. He began to utter entreaties of various kinds. Quinn stopped and stood staring at him. He was putting up no front at all. Perhaps that was part of his strategy.

"I really have to talk to you," Thomasson said. He was speaking in a low voice. He wasn't quite begging yet. "Come on. We can sit down on one of the benches over on the mall. Please."

Quinn shook his head. Mona would be sitting in that particular mall, eating her lunch. He didn't want Mona to see him with anybody except union members at this point.

"We'll walk to a store. You make this good."

They walked a few steps in silence.

"I want to ask you a favor," Thomasson said. "It has to do with Andy Deggan. I want you to lay off him for a month. Whatever it is between you and him. Just a month. After that—you can do anything."

Quinn cursed under his breath.

"He's my snitch on a couple of heroin deals," Thomasson explained. An angry and somewhat youthful excitement took over. "These deals are big. Nobody knows he's working for me. If I lose him now, four months of work go down the toilet!"

They were silent as a passerby brushed past. Quinn once again cursed softly. When he stopped he had his questions ready.

"You say he's your boy. Does that mean he's working off a case for you? That you actually went out and made against him?"

Thomasson's stride slowed perceptibly. Uncertainty and an unpleasant meanness flickered across his bearded face. "I didn't bust him. I didn't have to."

"On what?"

"Another heroin deal."

"Whose idea was it that he should be your snitch?"

"His."

"What else did he do for you?"

"He saved my life. Strange as that may sound."

"You're an asshole. If he saved your life, he did it for a reason. He was probably about to get killed himself. He's playing you off on me. How long have you been a cop?"

"One year on the street." At first he did not seem affected by the insult. But as they crossed a street he flexed his arm while clenching and unclenching his right fist. "They put me working dope because they thought I could look like a hippie . . . . "

Quinn detected a note of resentment. He wanted to be a street soldier—instead they made him an animal trainer in the City drug zoo.

"Deggan and people like him don't know what the truth is." Quinn lit a cigarette. "You have to lay it on the line to them. If you don't, you end up working for them instead of the other way around."

They reached the grocery store. Quinn bought an apple while Thomasson lounged around outside. A Latino stared at his sarape with loathing. He sighed like someone too bored to care.

Quinn emerged and they started back.

"Where did you get the idea I wanted to hurt Deggan?"

"From him."

"How much did you hear from anyone else?"

"Nothing."

He stopped and stared at him. Thomasson had put on dark glasses. There was no chance of eye contact. Quinn noted he had not seemed surprised at the last question.

They walked.

Quinn was wondering—as he had many times

before—if one answer to a great many of the world's problems might be a special day every so often during which you might break the arm of anyone who fucked with you. You could do it to anyone. You could do it at the exact moment they began to complicate your life. It would not be against the law.

"Jesus Christ!" Quinn exclaimed.

He felt himself losing control.

"I mean . . . " Thomasson began.

"Get lost!" Quinn said.

"Jesus Christ!" Thomasson said.

When he got back to the office, it was crowded with members. It was a question of setting up a schedule and taking care of things one at a time. It was also a question of listening carefully to each man. A long time before, Quinn had found that many people reported grievances but did not wish to do anything about them. They just wanted somebody to complain to.

Late in the afternoon he received a telephone call informing him that a safety hazard he had been concerned with earlier had now been corrected. He was mildly disappointed. He had looked forward to a row.

Finally he was alone in the office with Mona, doing paperwork. Every so often he would look out at the Bay and laugh to himself.

"So goddamn funny?" Mona asked sharply without turning around. "Let the help in on it."

"Just craziness."

He was thinking about Thomasson. Somehow he struck him as funny. Not that he envied him his job—not at all.

Mona left early to shop. "I don't suppose you want to say good-bye—" she said at the door with her back to him.

"Take it up with the Office Workers," he murmured.

He was somewhat irritated with her for taking off early. It seemed like she had been doing it all week.

He finished the coffee and vodka he had been drinking and poured himself a full cup of coffee. He sat staring out at the Bay. There were sailboats going slowly up and down in the shallow troughs of waves. The white of the sails was bright and hard. It was the clean fresh white of wealth—of sailing on a weekday when everyone else was dragging his ass on a job. Quinn could see a few of the faces on the sailboats and they were the same color. The hard-eyed rich enjoying the traditional good weather of San Francisco's early autumn

Don't complain. At least you have a view.

This was the City's magic time. Dog summer. Indian summer. September and October. The days were warmer and the light softer. The smells were richer and the colors as warm as the days. The Kingdom of Death became desirable, warm, romantic, and inviting. Sometime in November the rains would come and the illusion would be over.

The rich would go south.

The telephone rang. Quinn picked it up.

"Hey."

It was the friend he had met in the Embarcadero bar.

"No names," Quinn reminded him.

"Your guy is tops," the friend said. "Everybody says so. No funny stuff. A good straight shooter. Very rough— but you can trust him."

"Thanks."

"Rough though."

"I got that the first time."

"Watch yourself."

"Thanks again."

Quinn got into his pajamas early. The three of them ate dinner without conversation. Afterwards Dawn and Rozalyn sat watching TV. The jittery nerves of two days ago had been replaced by a deeper and more subtle tension. They were not even trying to talk to each other. It was as if they all struggled in silence with some staggering riddle the complexity of which they had just tonight became aware.

They were drained—exhausted. It was like a dream.

Quinn pulled out all the stops. He went upstairs with a bottle and a glass and passed out in bed.

Deep in the middle of the night the telephone rang. Quinn bolted upright. The house was in darkness. Rozalyn was sleeping beside him. She started awake with the second ring.

"What?" she said breathlessly. "Quinn?"

He grabbed her leg too roughly. "I'll get it."

"Who is it?"

He stood up. He was stone-cold sober.

As he passed Dawn's room he heard her moan. At the top of the stairs he flicked on the hall light and went back to her room. With the next ring of the telephone her moan was louder. He went in and shook her. Her eyes flew open like a doll's. The phone rang again.

"You were having a bad dream. Go back to sleep."

He released her. She stared up at him uncomprehendingly.

He padded slowly down the stairs in his bare feet. This was the way they did it to you. They got to you with the telephone. The aggressor could strike directly into the middle of everything that was private and special. If you didn't answer it, the ringing haunted you. If you did, you were already playing his game. Every time it rang it was another nail in the structure of the death game.

But he wouldn't let anyone bulldoze him with the telephone. People had tried. He took care to walk slowly down the dark hallway. He stopped in front of the phone.

He picked up the receiver. For a moment he heard nothing but the silence where the jangling bell had been before. He became aware of breathing.

"Hi," a voice said.

It was a lighthearted almost adolescent voice. It had a slight drawl. It dragged out the word as if it had two syllables or tones.

"How are *we* tonight?"

The nasality of the voice jarred him. For a moment it reminded him crazily of his wife's girlfriend Marcie's voice. But the mid-South accent set it off. It was a male voice with a disturbingly childlike tone to it.

"I was wondering when you'd call—you little cocksucker." He spoke quietly but with intensity. He was sure they couldn't hear the words upstairs. "Did your pal in narcotis dump you yet?"

"Well-l-l-l . . . "

There was a knowing and somewhat ingratiating laugh. Two men of the world.

"You know you just can't trust them John Laws no ways."

The voice oozed nastiness as thick as slow molasses.

It became suddenly businesslike. "Now looky here. You and I . . . "

"Fuck it," Quinn said.

" . . . we-all wanta talk."

"It ain't gonna work."

The voice slowed as though speaking to a-retarded child. "Now you. You're not the kind of guy to do something in cold blood—that you'd regret for the—"

"Cold blood is best. You can see what you're doing."

"I mean you're not the kind of—"

"You don't know *what* the fuck kind of guy I am." What he spat into the telephone was pure hate chopped into short tight words. "You didn't check me out very carefully when you dumped on my kid. Maybe you thought all the Dunaways were like Grace. That was a big mistake for you—wasn't it? That's what we're talking about—isn't it?"

Deggan gave him a short silence.

"You're real concerned about yourself. Ain't you, sweetheart?"

Quinn laughed. "Try that line on some psychiatric social worker. It ain't gonna work on me." There was no dynamic between them—no guilt or fear or awe—upon which to build such a hustle.

There was only pure hate on one end and a psychopath on the other.

"What's eating you," Quinn said, "is that something's going to happen and you don't know what it is. Or when. Or how. And you called me up to cry about it."

He waited for Deggan to turn. Fly into the bad-ass part of his act. He heard a sharp intake of breath.

"LISTEN you old fart I'm tired of FUCKING WITH YOU!"

Deggan's scream was a bad dream of adolescence. Also of losing control; and of course cold killer from Oklahoma.

"Crybabies always cry."

"I mean something can happen you dumb cunthair!"

Quinn knew most of this by heart.

"I'm scared shitless," he said.

"ANYTHING," Deggan screamed.

"Be my guest."

Deggan's voice shot up a register. He seemed to be choking.

"I know every damn thing about you Dunaway! You smalltime dipshit wino! YOU'D NEVER KNOW WHAT HIT YOU, something happened a you, do you UNNER-STAND THAT?"

"Unh-hunh."

Quinn decided not to point out the obvious corollary.

"It could happen a ANYBODY you fucker! It could happen a that half-breed TWAT you got there! On the way home from school!"

"Punks always talk."

"ANYBODY!" Deggan screamed.

"I'll be waiting."

Quinn hung up. Then he raised the receiver and left it off the hook.

6

Friday

Quinn sat in his office talking to a retired union member. Outside, the Bay was gray and windy. The retired member was an oldtimer who had spent his life on the waterfront. They were talking fishing. "Best place for striped bass is the Sacramento Delta though—" Quinn was saying. Just talking about the Delta made him feel better. "There's little cabins you can rent for fifteen bucks a throw—they have kitchens too . . . . "

That was the life.

The oldtimer nodded. "Been there. Got a big table and sink down by the dock? Where can you dress the fish?"

"Right." He could almost see it. "Come evening there's always a crowd down there—tellin' lies . . . . "

They laughed.

"The big one always gets away."

"Naturally."

Suddenly the door flew open. They started. It was Don Richards.

"Hey!" Mona said.

Quinn rose slowly.

"Can I talk to you?" Richards asked.

He was breathless and excited. Quinn was not

surprised. Anyone who lived with Grace at this point lived on the edge. If they were not already over it.

"Certainly."

He turned to the retired member.

"Excuse me."

The oldtimer bobbed his gray head. He was still fighting the striped bass. Quinn motioned for Richards to follow him. Mona watched them closely as they left.

"Didn't your mother teach you not to stare?" he asked her.

She shook her head.

He walked in silence with Richards to the middle of the parking lot at the foot of the pier. Quinn lit a cigarette.

"Deggan got Grace," Richards said excitedly.

Quinn nodded. "When?"

"This morning."

"How?"

"I went down to the corner for cigarettes. I saw the little maggot driving her off in her own fucking car."

"Did you try to stop him?"

Richards looked away. "Fucker had a piece," he murmured.

"Didn't you have one?"

Richards shook his head numbly. "It was in the apartment." Mellowness had fled from his smooth and peaceably aging face. His nostrils flared and the pupils of his eyes were huge with rage or dope. "This shit is out of the question! Out of the question! I never figured him for anything this bold. Right under my nose!"

One thing had to be said. Quinn sighed. "She left willingly," he said.

"He had a gun!"

"Come on."

Richards jumped with pain. "Look man—don't say that! I don't want to hear that shit!" He grabbed Quinn's arm. His nostrils opened like a horse. "She's your fucking *sister!* You can't say that!"

"I'll say it because it's probably true."

They stared at each other. Quinn leaned forward and smiled. When men pushed him it gave him extra strength. He was fully prepared to deck Richards.

Richards panted. "Naw—we don't know a damn thing for sure—"

"You want to help?"

Again Richards jumped with anguish. "Hey man—kiss my ass!"

"Then stop fooling yourself about the person you're dealing with." He shook his head. "She's not a prisoner. She's sick."

Richards bowed his head. With great effort he got control of himself. A moment later he glanced up at Quinn. Quinn waited. He had found long ago one secret of communication was that people spoke at different speeds. When they finished one they shifted to another—like gears in a car.

"Not *yet* she isn't a prisoner," Richards said.

They also spoke on different levels. It depended on how much they wanted to reveal (or were able to face). Nobody was completely honest. They were always outsmarting themselves.

"Not yet?"

"But Deggan could use her as a hostage," Richards continued. "That is if he got in a jam—"

Quinn threw away his cigarette. He stretched and looked at the Bay. Whitecaps and a couple of sailboats. Peace—or at least an image or illusion of peace. The water was too choppy today for sailing. Didn't they know small-craft warnings were out?

"A certain *kind* of jam, goddamnit," Richards suggested.

Richards was going to push. Quinn stared at him. He grinned and tensed his body. "Unh-hunh . . . " He made an outward-spilling motion at gut level. Richards shrugged.

"Explain that statement," Quinn ordered. "Or pack it in."

"He could use her as a hostage—if he thought someone was trying to get down on his case."

"How?"

"Make her his fucking mule. Make her carry his piece for him. That way he could keep her with him all the time." He glanced away in disgust. "Lotta dudes with records do that. They don't want to take the fall for carrying a concealed weapon."

"How does he know she isn't setting him up?"

Richards shrugged impatiently. "How does he know anything? He's crazy and he's bold. It's all a fucking mind game anyway. He makes his own fucking odds."

Quinn nodded. "Okay. What's he scared of?"

Richards took out a pipe. From a plaid pouch he tamped tobacco in the bowl. This enabled him to break eye contact. "He think somebody want to waste his motherfuckin ass," he said with satisfaction.

"Who?"

Richards lit a match and sucked at his pipe. "You."

"Me?"

"Might could be." He met Quinn's eyes briefly. "That's what Grace thinks."

"Why?"

"Don't know why."

"And to stop me he might put a gun to Grace's head?"

Richards lit another match. The pipe made a sucking noise.

"What do you want?" Quinn asked in a low voice.

"We can go partners. Blow him up together."

"No, no."

"Got to happen."

"That sounded like a threat."

"You gonna need help with Grace, my man—"

Quinn grinned and grasped the lower part of Richards's shirt. He pushed. Richards stumbled and grabbed Quinn's sport coat clumsily. It tore slowly at the armpit. "She told me you gonna blow his shit away!" Richards yelled.

"What else?"

Richards's pipe fell to the pavement with a clack.

"That's enough."

"Forget it. I mean for*get* it."

"We be partners and take him off together—or I blow the whole mothafuckin gig for you," Richards said.

"*That's* a threat."

"Be a fucking *promise.*"

An insane good humor overtook Richards. He shouted with laughter. Quinn was aware of the need to be careful.

"It won't get her back," he said.

Richards continued to laugh. "How do you know?"

Quinn regarded him closely. For all practical purposes the man was temporarily insane—Grace's work. He felt sorry for him. There was no telling about people.

String him along. He took his hands off Richards.

"Ever do it before?"

"In Korea."

"It's a little different in civilian life."

Richards laughed even more wildly. Across the parking lot a small middle-aged woman paused to gawk at them. She clutched her purse tightly.

Quinn stared. She ducked her head and walked.

"Well when?" Richards asked when he stopped laughing.

He stooped to pick up his pipe.

"Soon. Stay at her apartment. That'll make it easier for me to get hold of you. I want to know immediately if she calls you. Or if Deggan calls you. Right?"

Richards nodded. He gestured toward the torn sport coat.

"Sorry about that."

"Forget it."

Richards pumped his hand. He grasped it like a lover. His eyes glazed over in anticipation. He was already killing Deggan.

Quinn went to the bar on the Embarcadero. As the weekend got closer he felt the pressure building. So was his thirst. Old Escobar watched while he put the bourbon and water away. "Want one?" he asked him.

Escobar shook his head.

"Good man."

The alcohol stopped the slight hangover and put his nerves in order. He rattled the ice in his glass. "One more." He held up his hand. "When you get a chance."

Old Escobar smiled. They were almost alone in the place.

He checked himself out in the mirror behind the bar.

Still a strong face—the gray hard eyes and the mouth were still solid. But awash in the rising tide of red. Today the red nose was particularly bright.

It was one-thirty before he left.

When he got back to the office Mona was alone waiting. "You can go home if you want to," he told her.

"Maybe I ought to stay there."

He looked up. "You quitting on me?"

She sat with her purse in her lap. She had something to say.

"I'm not quitting on you. You quitting on *me*."

His coffee cup had disappeared. He went into the bathroom and got a glass from the shelf. He rinsed it out. He walked over to the file cabinet and withdraw the vodka bottle.

"Want some?"

She shook her head. "There's work to be done!" She was breathing heavily. "Turkey—it ain't no joke anymore!"

He poured himself a drink. When he had put the bottle away he turned to face her. "There is a little crisis—" he said carefully. "It's just one of those things."

Waves lapped crisply at the pilings beneath the office.

"What is it?"

"I can't tell you."

She sat staring at him. "Turkey—!" The short natural hair that framed her face gave it a firm and deliberate warmth. Anger—which with her usually accompanied concern—made her uncomfortably attractive.

"People are talking about the drinking."

"Let 'em talk. Bitch and moan and tell tales is what people are real good at on this front." He sat the glass of vodka on her desk. "Go on—have some. You can tell

Walter I tried to get you drunk!"

She knocked it cleanly off the desk. Vodka splashed across her hand. She was trembling. "We drink at night when people supposed to!"

The office rocked gently as a big wave rolled under them.

"Sure." He wanted to get their conversation on the kidding level—if that was possible. "You drink in bed."

"Sometimes." She stared at him. "That's okay."

"There—you see?"

"See what?"

He sighed and turned away. She was not going to smile for him. When he sat down behind his desk he saw she was crying. *So that was how it was with her.* Yes—and how stupid of him not to have known. In his own way he was as blind as the men who thought they were God's gift to women.

"Turkey!"

Sometimes a woman started caring deeply about someone with whom she worked closely. It was not dangerous if the other person didn't take advantage of it. "I'm sorry," he said truthfully. "Very sorry."

"Sorry doesn't make it."

So to his anger and excitement was added sorrow. She sat crying because she knew he had a problem; and she was nothing but a kind of servant in his small world of tawdry male games. And there was nothing he could do for her.

"Kid." He cleared his throat. "Cookie—"

A classic innocent bystander.

"Shut up."

He got up and stood behind her. He was careful not to touch her. "Don't cry for me. I'm serious."

"Okay."

As she got up she sought to touch his arm. Her purse caught clumsily on the edge of the desk. They laughed. She turned to go.

"Whatever it is—" she said.

Go on. Put some distance between us.

"You're gonna tell me to be careful."

She opened the door. "Naw, honey." She wiped her eyes and stepped out the door. She looked up and down the pier. "'Cause everybody else done told you that already."

Intuition? Or did she know something?

"Yes," he said wonderingly, "they usually do that."

"Except those who ought to be careful themselves."

"Except those who ought to be careful themselves."

Outside his window the Bay had gotten darker and windier. A single sailboat whacked stubbornly through the troughs of white-tipped water. Up—down—up—then a big one and all the way down. The waves came in threes and fours against the pilings beneath the office. First a heavy roller that rocked the whole pier gently, then three or four fast small ones like shock waves. It reminded him of the rhythm of a freight train (they didn't call them rattlers for nothing) slowed down and softer and without the hellish noise. He let the fantasy take him away. He was no longer in a union office but a sea train of the San Francisco Bay. They were pulling out for the weekend— bound not only for glory but for violence. The sea train would take him through the Golden Gate into the deep blue sea where the big waves were born. He would spend the weekend killing ghosts and demons. He would return stronger, and the danger that threatened him and his loved ones would be beaten.

He sipped his vodka. Dry like dry ice—and with the same slow burn. That was San Francisco. Everything inverted or hidden.

He missed the warm explosion of bourbon in his gut.

The telephone rang. He sighed and picked up the receiver.

"Quinn Dunaway?"

The voice was vaguely familiar.

"Is this about union business?"

"No."

"Then let me guess."

It was about Deggan—that much his gut told him. There were a lot of possibilities. It was a somewhat husky male voice.

"Give me your initials."

"Why the initials?" The voice was reasonable—too reasonable.

"My phone may be bugged."

Now he remembered who the voice belonged to.

"Why?"

Quinn laughed. "I'm not supposed to tell you that— am I?" He took another drink. "I'm an active trade-union officer who knows a couple of Communists. Or did once."

Telly Frahm—chairman of a prison-reform group associated with the Society of Friends. He had once been on a Farmworkers' support committee with him. He was probably also close to the staff of the halfway house where Deggan had first met Grace.

"I know you," Quinn said. "Never mind the initials."

Deggan's hustle—Deggan would try to play Frahm off

on him. The Quakers were easy marks that way. Grace
would be involved.

"Quinn—I need to talk to you," Frahm said.

"I don't want any names over the telephone. That's
important." He paused. "Just a time and place to meet."

"No rough stuff."

"Are you coming alone?"

"Yes."

"Then you have nothing to worry about."

Frahm was almost jovial. "The stories you hear—"

They laughed.

"Thank you," Frahm said. There was a pause. "How
about the park that looks over the Cliff House? In about
an hour?"

"Sounds good."

"All right."

"See you then."

"See you then."

He locked the door. He sat drinking coffee.

He smacked his desk with his palm. The Deggans of the
world! This was the way they ran their games. They
involved an everwidening circle of people in devious ways;
such people almost always became involved on terms different than they had imagined. In this way the Deggans
protected themselves. It also allowed them to create more
confusion and disruption—more lies and violence. With
innocents like Telford Frahm, they legitimatized their
machinations.

Deggan had probably told Grace to call him.

And Frahm? He was hopeless. Not only did he not see

the world as it really was—he did not *want* to see-it.

So people got hurt.

A big roller swelled up below. The office rocked gently.

Real people got hurt. Couldn't Frahm see that?

Somebody tried to get in the office. "Get the fuck away from the door!" he yelled without thinking. The door-knob was rattled vigorosly. "*Stay* the fuck away!"

Real people—

Quinn was aware of losing his perspective somewhat. The coffee was not helping. He put his head on the desk. There was male laughter from outside.

"Hey Mona! What's going on in there?"

Another rumor for the rumor mill.

"She went home!" he shouted.

There were steps going down the pier away from the office.

The telephone rang again. "I don't want to hear it," he told the telephone reasonably. "I don't care what it is."

More trouble—ignore it. At last it stopped ringing.

"Thank God."

The telephone said nothing.

"Damn you!" he said to it.

No one could know how he hated it. Over it came, no touch—no face. You could not hit the man whose voice threatened you. You could not embrace the people who loved you. If your phone was bugged, you could not see the man who taped the words. And what was recorded from the telephone? Only words. Denied was the rest of life—the only context in which human communication could be put. It was an instrument of Death.

He sighed and unlocked the door.

"Damn you," he told the telephone again.

The telephone rang loudly. He jumped.

He knew what to do. It was like he had rehearsed it all his life. He took the black cord firmly in hand. When the anger boiled over he ripped it out of the wall. It snapped across his neck like a whip. He picked up the phone like a punter about to kick downfield. He opened the door and sleepwalked the few steps to the end of the pier. He hurled the phone into the whitecapped Bay.

It sank like a shot. He bellowed in victory.

The ringing had been stopped forever. He stood staring at the spot where it had disappeared. He was vaguely aware of someone on the pier across from him staring in amazement.

You okay? somebody hollered.

He had done it many times before—in dreams.

Thank God it's Friday!

Now was real life.

Above Sutro Heights was solid overcast. Thick wisps of fog blew in at ground level from the Pacific. Out here the feeling of unreality was greater. It was something in the light.

He parked in the lot overlooking the ruins of the Sutro baths.

In the park the tall eucalyptus and Monterey cypress trees had been twisted by the wind. He walked slowly down the main path. The grass was green and gold with autumn. It moved softly in the ocean wind. A small giggling shoal of high school students shield a joint from the wind; their books were scattered around them on the grass.

Frahm sat on the remains of a collapsed arbor in the

center of a lush meadow. They saw each other at the same time. Frahm came slowly to his feet. Quinn left the path and walked toward him. The damp grass clung lightly to his pantlegs.

He stopped and looked around. It seemed safe enough.

"Nobody followed me," Frahm said patiently.

Quinn nodded. "Okay." He continued walking.

They shook hands.

"Hello, Quinn."

"Telly—how are you?"

Telford Frahm was about fifty. He had a gray beard and the intense blue eyes of an engineer or laboratory scientist. He was quite handsome. Even teeth and an aggressive smile—every inch the Pennsylvania Quaker. But the face was too bright and its good looks too quick. It presaged not compromise but capitulation.

"Glad to see you."

Quinn lit a cigarette. "I wish I could say the same."

They walked across the meadow. They started down a disused path leading through a grove of Monterey pines.

"Grace asked me to intervene." Frahm's voice belied somewhat the enthusiasm of his smile. He sounded tired. "She believes you want to kill Andrew Deggan. She wouldn't tell me why."

"Do you know Deggan?"

"From the halfway house."

"What's your relation to the halfway house?"

"I'm on the advisory council. I used to be the administrator."

"How's Grace?"

Frahm gave him a blank look. "Absolutely terrible. She's suicidal. She needs immediate detoxification, in my opinion."

"Except she won't cooperate."

"Correct."

Frahm had worked in the South with Grace years before. They had both been involved in voter registration. They had maintained their friendship in San Francisco. So far as Quinn could remember their relationship had not been particularly close.

"Okay," Quinn said. "What does Grace want?"

"She wants to set up a meeting between yourself and Deggan."

"Would she be present?"

"Perhaps. But she specified that Don Richards—the man who is now living in her apartment—was not to come."

"Then you can forget about the meeting."

"Why?"

"The only reason I would ever agree to such a meeting would be because maybe there's a chance of Richards talking her away from Deggan. The poor bastard really cares about her." They paused between two tall pines. The wind did not reach them here. "The poor bastard."

Quinn put out his cigarette and buried it under a handful of dirt.

"According to Grace you don't care anymore what she does," Frahm said. "She says you don't care whether she kills herself or not."

"Just because I don't respond to her threats doesn't mean I don't care. Or that I'm not willing to take reasonable steps to help her if I can. But I know there are practical limits to what I can do. Getting her away from Deggan is essential to her survival."

"Grace thinks you want to get her away for another reason."

"What's that?"

"So you can kill him without any witness around."

They continued their walk. The path led through high shrubs. A yellow slug lay in the path before them. They stepped over it carefully.

"Think of the legal penalties." Frahm's voice was resolute. "If nothing else. Think of what that would do to your family."

"You're being used."

"Think of what it would do to you—what's happening to you right now."

"Give me a break." Quinn cursed. "Psychopaths like Deggan always try to set up meetings. As soon as they do they start running off at the mouth about 'negotiations' and 'summit meetings' and every other goddamn thing that'll make them sound bigtime. There's nothing to negotiate with those bastards. They'll fuck up everything that's halfway decent if you let them."

"Every story has two sides."

Frahm had a way of smiling grimly when attacked. It made Quinn angrier. There was an element of self-congratulation to it. "People like you always want to run interference for these maniacs—"

Moral ascendancy. Worse—the longsuffering patience of the dissenter.

"You know our traditions. You were raised in the Society of Friends. So was Grace. She told me all about your family in Kansas."

"I left when I was fifteen."

"But you know our beliefs."

"Yes," Quinn said grimly.

The path ended abruptly. They found themselves upon an elevated concrete promenade that looked down upon the Cliff House and the broad expanse of Pacific beyond it. The wind here was quite cold. A few tourists made their way up a dirt path. In the bushes off to one side was another group of highschool pot enthusiasts.

They sat on a bench and spoke in low voices.

"As long as Deggan is running around free, he's hurting people," Quinn said. "Innocent people. People who can't defend themselves."

"You can't rehabilitate a man in a cage."

"Some people can't be rehabilitated at all. That's why they have to be kept in a cage."

"We'll never accept that."

"Wouldn't you admit the possibility that out of billions of human beings, the divine spark might die out in a few of them?"

"No. Not completely." Frahm folded his hands firmly. "We have the right to be subjective about that."

"No—no you don't."

"If I didn't know better I'd say you've been deradicalized."

"Bullshit. It's people like you who changed. You got in bed with the criminals." He paused. "I'm thinking of the men in my union. Family men who struggle to meet the bills. Pay the taxes. Keep their families together. It's hard. Everybody wants to push these men around. Can't any of you Typhoid Marys see that they're the real heroes in this country? That they need help? Why do the Friends and all the so-called progressive groups always want to help the rapists, the killers, the maniacs—?"

There was a silence.

"I have a message for Deggan. Tell him if he makes a full confession to the cops by tomorrow night—everything will be okay."

Frahm flushed. "My role will be useless if the two of you use me as a messenger for various threats."

"You tell him that."

Frahm said nothing. A group of Japanese tourists moved slowly from the dirt path to the promenade. The whirring of cameras reminded Quinn vaguely of grass-hoppers—or was it locusts? The children pointed to the barely visible seals on Seal Rock and spoke excitedly in Japanese.

A moment later a patch of fog hid them from view.

"I'll tell him. But if you're referring to any alleged offense . . . I don't think he'd cooperate." Frahm's tone was studied but strained. "You see—it'd be his third fall. He'd get life."

"How do you know this?"

"I counseled him at the halfway house."

"What was your impression?"

"Erratic—but potentially a good manager. He had a certain amount of influence with the other ex-cons." There was a half-smile on his face. "You think I'm naive."

"I think you worship violence—physical force. Most Quakers do. You're not aware of it. My father was like that. He had no common sense. That's why I left so young. That and the fact that he kicked my ass every chance he got."

"You can't blame all of us for the faults of your father."

"I've met very few Quakers in the last few years who didn't strike me as being fascinated by and attracted to violence." He cupped his hands and lit a cigarette. "Maybe it's because the scale of violence is so outrageous. People think they have to identify with part of it or go crazy."

The color in Frahm's face spread to his neck. It was apparent he was angry. "Of course you're above all that," he said.

"When people fuck with me—I retaliate. I don't hurt innocent people."

"And you get to decide who's innocent and who's guilty?"

"Only when the law doesn't."

Frahm closed his eyes and bowed his head. Quinn wondered if he had any idea how insulting this gesture was to him. But of course he wouldn't. He was too busy trying to tune in the Inner Light.

Quinn spat smoke into the wind. "Give me a break . . . "

The sight of Frahm praying was making him sick. There was something in the way he bowed his head that reminded him strongly of his father. It was not a happy memory.

" . . . I don't pray over you. Do I?"

Frahm raised his head and looked at him. "Loving your enemies." He stared at the rough surface below. "For two thousand years that single principle was the dream of Christianity. It was what made it different from other religions. A program for human survival. For three centuries the Society of Friends has tried to witness that principle in a practical and applied way—as you well know."

Quinn took a deep drag. He was starting to thirst for a drink. "There are enemies that love doesn't help. Psychopaths can only respond to love with contempt. It makes them more dangerous."

"Do we hate them then?"

"Sometimes. Probably." He was having difficulty controlling his temper. "Loving your enemies—it's just like any other principle, goddamn it! No principle works *all* the time. Modify it or throw it overboard. Admit that it doesn't always work." He gestured violently toward the ocean at which Frahm continued to stare. "That's what it's there for . . . this West Coast! It's where things in this fruity country end—although most people don't have the common sense to know it. It's there to show us our limits. Keep what's good and toss the rest overboard."

Behind the Cliff House two waiters threw bread scraps to the gulls. The gulls squawked loudly. The tourists were delighted. One of the smaller children clapped his hands happily.

Frahm turned his blue eyes on Quinn.

"What do you call this philosphy?"

It was not clear whether he joked or not. From past association he knew Frahm was not without humor.

"Common sense and a sense of common decency."

Both men were silent for a long time.

"I also call it survival," Quinn said.

Frahm stood up. "It's ironic we both have the same names for such different . . . ."

"Yes," Quinn said.

The family ate dinner. They had roast beef and the sweet beets Rozalyn bought at the deli on Twenty-fourth Street. The tension they felt was now complete. Consequently it threatened them less—they swam with it like fish in a tidal wave. The pain was ecstatic.

It was even funny.

"Why should you care what other people think?" Roz

had initiated a rambling discussion of Dawn's woes at
school. There were long silences and sudden spurts of
conversation. "Everybody learns at their own speed. As
long as you do your best—that's what *really*
matters . . . ."

It was clear this would become a question. First a long
pause ensued.

Dawn giggled.

"Isn't it?" Roz asked.

They laughed giddily.

"Well, *isn't* it?"

Tension had become the perfect family in-joke.

"I wish we had dinner at the kitchen table like we used
to." Dawn chewed stoically on her roast. "We could look
out the window at the lights."

Quinn started. That was exactly what he had been
thinking.

"Never mind—" Rozalyn snapped. "School—"

"Roz is right," he said. He felt laughter creeping up on
him. "Always do your best!"

Dawn stared at him with polite incredulity. "You can
get flunked even if you do your best."

They laughed. At the same time Quinn felt the tightening in his chest which was for him the presage of sadness. Out of the mouths of babes.

"Okay—so they flunk you."

"You can't go to junior high."

"So what?"

"The kids call you a flunko. Nobody wants to be your
friend."

Rozalyn went into the kitchen to start the coffee. He
sipped his bourbon. Dawn finished her food. "Want me
to take my dishes in?"

"I'll get 'em later."

She went to the TV. Quinn sat down in the Naugahyde recliner. She turned on the TV.

"Why don't you use the *TV Guide?*"

"It's easier this way." She flipped the channels.

"You never read anything. All the teachers say when you master reading the other stuff comes easier. Writing. Math—"

Her hand dropped from the TV like she had burned it. She turned it off and bunched her hand into a fist.

She stood waiting.

"You don't want to flunk?"

"No."

"Then you'll have to work harder. It's just that simple."

Instead of the usual amused interest, the look in her eyes was pain.

"The harder I try—the more mistakes I make."

He glanced away. Some people were vulnerable to pressure. But he didn't want it to become an excuse. "Every day from now on we want you to read at least an hour. Whatever you want to."

"There *isn't* anything I want to read."

"Then force yourself."

"Why?"

It wasn't a smartass question. She wanted to know.

"Why do you watch TV? Because it looks real to you? It isn't. Neither are books. But you have to learn to read better or you'll flunk. You don't have to like it." He paused for the punch line. "Just do it."

From the kitchen came the pop of Rozalyn's lighter.

"Is it a deal?" he asked.

A neutral good humor gradually replaced the pain in her eyes. She shrugged. "Okay."

He went over to her and extended his hand. She shook it silently.

He smoothed back her hair. The bruises had turned light yellow. A leprechaun face—with secrets. He wondered what went on now behind the unblinking almond-shaped brown eyes. Adopted children rarely challenged the adoptive parents on home ground. They were afraid of killing them.

That was what the experts said.

"You're a good kid."

Omnipotence fantasies—that was what the social worker had called it. If something happened to the adoptive parent they blamed themselves.

"I know," she said.

He wondered if it was true or another myth of psychiatrists.

"Good."

She caught him checking out the bruises. "They're almost gone." Her eyes drifted toward the door. "They don't hurt—"

He paused. "Bad dreams?"

She shook her head. "I don't hardly think about it anymore."

She seemed anxious to reassure him.

"Okay." He gave her a soft punch. "Tell us if you go off the block."

"Okay."

She ran outside into the dusk. It occurred to him he had forgotten to remind her to brush her teeth. That was his fault. She had few problems accepting the limits they set for her. They would feel less vulnerable if she gave them more reason to be angry with her.

Pain—

"Problem's all solved!" he called out to Rozalyn in the kitchen.

"Good."

"Smoking too much."

"Shut up!"

He watched Dawn from the window. A neighbor child was autographing her cast. It was getting dark. He sighed and began gathering up the dishes. He stacked them in the kitchen sink. Roz sat at the kitchen table with the *TV Guide*, checking the listings.

"Anything interesting?"

She smoked furiously. "Nothing much."

He shot a rope of Dove into the sink and turned on the hot water. He made himself a fresh drink. The sliding windows above the sink were open a crack. The breeze seemed less chilly now.

The air smelled clean.

"How was your day?" she asked without looking up.

"How much do you want to know?"

"One word will suffice."

"Disgusting. Strange. Ugly."

"That's three words."

"I want to keep you well-informed."

"*Sure.*"

The sound of running water filled the kitchen. He switched it off.

"How was yours?" he asked.

"Marcie Loeb came over. She wanted to talk about Harold."

"I thought they were getting a divorce."

"They're separated—but she talks about him more now." She giggled. "She talks about the woman he's dating."

He turned off the water and washed the pots. There was too much water in the sink. He pulled the plug to let some of it run out.

"Talk to you about something?" He lit a cigarette.

She lit another cigarette herself. "My God—what now?" Her sigh was so unintentionally melodramatic they both laughed.

She raised her hand to her forehead with a flourish.

"What's that? Camille?"

She liked to imitate Garbo. In face she resembled her.

"I can't tell you what's best for you," he said, "but I think you ought to consider going back to work."

He took a drink and looked out the window. On the Bay Bridge the traffic had thinned out. In the soft blue evening light the cars were tiny and unreal. He put his cigarette in the ashtray on the windowsill.

There were wet spots spreading along it where his fingers had been.

"You haven't had a job since the adoption," he pointed out. "We could use the money."

"What about Dawn?"

"What about her? You don't have to be standing there in the doorway wearing an apron to meet her every day after school. Give her a key. She could let herself in. You'd see her in the evening."

The tears were already coming. "You think I'm smothering her."

"You're smothering yourself." He paused. "You're trying too hard. It happens all the time with parents."

She snorted. "Except with you, of course."

He shook his head. "No. I'm worse. But I have somewhere to go every day."

There was a sharp intake of breath. Her face fell slowly

forward into her long red-nailed hands. He stood with water dripping helplessly from his hands. Her shoulders heaved gently.

It was exactly like being stabbed with a knife through the heart.

"What?" he shouted.

Their communications system allowed and even encouraged deliberate silence—when it enabled one partner to come to a conclusion the other did not particularly wish to put into words. But this he had to hear.

"Say it!" He stepped forward furiously. "I know what you're thinking. We never should have adopted. It was too late for us. We should have left well enough alone. Right?"

"I'm scared—damnit!" Her teary eyes widened. "this is just the beginning, you know," she added ominously.

"What's that supposed to mean?"

"We're a jinx!"

Two more steps to reach her. He knocked her hands away from her face. She screamed. Tears covered her face and hands. "Fuck you! Get away from me!" She was angry and shaken up.

"No—we're not giving up!" He pointed brusquely toward the front door. "We're responsible for that kid! I won't let you say that! Jinx—"

"It's the way I feel—sometimes anyway! Don't I get to have feelings?"

"*Feelings!*" He strutted with fury. "Now *that's* the big hustle nowadays. Everything gets justified because of some asshole's *feelings!* I couldn't care less how you feel. What's important is that we're responsible for Dawn. And by God we're not giving up without a fight!"

"Sometimes I just feel like something's going to happen to her—"

"Then don't talk about it."

She rose slowly and pointed at him. She crowed with laughter. "You're scared! Scared! Admit it—aren't you?" She remained standing and pointing at him. "Admit it! Admit it!"

He turned and went back to the kitchen sink. He picked up his smoldering cigarette and puffed furiously. He had not turned the light on, and in the darkening gloom the cigarette glowed fiercely. He glanced back at Roz; as he had hoped he could not see her face clearly from here.

He dropped his cigarette *pffft* into the dishwater.

"Quinn—"

He placed his elbows gently on the windowsill above the sink. Yes, this was the best time in San Francisco. Autumn evening. Lights twinkled below him like stars on Twenty-fourth Street and farther down toward the center of town. It was that special time in the evening when everything seemed too soft to be real. He sipped his drink.

City lights. Under each a painted lady.

"Sometimes being responsible isn't enough," Rozalyn said in the darkness behind him.

"That's right." Deliberately he made his tone conciliatory. "You need luck too."

Magic lights. Under each a dreamer.

"Sometimes it might help to admit you're scared."

"Tomorrow the kid may slip and fall in a well. Why should I cry about it now?"

Sad magic City lights. Under each a beautiful nightmare.

She laughed bitterly. "Terrific!"

That too was marriage, that she could laugh without hesitation or embarrassment at his deepest pain.

"Besides," he said after a pause, "if I start getting scared, the whole show will fall apart."

She walked over and put her arms around him tenderly. "Something's going on with you." She pulled out his shirt and rubbed his flat stomach from behind. It was a signal she wished to make love.

"I guess that's what I'm trying to say. I have other things to think about."

"And you can't talk about it."

She stood very close to him.

"Whatever it is—I want you to be careful, Quinn."

He was too tired to pretend. "It's everybody *else* who doesn't understand the importance of being careful."

"Well then—keep it simple."

She accepted so much about him—too much. "Do you think I'm getting old?" he asked her.

"Experience gets it every time."

She knew more or less what he was up to. At least on the level of emotions. On one level it would be exciting— a validation of certain things that attracted her to him. On another it would be only a dream. "You'll feel better when it's over," she assured him.

He turned and kissed her. One hand cupped her breast. He felt it tighten and her breath quicken. Violence excited her sexually—it was disturbing but true. He pushed this from his mind. The cornerstone of intimacy was vulnerability; right now he had no more desire to think upon her areas of vulnerability than he did upon his own.

"Um," she said. "Tough guy—"

They both heard the sound from the hallway. He felt a

great distance open up between him and his wife—it hit him like a sweat or electricity but had the coldness of space in it. The next moment the front door burst open. It was Dawn.

"Yes . . . ?" He was surprised at the anger in his voice.

"Hi," Dawn said.

Blessedly the wild humor returned. They laughed.

"Can we help you with something?" Rozalyn said.

"Yeah!" Dawn ran up the stairs. "My skates!" They heard her rummaging in one of the trunks where she kept her belongings. In a moment she came back down. She stood watching from the darkened hall.

Rozalyn lit a cigarette. "How long are *you* going to stand there?"

"Long enough!"

She ran outside.

Quinn reached for his glass. His hands were shaking. "Well . . . "

Roz inhaled. After a moment she walked away. He heard her going up the stairs. He turned back to the lights of San Francisco. *Star light star bright. First star I see tonight. Neon neon City lights. Can I make a wish tonight?*

"Honey," Roz called from the top of the stairs. "Honey?"

Let killing be done. That we may live.

"I'm coming!"

Outside, the neighborhood children were playing. The muffled scrape of their skates and their faint cries of laughter carried into the dark house clearly on the night breeze . . . .

PART THREE

Killing

7

Saturday and Saturday Night

Quinn woke late.

He was alone in the bed. From below came the voices of Saturday morning TV. He sat up slowly. Outside the sun was shining fiercely. One lace curtain furled slowly in the breeze. It would be warm today but not too warm. The best time—Indian summer.

Killing time.

"Good morning!" he said to himself.

He had no hangover.

Through the open window came the whirr and clatter of lawns being mowed. Below that the soft hiss of lawn sprinklers.

He had never been as ready to do anything as he was today.

"All you add is love!" said a Puppy Chow commercial downstairs.

He lit the first cigarette. He sat on the edge of the bed, facing the sunlit window. Power—you were king when you felt like this. The words were true. The brave died only once.

He grinned.

There was just nothing to compare with this feeling.

179

"Wow!" barked an appreciative TV dog downstairs.

He shaved and showered. He went down to the kitchen in his Birkenstocks and gabardine slacks. Rozalyn sat at the kitchen table reading the newspaper. The sleeves of her robe were rolled up to her elbows. At her right was a cup of coffee. She held a cigarette.

She smiled good morning.

He poured himself a drink and plugged in the coffee maker. There was the sound of a clock ticking—a commercial for a new children's game.

"Locked in combat!" screamed the TV.

"Lies!" Quinn said.

From the living room came the crack of a peanut. All he could see of Dawn through the kitchen door were her feet.

She giggled.

"How would you know what to buy if it wasn't on TV?" she asked.

"It'd be cheaper that way. We'd all be better off."

She didn't bother leaning forward to stare at him.

"We'd die," she said, "We'd starve to death."

It was a long-standing argument.

The Saturday morning cartoons were not like the Looney Tunes she viewed on weekdays. They had no wit. They were overrun with characters fleeing from ghosts. The sound effect of choice was a hollow running noise— an endlessly reiterated drumroll of spinning feet.

"Besides—it's only for kids."

Rozalyn yawned. A halo of tobacco smoke wound round her head. Under the table one furry-slippered foot poked at the other.

"Top of the morning," he said to her. "More coffee?"

"Um."

"Hang on."

He poured himself a cup. As he replensished hers she whispered to him, "Remind her to *read* today." She pointed at the living room.

"I'll talk to her before I go out."

There was a pause.

"When are you leaving?" she said in her normal voice. She did not raise her eyes.

"About five."

She nodded.

He stood in the living room door. Dawn did not take her eyes from the TV. She cradled a bowl of peanuts and peanut shells in her lap. The yellow bruises on her face gave her a wizened look.

"If you had all those toys on TV you'd get sick of them."

She appraised him coolly. "That's why they make new ones. For when you get tired of the old ones."

He set up the sprinklers. He spaded around the house. He weeded the truck garden. He did not rush. Yet time flew by.

Puttering around the house—today he loved it.

At four he put the spade away. His work gloves he threw in the toolbox under his workbench. He took the basement stairs two at a time. Excitement made him strong.

From the patio the grass seemed already greener. He decided to tie up his roses with sack. Nobody did that here. It would be fun. He could do it tomorrow—in between watching the games and reading the paper. He would feel good tomorrow.

A jolt of energy shot through him.

He took off his Birkenstocks. He shadowboxed, his bare feet scuffing on the uneven bricks. It felt very good. Perspiration patched his sweatshirt at the arms and back. Dobbs—his neighbor on the south—watched him from a hall window. Quinn waved to him.

The old man stood mutely staring. He did not wave back.

In the kitchen Roz sat at the table with her sewing box. She was looking for buttons. "Take it easy," she said. "It's Saturday."

"Let's both take it easy."

He poured bourbon over ice and took the drink upstairs with him. He had a second shower—this time finishing it off with cold water to close his pores against the night chill. When he had dried off completely, he put on an athletic supporter of the kind used by boxers. It had a wide elastic panel at the front and a metal cup. Inside it he sprinkled baby powder. That was to keep it dry. He fit the cup gingerly and ran in place to test it.

Just enough exercise to loosen up.

He put on fresh gabardine slacks and a thick cotton turtleneck. He combed his hair in the dresser mirror. He lit a cigarette and sipped his weak drink. Already it was mainly water.

But the gray eyes were not water. He stared at himself in the mirror. Nor the face. He was sure of it. Even with the red streaks and puffiness, it was hard underneath.

"Bloody but unbowed. Damn it."

He went to the closet. The seaman's duffle bag was all the way to the back. He jerked it out of a tangle of closet stuff and slid it across the bedroom floor. He sat down on the bed. It was a medium-weight sea bag—white canvas with a round bottom and brass grommets and a pull rope at the top.

There were many memories. *You ugly goddamn thing.* You opened it slowly. Part of the ritual.

On the top were the old black boots. It had been five years since he had worn them. He wiped off the fine dust with a tissue. The leather was still as soft (and the rubber soles as hard) as they had been twenty years before. You wore rubber soles when you shipped out; leather soles could kill you on a slippery deck.

He slipped them on over nylon socks and stamped the floor. The contact was solid. They did not pinch.

"Beautiful!" he said.

Next—the Cooper boot knife. It was wrapped in a stiff towel with his things from the time he had worked ship's galley: French knife, turning fork, spatula, a steel for sharpening.

He sat looking at the knife. Memories—

He had never gone on a strange beach without the boot knife.

It was in a sheath with a patch of Velcro sewed on one side. He slipped it into the right side of his left boot. Another piece of Velcro had been epoxied there. The two pieces caught. The knife came out cleanly.

It was only backup. Both knife and sheath could be ditched quickly. If you used it you had to throw it away.

He stood to practice the draw.

He lifted the pants leg with his left hand; he crouched. He drew with his right. The sheath did not slip. The draw felt good.

He sat down on the bed and put out his cigarette.

Next out was a woolen watch cap. It was stiff with

ocean salt. He put it on. It was as rough and scratchy as he remembered.

It was a good feeling.

He closed the sea bag and put it back in the closet.

He took a hundred dollars from his wallet. He fastened it with a money clip. In his pocket he slipped also a coin purse with loose change. He pocketed his house and car keys and a tube of Chapstick.

He did not take his wallet or ID.

He unlocked a small strongbox on the shelf in his closet. From it he took the pistol he had just purchased. He checked it carefully and stuck it in his belt in front. It was very uncomfortable. He took it out and checked it again. He was glad he would not be carrying a revolver. He did not agree with the popular idea that revolvers were safer.

His friend in government said there was no adequate safety for revolvers because the Irish needed their disability pensions. *They know how, but they won't develop it. Goddamn Holy Father's sitting on the patent.*

Quinn laughed. A lot of cops in this town shot themselves.

From the back of the closet he took out an old pea jacket. In the left pocket was a small brown paper bag. He checked its contents: a pair of thin rubber surgical gloves; six rounds of standard-velocity ammunition for Deggan's thirty-eight in case it was empty; and the room key he had been given at the Celtic Palace. He put the bag in the left pocket.

He put on the pea jacket.

He slipped the pistol in the right pocket. It had been razored open cleanly at the bottom. The pistol slid down through the opening in the bottom of the pocket and rode in the lining. He checked it out in the mirror. If he did not slouch the bulge could not be seen readily.

He looked in the mirror. With the pea jacket and the crusty watch cap, he looked quite dangerous. He was glad he had shaved that morning; with two or three days' growth of beard he would have been fair game for the cops—even in a town like this where they usually didn't stop people for looking outrageous.

He was almost ready.

The light outside was soft yellow. Already the fog was coming in. Slow rivers of white twisted across Twin Peaks onto the hills above Market and were parted by the high-rises. Toward Marin the fog would be pouring in like lava through the Golden Gate. The taste in the air that came through the open window had the electric quality it often did this time of year. Both wet and dry—like the vapor given off by dry ice.

He went to the window. Dawn stood with a small group of kids on the sidewalk down the street. One boy held something in his hands which the others examined with great interest. Dawn did not look at it directly. She maintained her distance and watched the faces of the others.

He saw one of the kids mouth the word *gross*.

Their current greeting and password. The clean soaring disgust of adolescence for the adult world. He had been denied that period himself. As a result, certain adolescent preoccupations had been distributed throughout his consciousness where they were least wanted.

He had discovered early that grossness could be exciting.

He sat down on the bed and lit a final cigarette. He finished his drink. The old Singer hummed on the back porch. He thought he heard Rozalyn curse.

Silence. Again the machine whirred.

Home—it was the refuge. Here were the people you loved. Before leaving, you went to a room and empowered yourself with things that could punch small and deathly holes in people in the twinkling of an eye. The stout yeoman put on his cross of mail. Then you essayed forth into the place of nightmares. You made the descent into hell. The intense pleasure came from the passage from one extreme to another—the incongruity of the two. Like a border raid. You crossed over into the territory of the enemy unknown (which was another world). Now you sat listening to your wife sewing. In a few hours you would be killing someone.

His heart beat very fast.

A deeply satisfying feeling. The old male feeling—the hunter and the warrior. Glory, the ancient poets had called it. Quinn felt sorry for the men who had lost all touch with it. When challenged directly they were helpless.

He stood up; it was time.

From the top drawer of the dresser he took two packs of Camels and a book of matches. He put them in his left pocket next to the paper bag. As he went down the stairs the crunch of the hard rubber soles echoed lightly off the hardwood steps. He stopped at the bottom to flex his shoulders and button the pea jacket. He went into the kitchen and stood where Rozalyn could not see him. The sewing machine was silent. He thought she had probably heard the boots.

"I'm driving up to Brannan Island," he said.

A resort spot in the Sacramento Delta. In their communication system it meant he would not be home early.

"I'll call you early if I don't get back tonight."

There was a long silence. "Good luck."

"Thank you."

"With the fish."

There was another silence.

"Why don't we go up there next week? The three of us? We can rent a cabin. For the whole weekend."

"Be careful," she said.

"I will."

"See you later."

"See you later."

Outside he did not see Dawn. She and her friends were probably down at the park. He was sorry he would not have a chance to remind her to read today. How much he wanted for her—! When you were a parent, you were responsible for a world.

Low-riding Latinos were dragging the main on Army Street. From Army he turned onto Third Street. Beginning at the drawbridge at China Basin he took the long bumpy curve of the Embarcadero. He parked near Jackson Square.

He felt like walking.

North Beach had Saturday night action. Old folks stumbled off the Gray Line bus at Finocchio's. There were pimps in leisure suits and their tense gum-snapping women on Broadway. Nasal hardsell barkers yelled obscenities at tourists outside the topless joints. On Columbus there were chanting Hare Krishnas with shaved heads and orange robes; they exuded incense and hysteria. It was the usual Saturday night street scene. He could laugh at it. Positively wholesome—compared to what he would get in the Tenderloin.

Thinking of the Tenderloin made him thirsty. Two blocks off Columbus, he entered a bar he occasionally visited.

The bar was long and narrow and paneled with old wood. A wide door connected it to a family-style dining room. Among the restaurant patrons he spotted a couple of people he knew. He smiled and waved to them.

The bartender was a man named Cicerone. He was another friend from around town and from Democratic Party functions.

"Bothering decent people!" he shouted when he saw Quinn. He liked to do broad impressions of the Irishers who flourished in his business. "How's the boy?"

"Looking for entertainment. Let's see you jump over the bar."

"Not until they make me a partner."

Quinn laughed. Cicerone was at least a partner, probably an owner. He owned several bars and restaurants. He was a smart but smalltime mover and shaker out of the Salesian Boys' Club.

He drew beer. Quinn started.

"Get your hands off that horse piss!"

"It's for me. You're buying—right?"

"I never bought a drink for a bartender in my life."

The crowd was sparse but finely mixed. Longshoremen, elderly Italian-Americans, a drowsy superfly at the end of the bar, professionals from up the hill. Cicerone moved away to serve a couple from the restaurant. He was slightly drunk.

When he finished with the couple he came back and shook the lapel of Quinn's pea jacket.

"The last time you wore his charming apparel you got

into a little trouble, remember?" He leaned over the bar and looked downward. "The fucking boots too," he said wonderingly. "Sometimes I think the feds should have tossed the key on you."

"They tried," Quinn said.

Cicerone tucked his chin and poked jabs at him. Quinn slipped them, smacking hard with his right palm. He was pushing the punches heavily away in a wide flying arc around his head. His biceps felt good. Hair-trigger sharp and firing like a rifle. Cicerone was impressed.

"Training. You're in fucking training."

"Just feeling good," Quinn said.

Cicerone blew air like a horse. "A rough boy."

Quinn wondered if his friend noticed the deterioration in his face. Possibly Cicerone was too drunk.

"A legend in your own time," Cicerone said.

Cicerone's face was flushed. He was almost bald. Quinn thought he must be fifty, if not more.

"I try," Quinn said.

Cicerone moved off. He was smiling and blinking rapidly from the excitement of the jabs.

At the end of the bar the superfly was winging. He stood pointing at his drink, muttering, his feathered slouch hat dipping like a beak. The sparring had set him off. He threw some weak punches. Cicerone spoke to him in a low voice, like a man calming a horse.

Quinn lit a cigarette and thought about being a legend.

Smalltime—like Cicerone. But a fantasy people liked. What did they see in him, of what was he the idealized version?

There were two parts to it. The first part was the 1950s. He had refused to give a congressional investigative

committee certain lists, had refused to testify about
certain people. For that he had done time. People
respected that.

And the other part . . .

He had arrived in San Francisco at the age of fifteen
and fought amateur for six years, then a year professional
on the circuit to LA and Las Vegas. Without the big
punch—a heart fighter who took the punches. During
those years he had shipped out regularly, making friends
with some Communists and fellow travelers in the mari-
time unions, who had given him a leg up in union politics
on the beach. The union he had settled into was a
remarkably democratic one, free of mob influence, but
controlled by radicals. This led to jurisdictional tensions
on the waterfront. In the late 1940s a new leadership took
over the union that organized cooks and stewards on the
ships, kicked out the CP, and began to wage war against
Quinn's union. Organizers from Quinn's union were
thrown overboard. Bad feelings escalated. Death threats
were made. A faction in the rival union made a play for
some expensive equipment in the office of a CP front just
padlocked by the IRS. Quinn intercepted them. One
man was in the hospital for six months.

Later, there were other incidents. An employer who
had threatened people in San Pedro. A picket-line
incident near a cannery organized by the warehouse
division, during which a company man had swung on
him with a tire iron. A Hell's Angel looking for trouble in
a bar. There were a few others. Always, these people Had
It Coming, they Went Too Far. Always, he made sure
these situations lent themselves well to an interpretation
of self-defense.

Brawling became part of the legend. The popular

image was of a rough but honest labor type, a two-fisted and likeable drunk. But the image was phony. People did not see the larger reality of respect that fighting taught and without which fighting meant nothing. Furthermore, the rich Democrats who ran the City, who had encouraged this legend, had nothing but contempt for labor. Their celebration of him was a form of patronization.

A civilized town on the surface, beneath which there were deep divisions. Papering them over were slogans and fantasies.

Cicerone came back with a drink in his hand. The superfly had sat down and resumed his nod. "Why," Cicerone wanted to know, "do we put up with you? Bothering day-cent people?"

Stagnation or death, when cities got to believing their own fantasies.

"You need me," Quinn said.

He had a steak and salad. Afterward he sat drinking until seven. He could dawdle. He was in control.

Outside, it was night. There were wet circles around the beckoning neon ladies above the clubs on Broadway. They crackled with moisture as he passed beneath them. The mist was still fine, but blew faster and harder. It felt good against his face. Cotton candy driven by a sea wind.

There was solid noisy traffic on Broadway. He flipped up the collar of his pea jacket and hustled across on a yellow light. The pistol rode easily in the lining of the jacket.

He angled through Chinatown. From the sweatshops

came the metallic snicker of sewing machines, punctuated by gongs from Chinese opera on the radio. On Stockton he decided to walk the tunnel. Halfway through, a patrol car cruised by him, but the patrolmen did not look at him.

He was on Post walking toward Taylor when he first felt the Tenderloin. On Geary he saw the first street-walkers. He could spot the ones from the Tenderloin. They had the junkie dip of the hips when they walked, the distinctive junkie manner of gesturing with the forearm and wrist held stiff, the wasted heroin eyes, the pasty faces in which the features were slowly coming unglued. As he approached Jones on Geary, the full shock of it hit him. He could feel it coming up through the ground through his feet and striking him in the stomach.

The Tenderloin—

As soon as he turned the corner things were different. There were certain things you spotted if you knew what to look for. Many of the stores were run-down and some were abandoned. The window of a second-hand shop with a bullet hole in its center had been taped in such a way that it would not shatter. There were iron gates protecting some of the businesses. The storefronts smelled of urine.

He was not particularly conscious of the route he took. He was being pulled toward his destination like a magnet.

Dead ahead was the Regina Hotel. It was in the next block. On the corner ahead of him was a small mob of streetwalkers. They stood in front of a mom-and-pop grocery. As he approached he muttered to himself in the manner of the certifiably insane.

"You wanna party?" a pale girl with undersea eyes asked him.

He barked like a dog. She stared but said nothing.

The mom-and-pop grocery was manned by unhappy-looking Arabs. The door was wired so they could look over patrons before letting them in.

"Stop killing me," Quinn said as he waited for the light to change. "Killing me. You're all killing me."

He crossed slowly. The streetwalkers on the other corner fell back when they saw him talking to himself.

He stepped into a doorway a few doors down from the corner. It was unoccupied and partly protected by shadows.

The Regina and Southern Home hotels were half a block away on his side of the street. In front of them were twenty or so dealers and junkies. Iron grates had been pried loose from certain doorways and in their shadows were other shadows that moved like men. About half of the men trafficking dope on the street were Black.

Across from the two hotels was another and smaller hotel above a bar. From the bar came jukebox sounds and the burble of Saturday night voices. A row of bikes had been parked outside. A crude glitter sign in the window said TRAFFIC JAMMER.

Traffic was light; the streetwalkers on the corner were getting restless. When a car driven by a man passed and did not stop, they cursed. On a corner diagonally across from them were men dressed as women. Most of the drag queens were Black.

It was cool but not yet cold. The sky was black and there were slow-moving low clouds. They had faint pink linings from the City lights.

He edged out to check out the Regina again. On the corner a Black streetwalker started toward him suddenly, her nostrils flaring. Her face was crusted with green eye shadow, and at first he thought she was a drag queen. She had red hot pants with a wide red plastic belt. Her right hand was half open at crotch level. She made rough motions with it, as though rowing a boat.

"Pussy!" she demanded in a dangerous voice.

Probably angry because of the slim pickings on the street. At the same time it occurred to him that something in his psycho act might have set her off.

"Watch out," he warned in a noncommittal voice.

She had rings on every finger. Her fingernails were green.

"Pussy," she repeated.

Her eyes were small and mean. Quinn tried not to meet her eyes — to look past her. She saw something in his face that caused her to blink. But she did not look away.

"Not tonight."

"Say *pussy*."

For emphasis she rapped on the window of a parked car with the back of her hand. The rings made a clacking sound. He stepped backwards into the doorway and the shadows. She took a couple of wild steps toward him. She was close to some kind of hysteria.

"Say now! Pussy feel good." Her chest was heaving. "Don't be here on my corner unless I'mo sell you something. That old way you got! Talkin to yo self! C'mon. I'mo sell you a party. You can make *love* to *my* sweet ass!"

He saw how it was. She wanted to read him as a john, no matter what he did. Crazy people could be like that. To change the subject he pointed at the drag queens on the opposite corner.

"What happens when they take some sailor home?"

She snorted. "Sailor find out — and they fight and feud. Drag queens love to fight. Shelly don't treat you that way.

Shelly make you feel all nice down around yo pants, honey."

He nodded at the small hotel above the Traffic Jammer bar across the street. It was almost directly across from the Regina.

"That your trick hotel?"

"Around the corner."

He shook his head. "I want that one across the street."

"Twenty for the party. Five for the room."

"Okay."

She wanted to walk directly across the street to the hotel. Instead he made her walk to the corner, where he ducked into the mom-and-pop to buy a pint of Bourbon Deluxe. Her impatience was pathetic. She would gladly have run.

The hotel was unnamed. Inside on the second floor the white room clerk was a poster boy of dope, jail, and probably bad sex in cages. Slow broken adolescent coordination, acne scars, terrified sneer, squirrel eyes without depth. Over a chair behind him was a cheap black leather jacket with a sizable Iron Cross on a shiny silver chain.

"You her parole officer?" he asked Quinn.

His laughter sounded like the gasps of someone drowning. He was begging to be hit. Quinn laid down five dollars and pointed at the keys on the wall. The boy stared at him. Eventually he gave him a key.

"Eat that cheese," the kid said as they went upstairs.

When Quinn did not come back and beat him up, he began to laugh uncontrollably.

"Mothafucka talk more shit than the radio," Shelly said.

There were fast roaches on the wall in the hallway.

Inside the room she flipped on the overhead light and stepped toward him like she had done on the street.

"You a cop?"

He turned off the overhead. The room was well lit from the neon signs outside. From here he could see everything going on in front of the Regina Hotel.

"Will you take it easy?" he said in a placating tone.

He took out twenty dollars and laid it on a dresser. She began to unbutton her shirt.

"Wait," he commanded.

She started looking for the door. At the same time she looked at the twenty dollars. She wanted to grab the money and run, but he stood too close to it.

"No—I'm not going to beat up on you."

She fronted a staunch cool by slowly lighting a cigarette. She was going to wait and see what he wanted. "Pussy," she explained, "ain't nothing but meat on the bone. You can fuck it. You can suck it. You can leave it alone."

"Well, I'm a talking freak. I have to talk to someone." He motioned across the street. "Go over there and tell Andy Deggan that someone wants to see him at the bar downstairs."

Apparently she knew Deggan by name. She was angry.

"You can't come down here with that old stuff! Things is stormy down here."

"You can get the message to him."

He picked up the twenty and handed it to her. She blinked and took it. Tonight she had not been scoring like a star.

"Want some bourbon?" he asked.

"Why'd you act all crazy before?"

"When?"

"You know when."

"I wanted to be left alone."

"You a party all right."

She made no move to join him in a drink. From the bar below came male screams and a crush of running feet. It was hard to tell whether it was playing around or deadly force.

"They likes to give each other baby slaps," Shelly explained.

Quinn was glad she knew Deggan. He wanted it to be simple. He sat down on the bed and had a drink from the pint of Bourbon Deluxe.

"Somebody want to see him at the bar," she repeated.

"Come back and tell me what happens."

"*That's* another twenty dollars."

He wanted to put the look of fear into her face. Something vaguely like respect was not enough down here. But he had her figured as a potential slasher. Besides, pity had completely swamped his will. That was a mistake, but there were limits. She was too pathetic.

"Ten," he said.

She nodded and left.

Andrew Deggan saw the rat before it saw him. It was on the fifth floor of the Regina Hotel, and it was making good time; it was scurrying from one empty room to another on the other side of the hall. In its excitement it nearly ran over Deggan's foot. He released his brass belt buckle, which he had been fumbling to close, and concentrated everything on a kick. The rat squeaked and put on a burst of speed. The kick missed by inches. It had a long pink bone of a tail, and it took a long time for the tail to disappear into the darkness. It looked like a bony arrow bouncing along the floor amidst the paper and garbage. For a moment it reminded Deggan of something else, something he had once seen at an animated cartoon festival in San Quentin. He tried to remember, but couldn't. He cursed disgustedly.

"Lord Jesus the Son of Man!" he cried.

Deggan had once heard that rats were the first to abandon a sinking ship. Actually, they made very little impression on him except for the satisfactory fact that they usually ran whenever he approached. He wished he had his Okie credit card. Many people shot at rats in this hotel. The roaches made poor targets.

"Stay back!" said a surprisingly lucid voice from the interior of the darkened room into which the rat had just fled.

Whoever was in there would be afraid he was about to shoot into the room at the rat.

Deggan was momentarily at a loss for words. "Stob you with my knife!" he warned at last.

The voice shrieked with laughter. "You mean you forgot your gun, you poor bastard," the voice said happily. "You don't own no knife."

The voice was distinctly familiar. Deggan peered cautiously around the doorway. All was darkness. Paper, food, and cat litter covered the floor. The blind was taped shut. There was an old mattress on the floor. From beyond it came the voice.

Deggan hesitated. "Ralph?"

Ralph was one of the Crazies who roamed the upper floors. These were people who had run away from Napa State Hospital for the Insane and other mental hospitals.

"Swamp digger?"

It was an expression that had come to mean anyone from Oklahoma.

"Fucking A, I am," Deggan said.

"How come your pants is falling down?" the high and still-disembodied voice of Ralph asked innocently.

Deggan was severely nettled. "Man tries to fotch up his fuckin belt after he takes a shit," he explained testily. "Man can't even take a shit around here without some furry little bastard tryna fuck with him!"

The hall bathroom on the sixth floor had been over-flowing. He had forgotten that the Crazies on this floor always took the paper to sell to winos. Next time he would skip the fifth floor altogether.

The voice giggled. "Well why didn't you fasten your belt?"

Deggan buckled his belt suddenly. "That," he said with as much dignity as he could muster, "was a little oper-ation that was interrupted by Mister Rat."

Several things were coming together to make him dangerously angry. Lately he had embarked on a campaign to turn Grace out, but whenever he talked to her about working O'Farrell Street she laughed at him. Hitting her did no good. She could no longer feel any pain. He had to school the bitch, put a move on her that she couldn't ignore. Her ungratefulness stupefied him. Here he had shown her all his heart—and what did the bitch do? The frustration and unreasonableness of it all had already caused him to get mildly drunk and take over twenty street whites of Benzedrine.

"I wount brag about noth'n I was you," Deggan con-tinued defensively. "Hidin off like that with the rats and shit."

"Tryna kill me."

Deggan had the stirring of a bright idea. "Who?"

While he waited for an answer, he moved a few feet down the hall. It didn't take much to tip a Crazy.

"The Indians," Ralph said fearfully.

Deggan had figured that might be it. There were two Utes on the fourth floor who went on rampages. They did not like Crazies. Other people they attacked for even less reason.

"Fuckers on the warpath?"

"Cochise—" Ralph began. "I forgot," he concluded in a chastised tone.

He had to put the boots to Grace. The Indians would be perfect for that. The Benzedrine and his rage made him daring.

"Stay in your room!" he said threateningly to the darkness from which Ralph's voice had been coming.

From a room all the way down the hall came rhythmic, muffled female screams. Some mack man tenderizing the sweet meat a little. The screams made Deggan angrier and more excited. Hadn't he tried to raise Grace right? Damn straight he had. Many a time!

"What'd I say?" a male voice kept asking in a neutral voice after every blow.

Deggan made his way cautiously down the stairwell to the fourth floor. Nothing was happening. He went back into the stairwell and ran down to the third floor. He thought he heard footsteps following him from above, but paid it no mind. He had to keep the momentum going or all would be lost.

He found the Indians halfway down the third-floor hallway. They were drunkenly building a fire out of candy wrappers and fastfood cartons in a wastebasket.

Apparently they were trying to smoke someone out of a room. In addition to Crazies, the Indians did not like senior citizens. When they went on rampages, they frequently attacked the rooms of old people in the hotel and took their money.

Terrified shouts came from within the room. It sounded as though there was more than one. From within also blared a TV at top volume.

"*HO-lee SHIT!*" he screamed.

Basic con signifying and the momentum of the moment dictated that he scream on them. If he just walked up cold they would beat him unconscious before he could say anything. This way, he could say something.

"Indian Nation!" he hollered. "On the warpath! Ride my pony with the best of 'em!"

The Indians looked up in surprise. The cries of the besieged tenants within the room ceased. The fastfood cartons were sticky with sweet sauce and were beginning to smolder.

"How'd you brothers like to pull a train on my old lady?"

The one called Cochise wore a red bandanna around his neck. The other one had a badly burned face, the victim of Cochise's rage. He was known only as "Cochise's partner." They stared up at Deggan with dull brown eyes. Their mouths were open.

"When?"

Over the smoke Deggan could smell the wine they had been drinking. Their checkered hunting shirts were stiff with dirt, grease, and wine stains.

"Right now."

They looked numbly at each other, like a couple of drugged bears. They were flying.

"Now?" Cochise asked, frowning.

Deggan felt they were going to beat him up.

"No—ten fucking YEARS from now!"

Deggan felt the thing penetrating. They did not return to their fire. He danced down the hall, beckoning.

"Ain't but two floors up!" he yodeled. "Whoop 'n holler away!"

The Indians were momentarily distracted by muffled cries from the room. They stared at the door with open mouths.

"Go away!" a terrified senior was croaking. "Hey you people!"

Deggan cursed. He stopped to fire a question at the unseen speaker. "Can you believe this? Here I am BEGGING these brothers to have a FREE piece of ass!"

At last the Indians followed. They did not put out the fire in the wastebasket. Deggan decided the people in the room would put it out. He ran up the stairs ahead of the Indians.

"Wally whoop of a party!" he enticed.

It was a common practice in the Tenderloin for a man to preside over the gang rape of a woman he wished to put on the streets. It broke her spirit and made her more manageable.

"Drill the squaw! Drill her!"

The Indians said nothing but followed him mutely. Deggan was turned on by them. They had the slow rolling craziness of maddened animals. When they fell down in the stairwell it was like the crashing of elephants.

At the sixth floor they were all wheezing. It was important not to hesitate. He rushed into his room, knocking a couple of wine bottles off the dresser. Grace lay on the bed staring up at him through the bliss of a heroin high. She wore nothing but panties. When she saw the Indians she screamed. Deggan whooped with satisfaction.

"Cochise! Get your red ass some pussy!"

Grace rose halfway, then fell back with a cry of disgust. She clenched her fists at her sides fiercely. Cochise fumblingly unzipped his pants and pulled them down. He staggered sideways onto the bed on top of her. When he fell on her she closed her eyes tightly. Her back arched and she coughed.

Deggan slapped his knee and shouted encouragement to Cochise.

"Piss hole! That's right! Piss hole! Piss hole!"

When she did not take her panties off quickly enough Cochise began to strike her. He struck her as methodically as someone pounding a nail. From Grace came a long sigh that made her entire body shiver. The spasms became regular, like dry heaves, as though she were trying to vomit but couldn't.

Deggan strode importantly around the room. His nose was open good now. *Hadn't he tried to let her do the right thing? Like a mighty he had!* Maybe now the bitch would listen—

Cochise's partner slumped against the wall. "Doncha have yourself a mess a that wine?" Deggan opportuned his guest, pointing at the wine bottles on the dresser.

Cochise's partner closed his eyes and said nothing. Deggan helped himself to more wine. He continued to march around the room, yelling insults at Grace.

"Tryna fuckin bang me out! Doncha talk now bitch?" He recited a poem he had learned in prison:

Gotta *fool* that bitch!
Gotta *tool* that bitch!
Gotta *school* that bitch!
Gotta *rule* that bitch!

Cochise was having difficulties. He couldn't get an erection hard enough to enter her. In his confusion he turned her over. Her body was still. She allowed herself to be turned in his big clumsy hands like a chicken on a spit.

This struck Deggan as funny. "Bet your sweet ass he got something!"

Cochise tried laboriously to enter her from behind. Grace laughed harshly at him.

"Round eye!" Deggan whooped.

Cochise was not in her, but he rode her like he thought he was. Deggan was excited by the hugeness of his body. When he was drunk Cochise's eyes looked like poured glass. There was slow awful menace in everything he did. To be handled by him was to be handled in something already dead.

"Go on and bunny fuck her in the back door!"

Deggan laughed so hard tears formed in his eyes. Had he ever caught that bitch up good—

"Back door! Punch her in the *back* door!"

Frustrated, Cochise began to slap her buttocks. He worked his way up her body until he was slapping the back of her head. This was so much satisfaction for Deggan all at once that he almost fainted. Grace was covering her head with her arms.

Suddenly it was all over. Cochise shifted off her and staggered to his feet. He stared with loathing at Grace's naked body and zipped up his pants. For a moment it appeared he would do something else to her; then he wheeled on Deggan.

Deggan shook Cochise's partner awake. He was almost sure they would beat up on him. He would have to lure them out into the hall. He picked up a bottle of wine and danced out through the door, still charged up by what he had just done.

"How bout a taste?" he asked Cochise.

He waved the bottle. He was not particularly upset by the probability that Chochise would hit him. He found that rather exciting.

In a Black hangout around the corner, Shelly the street-walker sat talking to her old man. He was a Black man called Sonny Mac, Sonny Mac Man, Sonny Main Man, and Sonny Main Money. He preferred Sonny Mac. He wore modified superfly threads that made him look younger than his thirty-four years. He was a dealer and user who felt he had a stronger handle on his habit than his woman.

They drank red wine. They were the only people there except the bartender, but they spoke in low voices.

"He don't *sound* like the heat."

"Don't make no sense."

Shelly had just told him about Quinn. Sonny was trying to figure it out. A guy Deggan knew would be making a big heroin buy later in the evening—that much he already knew.

"If he's the heat," he reasoned at length, "might could be he's *different* heat."

"Might could be."

There were endless possibilities. It was a good way to pass the time. He picked his teeth with a small silver toothpick.

"Might could be the heat fightin among themselves. Ain't that a kick?" He laughed with relish. "Maybe the mothafuckas gonna get him in a middle and squeeze his nuts til he drop dead."

Shelly snorted and plucked a cigarette from the pack on the bar.

"Deggan don't do a damn thing."

"*Been* doing it nigga," the pimp called Sonny said warmly. "He work for Raffo."

" . . . that old stuff."

Since Sonny had a woman on the street and Deggan didn't, they naturally looked down on him as a loser. The fact that he did deals with the police legitimized him only slightly.

"Ain't nobody in his room but a little bitty girl layin' on the bed," Shelly continued. "An don't say nothin cause I done tol her the message already."

"Shit sakes woman."

Talk. It was all talking that talk. The real action was always beyond them. Sonny Mac accepted the fact that he was smalltime. Still—it was not unusual for him to be the conk man in various operations. And this was curious.

"What the fuck he *really* want?" he demanded.

She snorted. "If I don't know *what* the mothafucka be doin, how can I be tellin you what *for?*" She paused and blew smoke, anger boiling up like a storm in her green-painted face. "Nigga why don't you give me some a them reds you holdin?"

"Ho—don't get yo small ass in a uproar."

"Be small but it make money."

He knit his brow and let his right hand float languorously downward. It was a signal for her to shut up. Like her, he had rings with glass jewels on every finger. The hand went *clack* on the bar.

She persevered. "Why don't you ever give me a nice bath with all them salts in it like that guy in the book? Iceberg Slim."

She pronounced the name lovingly. The aging Black bartender standing down the bar laughed.

"Fuck Iceberg Slim!" Sonny Mac said with feeling. "That man come anywhere round me he better get some insurance on himself, cause that nigga's more trouble than he's worth!"

"*Sound* good," the bartender said.

The bartender was an old juicehead. In sober moments he thought himself an informed critic of pimp styling.

"Shut your mouth," Sonny said.

"*That* sound good *too*," the old man cackled.

Shelly drank her wine and pouted. "Daddy, I don't want to go back to that paddy. He look like a roller to me."

She was all sweetness and light. Sonny looked at her with contempt.

"Like a shot you goin back. I got to know something."

He fished some reds out of the cigarette pocket of his shirt and gave her a handful. She got up off her stool and started toward the bathroom. She paused at the door.

"I ain't goin back to that dude to deliver no funky message," she challenged. "He can kiss my sweet ass!"

So he would have to kick her ass. As usual, the old man behind the bar was checking out his slack styling. Sonny liked to go with slack. Let the bitches dig a hole.

"Yeah, you bad all right," the bartender said sarcastically.

Sonny Mac was in no hurry. He went to the jukebox. This one had all the soul specials from times past. Etta

James. Johnny Otis. Nappy Brown. The Flamingos. Jam, juice, and jelly. When he was young and running wild on the South Side (where else but Chicago—home of the hawk?). Soul, style, and sass.

The mellow mood passed. Time to work.

"Didn't I let the bitch drop the reds before I kick her ass?" he inquired of the bartender. "Who says I ain't Sweet Daddy Sugar in real life?"

He entered the bathroom. Words were exchanged. There was the sound of a blow and a sharp scream. The old man stopped wiping the bar and leaned forward attentively, listening to the rhythms of the man's style.

The Indians had been lured away and they were alone in the room. Deggan sat on the chair next to the washbasin, looking at Grace. His face shone with ecstasy. New heights had been reached.

"Sorra honey child," he sighed, "but you made me do it."

He shook his head mournfully. He had the paternal look of a teacher putting over a difficult point.

"Your understanding knows no bounds," she said.

She no longer felt like dying. Total war gave her freedom.

He guffawed and nodded shyly. "I guess I just knowed what you needed," he allowed.

She was going to kill him. She had to kill him. Why had it taken her so long to know that? To really know it?

"I guess that's what they all need," she said. "Women, I mean."

Deggan slapped his knee. "Cept they don't admit it!"

He got up and started pacing back and forth. "Come on. Get up. I want to see you out there working."

She made an O with her mouth, and nodded slowly. "Can I have a couple of hours to clean up before I go on the street?"

He was stomping up and down the room in a frenzy of self-importance. "Allright fuckhead—but I want you out on those cuts in two hours!"

"Okay, Daddy," she said.

He almost passed out with the power of it. She knew the *Daddy* would get him. "Better don't hold out on me bitch! Stave in your fucking head, you hold out on me!"

Enjoy yourself. His last night on earth.

"Oh I won't," she said. She found her panties beside the bed and put them on. "Never-never-never."

Killing Deggan before Quinn got to him was the only way to free Quinn of his obsession. She owed him that. But there was much more. She had to kill Deggan to go on living herself. That was the equation. If she killed him with her own hands, she would receive like a gift of heaven a whole clean new life. If for any reason she couldn't—she had to perish.

"Now don't bang me out," he warned. He stopped pacing and assumed a threatening stance. "Don't ever bang me out!"

Of course she would do time in prison. She would like that. Was her life bad luck, or she was evil? It made no difference. This way she could take responsibility for it, regardless of what it was.

"Won't ever bang you out Daddy. Ever-ever-ever." She paused for effect. "If I do you can kick my ass."

It awed her to remember that just a few years ago she had been part of a radical collective that followed the

New Left line that criminals were victims. The convicted class, they had called them.

"Better believe I'll kick your ass." He took a long drink of wine in his excitement. "Kick your ass *righteously*. You can believe in it!"

She stared at the man whose life she would end. She wanted to remember him as he was now. Bright blue jeans. Childlike stubby legs and short forearms (ghost echo of Mickey Rooney as a psychopath). Jerky unhinged stride. Thin-striped cotton printer's shirt which somehow —in her mind—went with the fiery carbuncles at the back of his neck. The dark walleye that never quite closed at night (to watch her always) with its suggestion of an ability to see more than one thing at a time (second sight some called it). The doughy unformed face whose features could not be molded together into a coherent whole even by the sweaty exertions of gang rape.

His sleeves were rolled to the elbow. On the right forearm was a tatoo that said GOOD BUDDY THE DEVIL. The other forearm had a crude prison-made job of a pony. Above it was the curved legend SWAMP DIGGERS. Below was the line HATES NIGGERS.

Efforts had been made to burn off the bottom line. Probably by one of the numerous Black prison gangs, she decided.

Soon this flower of the convicted class would indeed be a victim.

But first she needed the mighty Dutch courage of her medicine. The decision had been made—the consequences joyously faced. Now she needed the blinding momentum that came from successive waves of speed rushes.

"I'll need lots of speed," she said casually. "Lots and

lots." She hummed to herself. "Lots and *lots.*"

She went to the dresser. In her little gum-wrapper stash there were five amphetamine sulfate tablets left. Wedged between the mirror and the wall was a sizable amount of methamphetamine hydrochloride wrapped in aluminum foil. That was the ticket. She was going to get higher than she ever had before in her life.

A wealth of paraphernalia lay on the dresser waiting. She carefully spilled some drops of water from the washbasin tap into the bent spoon they used for cooking smack. The crystal dissolved immediately. She drew it out into the nose dropper and picked up the rubber surgical tube. She had never shot anywhere near this much before.

"Class," she said.

"Could be," he conceded airily, "you have a mind to be a righteous bitch from the ground up."

"No. I mean the rubber hose."

She sat on the bed and started tying up. She slipped the hose around her left arm and tightened it. It felt good. First the soft little rubber caress—then the welcome numbness.

"Whyncha ever wrench out my works," he was complaining.

She laughed. They had always been her works.

"*Your* works," she said.

She was reasonably sure they both had hepatitis.

"Well next time wrench em out good anyway," he grumbled. "*I* don't want your fucking disease."

He resumed his seat on the chair in the corner and sat watching.

"Got to get high to work those streets," she reassured him.

She took the tube in her teeth and pulled. The vein came up, soft and fat as a caterpillar. She caught a glimpse of herself in the slightly tilted mirror above the dresser. With the tube in her clenched teeth she looked like a disheveled animal gnawing on its leash.

She pressed the needle firmly home, relishing the slanting downward pressure into the fat ripeness of the vein. She had to push stubbornly through hard scar tissue. When it pierced in sideways she moaned. She dropped the tube from her mouth; it snapped and uncoiled like a snake. She relaxed the pressure on the bulb. A bright red spout of blood exploded up into the dropper like a tiny firehose being turned on. She shot some of the crystal with good steady pressure, then drew back some blood. She flagged it several times.

"Stop jacking off," Deggan said disgustedly.

She shot in the last with such firmness that she almost broke the dropper. Her body stiffened as it came pounding through her heart. She leaned forward in joy. The works fell from her hand to the bed. Every inch of meat on her body glowed with pleasure. The pleasure was so palpable it could be cut off her body like flank steak. She put her hand out on the wall to support herself. Her mouth opened slightly and her tongue came out; she made a soft birdlike cawing of euphoria. All the tissues of her mouth and nose were turning dry. She grasped her left breast with her right hand, pressing the breast and squeezing the nipple. Behind it her heart sang in staccato.

Again she cawed or moaned. The power was almost too much.

"Thank you," she whispered hoarsely.

Speed—the power to kill. She was seeping everything

with incredible clarity. She was in complete control.

"Next time wrench em out," Deggan was still complaining.

"You can take it for granted that I have befouled your works. You never do. It is always other people who are poisoning you."

He ignored this. "Fucking eyes get yellow."

She felt dirty from where Cochise had handled her. She felt as if his thumbs had left prints on her arms that could not be wiped away. She hated wearing the panties he had touched and wanted to take a shower. She was glad there was no semen.

"Maybe you can get some smack for later," she said with a trace of a whine. She was careful not to overdo it.

"Woman is a slave for doojee."

The speed had the effect of both intensifying her anger and allowing her to control it.

"You wouldn't be alive without it," she snapped.

So different than heroin. Heroin swamped the killing nightmare with dreamless sleep. It let you kill yourself. Speed let you go ahead and kill someone else. It let you plan, because you could think of three or four things at once.

She stooped to pick up her clothes from the floor. They were stiff with dirt. How many days had they lain there? How many days had she been here? Three—maybe four. She put on the jeans slowly. Gray prickly bra and dusty sweater. There were boots too, somewhere. She found them under the bed. Her body stank.

She put the works on the dresser. "Coming out tonight," she murmured.

Deggan got up and lay on the bed, his eyes half-closed. Grace sat on the bed beside him. She knew what he was thinking. Success was his. The criminal and prison ideal that women existed to be punished—to be fucked like sheep and beaten to death. Reinforced, of course, by the ghetto game of the pimp.

"Build a fire under your ass," he said dreamily.

The pimp was the hero. Why was America set up so that the whites always picked up only the negative things from the blacks?

"Stand em all on their heads—"

"—and they all look alike," she finished for him.

But hadn't she done the same with Richards? Made a deliberate joke of doing things that hurt him? She blocked out the thought. She had to take care of first things first.

"Humping for me," he was muttering.

That was the world that men had made. One long sadomasochistic adjustment. And how quickly she had joined in.

"Yes," she said. "Your righteous slave."

"Niggers are runnin this country," he said abruptly, rousing himself to look at her.

She was startled. It was as if he were reading a part of her mind.

"Boog-fuckers like you encourage em," he added.

It was necessary to start planning how she would kill him.

"I'm hanging out with you, aren't I?"

"How come?" he wanted to know suddenly.

"I've been waiting for tonight."

He was delighted. In a moment he drew himself up on his elbows.

"Guess I showed you."

"You showed me."

"Fuckin A."

"Saturday night," she said.

"Fuckin *A!*"

The pistol would be in the closet under the floorboard. To get to it, she had to get him out of the room. Now was the time to give him the message. She had almost forgotten about it.

"By the way—" she said casually. "Somebody named Shelly came around with a message when you were down the hall before."

She stood up and went to the mirror. She watched him go through changes in the mirror. "What?" he demanded.

"You heard."

He sat up jerkily. "I mean what was the *message?*"

She fooled with her hair. It was too matted to comb. She would have to wash and brush it.

"Said somebody wants to see you across the street in the bikers' bar. Traffic Jammer."

The new control she felt was amazing. When he came over and hit her, it was as if she were ordering him to do it. All part of the plan.

"What in hell you mean?"

"That's what she said."

"Fuckin meet wit *who?*"

"Didn't say."

"What was her name?"

"Shelly. That guy Sonny Mac's woman. You know her."

"*Jesus.*"

There was silence. She enjoyed his uncertainty.

"Why'd *she* bring the message?"

"Didn't say."

"Why dincha tell me before?"

"I didn't exactly have a chance," she said sarcastically.

There was another silence. There were street sounds drifting up through the open window. The blind fluttered in the night breeze. From several blocks away came the sound of three gunshots in rapid fire. Deggan started.

"At the Traffic Jammer?" he asked.

"Right."

"She didn't say who it was?"

"Nope."

"Right now?"

"I think so. Yes."

Slurred and throaty junkie laughter drifted up from below.

"Could be trouble," he said unnecessarily.

He stood at the closet door. At length he fell down on his knees and began to pull at a floorboard. The possibility that he might take the pistol with him had not occurred to her.

"It'd be safer to take your blackjack," she said. "You'll be in a bar surrounded by people."

He arose and went to the dresser. He jerked open the bottom drawer and took out a nine-inch black flat sap. He hit the wall with it. A large piece of plaster fell out in two pieces.

The blow made a shivering crash of the kind that travels through walls.

"Awwwwwww man," said a faint muffled voice in an adjacent room.

"Don't mean nothin," another faint voice said.

In his room above the Traffic Jammer bar Quinn sat drinking from his pint of Bourbon Deluxe. The overhead light was out. By leaning forward slightly on the bed he could see everything that was happening on the street.

Presently he saw a man with a cut on his forearm run by. The man wore black wristbands with studs. A moment later a patrol car cruised by, moving at the same speed as the running man. It was the first time he had seen the police since he entered the Tenderloin. Some of the dealers fell back in the shadows. The officers did not look at the running man with the cut on his arm.

Most of the people on the street had not bothered to move when the patrol car came by. The police seemed to be trying hard not to see anything that would require them to stop.

He wouldn't blame them. There wasn't much worth saving here.

From the bar below came a sudden crescendo of shouting. Unmistakably a fight. It moved gradually out into the street. Accompanying it, Quinn heard a distinct riff of Cantonese.

The Cantonese sounded strange. Out of place in a leather bar.

For some reason, this caused an image of Grace to jump into his mind. He wondered if she was still alive. Almost inevitable, her ending up here. People like her had to go all the way to the bottom. Perhaps it would give her the strength to do whatever she had to do to walk away from it. But not likely.

She hated Deggan as much as he did, but some terrible imbalance inside her turned it into a self-hating attraction. The Quaker orthodoxy of accommodation was burning her alive. It robbed her of her anger and her right to strike back. He had seen that before with Friends. The Inner Light led them not to separate the sinner from the sin, but made them accomplices to both. By submitting to violence, they encouraged it. It could easily become a kind of masochism. In the worst cases the excitement of submitting to violence became a substitute for a dying God. It replaced the ecstasy that faith had once given them. They became worse than accomplices; they became worshippers of Death.

Some fine day Grace would wake up and try to kill someone. It would be just as well if she was in an institution when that happened. If she couldn't kill someone, it would doubtless lead directly into another one of her suicide attempts. An extraordinary number of people had taken advantage of her.

There were slow steps coming down the hall. They stopped at his door. There was a knock. Quinn took another drink and put his bottle carefully down on the floor. He put his hand in his right pocket and went to the door.

It was the streetwalker Shelly. He motioned her into the room. She poised like a cat and looked both ways. Exactly halfway through the door she stopped and looked a second time.

"You can't be too careful," he said.

He wondered who she had been talking to.

"Not around here, honey," she told him.

He went back to the bed. That put enough distance between them for her to come in the door.

"Please close the door."

She reluctantly complied.

"Well?" he asked.

"Nobody in his room but a girl," she said finally. She

nodded with the sharp automatic anticipation of someone who is generally asked too many questions. "Yeah *I*
give her the message all right. She say she give it to him
when he get back."

He stood up and handed her ten dollars. She put it in
her purse without moving off. He offered her a cigarette.
She snapped her gum in a way that indicated it was
enough for her.

"What you want with Andy Deggan?" she demanded.

Her stance had widened. Her small eyes had gone hard
and challenging. She really was unpredictable. Yes, she
had been talking to someone.

"Who are you in with?" he asked in an equally
aggressive way.

She made the All Safe sign of a baseball umpire. "Unh
unh, baby! Don't put me in that shit!"

He turned his back on her and stood at the end of the
bed. He looked out the window at the street. He was
going to scare her off, but wanted to do it with words. He
opened his mouth to spit out the first threats but stopped.
He had just seen Andy Deggan come out the front door of
the Regina Hotel. He remembered him from the picture
Monahan had showed him at the Hall of Justice.

Deggan was uptight and checking out the street from
every angle. It took him a full minute to get across the
street. He headed into the Traffic Jammer below.

So he had gotten the message.

"If you is the heat," Shelly was saying, "you *know* you
can't trust that monkey—"

He looked back at her and noticed the door was open
again.

"Either close the door and come in the room or leave."

"Don't mess around with people."

She stood in the doorway glaring at him. Courage, insanity, or junk? Whatever it was, he was supposed to walk over and smack her. That was the form his answer was supposed to take, to mean anything. But he couldn't. Poor green-nailed wretch, hitting her would be as wrong as hitting a retarded child.

Instead he said, "Stay out of my way and I'll stay out of yours."

She gave him a contemptuous downward glance. She hiked up her purse and left, smirking. He waited until the steps had faded and took another drink. Then he pocketed the key and went to the hall telephone.

Surprisingly, it was in working order.

He dialed Grace's apartment in the Mission. After three rings Don Richards answered. There was TV action music in the background.

"Listen carefully," Quinn said.

"Just a minute."

The volume of the TV was hastily lowered.

"Okay," Richards said.

"There's a hotel in the Tenderloin called the Regina Hotel." He gave him the address. "Grace is in room six-eleven. Six-one-one. Deggan is out. I want you to come and get Grace. I want you to go right in and get her. You have to hurry. I'll be covering you from outside."

"Okay. Shall I . . . "

"Talk to her. Try to get her to go willingly. If she doesn't, use force. And don't take too long. Take her back to her apartment and stay with her.

"Where's Deggan now?"

"No time. Now hurry. I'll call you after you get her over to her apartment. Go."

Richards fumbled the receiver when he hung up. He

sounded like he had been drinking. Quinn shrugged.
Who else was going to come and take Grace Dunaway out
of the Tenderloin?

He went back to the room and sat on the bed where he
could see the front door of the Regina. If Deggan
returned before Richards arrived, he would have to run
down and stop him.

It was all poker. But the stakes . . .

Mortal stakes? No, when you gambled like this it was
more than mortal. The secret was not to fear losing. That
allowed you to bluff like a god.

Grace knelt in the doorway of the closet. The floorboard
was already loosened. She pried it off with her nails and
stared into the dark rectangular hole. The overhead light
was just strong enough from this angle to reveal the dark
blue outline of the pistol. She picked it up. It was covered
with fine vellum-colored dust and was heavier than she
had anticipated.

She laid it down and replaced the floorboard carefully.

She got up and sat down on the bed. She held the pistol
in her lap and examined it. With this simple piece of
mass-produced modern technology she would change the
entire course of her life. She loved the hard coldness of it.
It made her more excited than she would have thought
possible.

She looked for the safety, then remembered revolvers
had none.

She blew away some of the dust. She aimed at the
window. If you were close you couldn't miss. It helped if
your hands weren't shaking, if you squeezed instead of

jerked, if you were cold and calm about it. But most of all it was wanting and needing to make that person die when you pulled the trigger. The bullet went right from your hand into that other person and made them die.

Bang: everything changed then.

She fished her purse from under the bed. The pistol fit easily. She hadn't been carrying a lot—money in a pocketbook, tampons, tissues, a couple of unpaid utility bills, lipstick and other makeup, broken comb, a pencil, her house key, and an extra set of keys for the Volvo. With the pistol inside it the purse closed with no trouble.

She put the purse on the bed. "Don't go away!" she told it.

Having a gun inside made it a magic purse.

Grace stripped and washed herself with a towel, using water from the tap. In the emptiness of the room sound was magnified. Also the speed high and the excitement of the pistol were making her extremely sensitive to sounds. Water hitting the brittle enamel of the sink. The separate threads of street noise from the night outside (voice, tire, backfire, scream or sequence of screams). Coughing of old men in the rooms below. The sharp exclamations of people fighting, the kind that traveled up through the floor and entered through the skin. the plainsong drone of TV news from a room down the hall.

Two people were arguing somewhere in the hotel in the practiced way of people who had fought a long time, as steadily and as insistently as November rain. She couldn't make out the words. She didn't have to. What was important was the way the exclamations kept bouncing back and forth in perfect equipoise, one bringing on the other, almost as if the argument were creating itself separately from the people fighting. The fight was real;

the people were actors.

Or prisoners.

A private long-running theater. Except you couldn't stop it, couldn't get up and walk out. That was not purgatory but hell.

Forever: fucking up again and again—no way out.

That *had* been her life. Tonight she would change all that.

She couldn't wash off the feeling of dirtiness, but the excitement allowed her to ignore it. She dried herself with the sheet from the bed. In the mirror her face was chalky white and the hair badly matted. She couldn't comb it.

"You'll pay for this," she said to the mirror. Craziness. She giggled. She meant Deggan would pay. "*You* know what I mean," she told herself in the mirror.

In prison she would brush her hair every day. Not ostentatious about it, but a goddamn model prisoner anyway.

"I'll make that bastard pay for things he hasn't even *done* yet," she declared forcefully.

Again craziness: if he was dead Deggan *couldn't* do anything.

"Either way," she said.

In prison she would bask quietly in the charisma of murder. That would cause the others to leave her alone. If it didn't, she would probably sleep with one. She would take her time with that, but how could it be any worse than what she had gotten out here?

"Fuckers," she told the night.

When she was dry she put on the boots and stiff clothes. She kept looking at the purse on the bed. When she had dressed she sat with the purse in her lap.

"Now it's just a matter of waiting," she said.

Immediately she was sorry she had said it. All she had to keep her company were the sounds of the lost battalions of bums and crazies who inhabited this hotel. It occured to her that she would need another hit of speed. Just to put her over the top.

She hummed as she dissolved the crystal in the tap water.

"Lost battalions," she murmured with a laugh.

She liked the sound of that. She was quoting something —but what? A movie? Something about the Foreign Legion. Gary Cooper in *March Or Die.* Gary Cooper who had spilled his guts to HUAC. Tough on the bad guys in the desert, but not so tough when it came to a shakedown by the government. But in the movies a natural gentleman.

"'. . . of platonic conversationalists,'" she continued without meaning to. Ginsberg. She was amazed at her recollection.

"A lost battalion of platonic conversationalists . . . "

Exactly the image of talking to yourself. The last word in the platonic. Followed by an image of people going crazy. In Ginsberg they were always jumping all over each other, vomiting, telling final secrets, and plummeting off fire escapes.

She drew the liquid speed into her dropper.

Ginsberg and Kerouac. They had already been well established when she was just getting interested in the civil rights movement in the late 1950s. Better if she had gone with the Beats. Better if her fatal attraction had been for homosexuals, like some women she had known. Homosexuals were at least victims and not executioners. But she had always thrown in her lot with the executioners. With Deggan she had wanted to do it one last time, just to see how bad he could be. Curiosity—or so she had thought.

To what extent was that hatred of all men?

She was not quite ready to shoot up. She sat cross-legged on the bed with the dropper in her hand, the rubber surgical tube lying beside her. In the tilted mirror her sweater looked strange with the sleeve pushed up to the shoulder. Poor white face. She really must try to comb her hair, teasing each tangle one at a time.

She loved this moment. Everything was ready. There were sensations of pleasure in the crook of her arm. It was like getting hot with foreplay, then waiting that extra moment for more.

She hummed the tune from the duet of the cranes in *Mahagonny.* That was the ticket. Weill, Brecht, Kollwitz and her starving kids, the Lang films, Grosz. Doctor Mabuse. Not to mention Caligari. Isherwood's *Berlin Stories. Zeitkunst.* Most of all the music of Kurt Weill, *Dreigroschenoper* and *Mahagonny.* Singing it, a chain-smoking Lotte Lenya. In the background a workers' choir . . .

Germany in the 1920s. That was the mood she wanted. *"Wohin ihr?"* she sang from *Mahagonny. "Nirgendhin! Von wem entfernt? Von allen!"*

She knew the mood of that time and place in her bones. She had no idea why; it was just an overwhelming emotion. A secret fantasy was that she had lived then. She had been a singer in a *Kabarett,* a Communist, a drug addict, and beautiful . . . .

"So sind sie Leibende, Liebende, Liebende!"

At Cal she had studied German. She loved the long glutted words with one sound jammed on after another, like a train. Time was the switch-engine. As new horrors and delights arrived, new syllables got added onto the old words.

"*So sind sie Liebende, Liebende, Liebende . . .* " she sang again, softly this time.

In German she had wanted to find words for certain things she felt. She thought you went to the language of killers to find the right word for the killing thing in yourself. Now, that embarrassed her. Superficial. Not unlike the people who came west shopping for salvation.

California was their supermarket.

She liked the image. "Prices slashed!" she yelled vaguely to the night outside the window. She put the tube around her arm. *Must close tonight! Everything has to go! Two Karmas for the price of one! Let our loss be your gain!*

What was the word for what she was feeling now? *Bittersweet* was close; something about killing, mixed with an odd and powerful gentleness. *Power* was another word. Pleasure. Drugs were a part of it. And in the Tenderloin the words would be essentially raunchy, with certain secrets of the heart and body exposed.

It was the heart's needle, blunt but endlessly piercing.

"Handgun!" she shouted suddenly without meaning to.

She tightened the rubber tube. The vein stood out. She did not put the tube in her mouth. She felt like taking her time.

"The Great American Handgun."

To herself she sounded like someone in a trance.

"Fingerprints," she continued.

She had no idea what this was supposed to mean.

On the bed two feet away from her lay her purse with its wonderful secret freight. She wanted to stroke it. Touch it, with the hand that held the dropper. The power would flow out through the purse and right into the dropper, and she would put it into her arm.

She was leaning forward to touch it with the back of her hand when she heard footsteps outside her door. She hastily drew back.

There were two knocks on the door, three beats of silence. Two more knocks.

"Open up goddamn I'm serious!" said a voice that she instantly recognized as Richards's.

Quinn would be in on this. It would be tricky.

"It's locked. Go away."

She realized much depended on shooting up before anything else happened. She flexed her arm and put the rubber tube in her mouth. Her movements were precise —a clockwork dream. The tissue of her arm was tough but she felt her body willing the needle in. She angled it, pushing. The flesh pricked up, waiting for the ride. There were impatient noises outside the door.

Richards knew what she was doing.

"Pump in that fucking dope," came his hysterical muffled cry, "you don't feel a damn thing til you come down! Go on!"

The needle punched home. She flagged and shot. She released the rubber tube. She shot it all.

"Right!" she yelled. *Until you come down*. She yelled that too: "Until you come down!"

From the hall came an infuriated bellow. There were two heavy running steps and a crashing kick at the door. The needle slipped out of her arm. The door was struck once again. This time the lock ripped off the wall with a small explosion of plaster and the door swung open with the force of a whiplash. It banged into the dresser, cracking the mirror and knocking over wine bottles, and stopped dead. She laid the dropper down beside her and leaned forward. The speed was hitting her heart. Richards walked slowly in.

"See what I mean?" he said bitterly.

He sat down beside her. He almost sat on the dropper. He saw it at the last moment and picked it up. He tossed it across the bed.

"Dynamite."

This was the best of her life. A hundred orgasms. Her left breast tightened like a vise. She ran her hand roughly over the left side of her body. The nipple hardened like a jaw clenching. Her back arched like a bow; for a moment she thought her spine would snap. Her mouth turned to cotton. She gently broke wind. Behind her tightly closed eyelids sang green bullets.

"This is terrific," Richards was saying disgustedly.

From far away he seemed afraid to touch her.

Three times she shouted. Between each there was a long pause. The rush was going down from her chest into her arms and legs.

Finally she opened her eyes. Richards was staring at her. He was unshaven and nervous. He pointed at the dropper.

"What are you shooting?"

"Speed."

He sensed the great change in her. She was thinking with the speed of light. She wanted to do something that would throw him off. Change up on him.

She looked directly into his eyes. Her hand floated forward.

When she touched him he jumped. He looked at her as though she were a talking dog. His bleary eyes widened.

" . . . come to save Gracie."

He looked down in astonishment at her hand on his leg. She wasn't letting go.

"Save Gracie from *whom?*" she demanded sternly.

"What?"

"From Andy Deggan."

"From Andy Deggan," he obliged her.

He nodded slowly. He wanted to help her get the story right. He was also getting very angry.

"Look." She pointed at the cracked mirror above the dresser. Her face was split by the crack. "That's your boy Deggan."

He shook his head. "Come on."

"Without me people like Deggan couldn't exist."

"Then get away from him."

She watched him dispassionately. He was about to get rough with her. Her purse was not three feet away. She leaned over casually and pulled it over beside her. He hesitated for only a moment.

"Let's go."

"I'm not going with you."

"Yes you are."

In about twenty seconds he would hit her. She could see the pain in his eyes. First he had to talk about it.

"You just have to drag us down—" he began in a proprietary tone.

But there were steps. Quinn appeared at the door. He entered the room without hesitation. Grace jumped up.

"You bastard!" she screamed at Richards.

Quinn stopped five feet away. His eyes stayed on her face.

Richards's mouth was open. He spread his hands. "I don't know what this is!" he told her.

She had only seen Quinn in a pea jacket and watch cap

once before. He looked dangerous in them. His face looked different.

"I don't believe you people," Richards was saying.

Grace caught her purse by the strap and hoisted it.

"Fucker!" she yelled at Richards. The anger came without effort or contrivance. "You *better* believe this!"

Richards turned his back on them. "Completely fuck this shit!"

"I told you to *hurry*," Quinn said in a low voice to Richards.

Quinn's gray eyes had never left her. In them was neither anger nor pity. She opened her purse. He stepped forward: she saw the fist coming up. It hit her on the point of the chin.

Richards followed Quinn onto the roof. Part of the way he was dragging Grace. There was no time to check anything out. Quinn kept waving him on. Quinn apparently knew the route.

At the edge of the roof Quinn stopped.

"I'll take her across."

Richards saw that about two feet separated the roof of the Regina Hotel from the Southern Home. Exactly the kind of short haul that would fox you, if you stopped to think. In his excitement Richards decided that wasn't going to happen. A pace had been set.

"Go on across your own self!" he hollered at Quinn.

He judged the stride necessary to get him across. He gathered Grace into his arms; her body was all bones. Three long running steps carried him across easily. It wasn't even a jump.

Grace moaned. "Quinn?" Richards asked.

The light was faint pink neon, reflected from low clouds.

"Over here."

Quinn had opened the door to a stairwell. He propped the door open with a piece of wood. Richards stumbled over debris; the roof was littered with it. Going down the stairs the two men took turns carrying her. At basement level they were panting like horses. No one had seen them.

Quinn handed her over to him. "How are you?"

"Okay." Richards stopped to pant for a few seconds. It was hard work, even though she was relatively light. "I already fucked my back up a long time ago anyway. You know?"

"I know."

There was no door separating the basement from the stairwell. It was pitch dark. Richards smelled garbage and rats. As his eyes adjusted slightly, he saw shapes that he decided were furniture.

"Which way?"

Quinn pointed. Richards bore her forward, bumping into couches and tripping over mattresses. He heard the scrabble of rodents. The gray outline of a door appeared. Quinn opened it and made way for him. The Volvo was in the alley.

Richards thrust her in the back seat roughly. Her eyelids flew open and closed; he saw white. He fired up the engine. He wanted to get away quickly. The stuff Grace had been taking would wake her up.

"She's shooting speed," he told Quinn. The window was open and Quinn was leaning down, looking into his face.

"How do you know that?"

"I saw her."

Quinn hesitated. "What did she tell you?"

Richards glanced back at Grace. There was no time.

"Give me a call," he said. "Right?"

Quinn straightened. Richards pulled out. He was still breathing hard. He got out of the alley and into traffic. It was hard to concentrate on driving—the Volvo was skittish.

He checked the Saturday night special in his coat pocket. The pistol they had taken from Grace's purse Quinn had kept.

Once across Market Street he leaned over to open the other window a crack. He was not afraid of her jumping out. It was a two-door and he could probably stop her. If he couldn't, he would run over her. And enjoy it.

There was stirring in the back seat. Grace moaned.

"Killed while trying to escape!" Richards said threateningly.

"What's that?" came from the back seat.

"What might happen to you."

Behind them was a patrol car. He slowed without appearing to slow down too much. He hoped Grace wouldn't sit up where they could see her. Cops weren't crazy about salt-and-pepper couples, even in this supposedly liberal town. It would be hard to explain the gun in his pocket if they got stopped.

The police dropped back when he got into the Mission District. He turned around to check out his passenger. She had her eyes open but seemed to be drifting.

"You hate my guts," she said in a small voice.

"Take it easy. Just rest."

His mother used to say that when he was a kid and

couldn't get to sleep: *just rest* —

"No," she said. "It's okay."

He heard the snap of her purse. She was looking for the pistol.

"Thanks," she said.

The way she said it was as hard as he had ever heard anyone say anything. The word struck him like a slow air hammer. He was overcome by a need to do something crazy. He didn't care whether she was awake or not.

"You bitch. You bitch."

Ahead was a driveway attached to an auto-supply store. He pulled into it. He took the car out of gear and left the motor running. He turned around violently.

There was thick blood on her teeth where Quinn had hit her. Below her chin was a dainty string of blood and saliva down the length of her sweater. She was staring into his eyes without the slightest fear.

He took her chin in his hand in case she tried to look away.

"Listen," he said.

One pale cheek flinched slightly. She thought she was about to be hit again. He was glad of that.

"Listen quick now. You have a great kid. You know that? You want to save that kid's life? You got to make a home for him."

He paused. He couldn't tell from the steady gray eyes whether she knew what was coming or not.

"You got to marry me. Just fucking go down to the courthouse and marry me. You always want to take chances. Take a chance on something that might do somebody some good for a change."

He saw with great satisfaction it was the one thing she hadn't expected. Her eyes slowly closed.

"Let's go," she said in pain.

He let go of her face. He turned away and waited. There was a wracking sob from the back seat. He wanted to be angry, but as usual he felt pity.

In a moment the anger he wanted came rushing in.

"You're a freak. But if I *want* to do it—"

There were to be no tears from the back seat. There had just been that one great sob, like an explosion in a soundproof room.

"Don't talk about it."

He glanced back at her. She was leaning back and staring at the ceiling. There was no trace of emotion on her face.

He put the Volvo in gear and pulled back into the street.

"When you ask me to marry you," she said in the same small but determined voice, "I feel contempt for you. What do you call that kind of personality?"

"Sick," he said without hesitation, "but I already knew that."

He leaned out the window and sucked in air.

"If only you could hit me." She was laughing bitterly.

"I can do that."

In the rearview mirror he saw her shake her head.

"I mean really."

He thought about hitting her. They could use ordinary household items—knotted towels and sheets, old celery from the icebox, the telephone cord. Afterward he could tie her up and fuck her on the kitchen table like a piece of meat or cantaloupe. Is that what she wanted? No, she wanted him to *really* hit her.

He was awed and disgusted. The distance between the two was like the chasm between the Regina Hotel and the

Southern Home, which he had carried her across a few moments before—so narrow and yet so deep.

He shuddered.

"Anyway it's too late," she said.

They had reached her apartment. He started looking for a place to park. He found one at the end of the block.

"Remember Jacob Nance?" she asked in the middle of parking.

Nance was the father of her son Martin. He had been involved in union politics at the Post Office. He had also been collecting evidence for the government about an illegal strike. Grace had fallen for him. By the time she had found out who he really was, she was already pregnant.

He was the whitest Black man she had ever slept with: a perfect double agent.

"Aw man—" He strained to cut the wheels. "Don't talk about that. Don't even *think* about him is my advice."

"I wonder if Martin will ever want to see his father."

Richards snorted. He had knifed the wheels too sharply. He would have to pull out and park again.

"I wonder will he ever see his *mother*."

This time he got in the parking space. He cut the lights and motor. He turned to look at her. He reached down and took a tissue from her purse.

"There's blood on your teeth."

She took the tissue and used it. "Nance was a metaphor for my life. I've never been attracted to a man who wasn't a bastard."

"Bad luck is what I call it."

She came at him with a soft shriek. *"Bad luck!"*

There was still blood around her mouth. It was disturbing. He took the tissue and finished the job. "Yeah *bad luck!*" he said angrily. "Don't they teach *bad luck* over at Berkeley? Why do educated white people always say it must got to be some whole other thing like a *metaphor—*" He couldn't remember the other word they used. *Symbol,* that was it.

They wanted everything to be a symbol for something else.

"It wasn't just bad luck," she said forcefully.

"Sooner or later bad luck happen to everybody."

But he knew what she meant. There was a pattern. Even a common street idiot could see she regularly got involved with losers. And deeply so.

"You think I'm crazy to want to marry you," he sighed.

He turned off the car lights. About half of the pastel-colored houses on the street were dark. It was getting on.

"I think," she said, "I keep forgetting how you must feel."

He turned to roll up the window.

"That's the nigger's occupation in life," he said bitterly. "Not having feelings."

But it wasn't racism. If he didn't cut it for her, it made no difference what they were.

"Let's go," he told her.

Crossing the street he kept his hand on her arm. She was limping slightly.

The apartment was as he had left it: books neatly shelved, dishes washed and put away, floors swept, blankets folded at the end of the couch. Grace looked around.

"Stepin Fetchit," he said shrugging.

She turned on him angrily. "None of this was my idea."

He laughed and ushered her grandly toward the kitchen. After a moment's hesitation she followed.

"Let's have a drink."

She poured him a glass of wine. For herself she made tea. All her movements were precise. He had never seen her move this way before; all hesitancy was gone. Yet halfway through the tea-making she leaned forward. Her shoulders shook.

"Okay," he said. "What is it?"

She waited until the tea was done. When she sat down across the table from him, there were tears on her cheek. Yet there was no despair. Her damp eyes did not waver.

"My son. Martin."

She got up to examine herself in a small mirror above the sink.

"You know what Jacob told my brother?" She apparently thought he knew. He said nothing. "That I had a Black child because they kicked me out of the Movement."

He shuddered. That kind of mindfucking was meant to cripple.

"I've taken so much out on that kid. So much anger."

"Sound like something he'd say."

But the thought shook him up. He was glad when it passed.

She resumed her seat across from him. "Remember what happened at the Pacific Liberation School?"

He nodded. It had been a New Left school run by feminists. Deggan had gotten himself a job teaching a class on "prisons, jails, and concentration camps." They were thrilled to have a real ex-con on the staff. When he stole equipment and held one of the female staff prisoner for several hours with a knife, enthusiasm had waned.

"So what? What does all this have in common—except it's all some kind of trouble?" he wanted to know.

"It's a cycle of shit. Everybody hurting everybody else. Ignorance or malice, it makes no difference. It's just an orgy of people hurting each other on different levels."

"So?" he pressed grimly.

"I'm getting out."

He sensed danger. She wanted to rise up and smite the enemy. Who? How? He didn't know. Maybe he would have to barricade her in the closet.

"Come on with that old stuff," he pleaded. "You sound like that mangy-ass old man that calls himself a preacher in my mama's church."

Richards's nightmare was that the universe would turn out to be exactly the way Baptists said it was.

"My father used to read the Bible occasionally," Grace said. "Before supper. I always pretended to be listening."

"*You* were listening. You heard every word. And believed it. That's the dangerous part of that Bible reading and Sunday school bullcorn. Some fool might actually believe that stuff."

"What happens then?"

She was waiting for his answer.

"Ahhh . . . some kind of trouble," he said tactfully.

The wind picked up. The windowpane above the sink creaked. He glanced at his watch. It had stopped, but he guessed it was around eleven. The long silence deepened.

"Ever do any guilt hustling?" Grace asked at last. "In the sixties? All those nice civil rights ladies . . ."

He wearily took out his pipe and tobacco pouch.

" . . . just dying to prove how liberal they were?"

The skin game had penetrated to her bones. Probably even beauty came across to her as a hustle of some kind. That was why she hated the small bronze Adonis who was her son.

yodeling ceased.

"Grace you dumb crazy bitch," the voice began after a pause.

At that moment Quinn realized in his excitement he had left the door open.

" . . . leavin the door open allaways like that so any a these puny-ass thieves could walk dreckly in an help themselves!"

He suspected someone was in his room. Quinn cursed silently. The killing had to happen inside the room. If Deggan wouldn't come in, he would have to drag him in.

"Grace?" the voice inquired. "Is that someone in there with you? Where bouts?" Next came the adolescent snarl. "All right, somebody is SHIT OUTTA LUCK!"

Amazingly, he was slowly pushing open the door.

"Blieve some uns behind the chester drawers," the voice snickered.

Quinn jumped. The motion was wrong from the beginning. His thigh caught on the edge of the dresser. The intruder was already moving out. Quinn saw nothing of him but a blur. When he cleared the room the intruder had reached the stairs. Quinn remembered to hide the pistol by jamming it in the pocket of his pea jacket.

The intruder stopped at the stairs and turned around. It was the same man Quinn had seen crossing the street.

"Deggan?"

He hooted.

"Don't get rambustious old man," Deggan said scornfully.

He was a good thirty feet away. Down the hall a door started to open. It slammed shut quickly.

"Let's talk!" Quinn said breathlessly.

Get him back in the room.

Deggan's head jerked *no* furiously. "I know who you are!"

He was off like a shot. Quinn didn't bother chasing. The steps faded. Quinn looked down at his hands. One of the thin rubber gloves had been torn at the wrist.

Deggan's voice crowed up the stairwell. "You are *lame!*"

Richards kissed her a long time. Only the table between them stopped him from melting into her. The gun was making both of them excited. In her hair he smelled a sinister bouquet of dope and sex. That simply added to the excitement he felt.

"Grace—"

He put the pistol in his lap. She had won again.

"*Amazing* Grace," she murmured.

He drew back. The gray eyes opened. The were still wonderfully controlled, but beneath strained the usual insanity. It was like kissing the sea. In fact, there had been salt in the kiss. There was still blood in her mouth.

"A hymn," she explained.

"Tell me about it. We sang that when I was a kid."

"Bad nigga don't like no Calvinism?"

"I don't like to hear no names about it either."

She was giving him a slight smile with a pout.

"Is that an order?"

He shrugged wearily. He smiled for no particular reason.

"Hop to it."

"Miss Ann."

"Who got to keep a whip hand on the help—!"

"My God."

They laughed.

"I always preferred 'Blessed Be the Tie That Binds,'" Grace said.

She was playing a part. She was too damned much in control for a crazy person. The gray eyes were not supposed to stare in so calculated a fashion. She wasn't even blinking.

"Did the Friends sing hymns?" he asked politely.

There was something else Richards wanted to ask. He was afraid to say it. With some people you had to say too much.

"At this one particular meeting we did. For fifteen minutes at the beginning. The rest was silent worship."

She went into the front room and turned on the FM. Soft jazz from KJAZ floated back. There was a pause between tunes.

"Speaking of music," she explained.

She did not return to the kitchen. He heard the shower go on. When he opened the bathroom door he was surprised to find her showering. She sang for him.

Blessed be the tie that binds . . .

She added some words about sadomasochism. He went back to the kitchen. When Grace reappeared she wore fresh jeans, a clean sweater, and sandals. He was surprised and disappointed she wasn't dressed for bed. She brushed her hair in a businesslike manner.

"You had your chance to blow out my brains," she said.

She lit a cigarette and stood looking at him.

"You *couldn't*," she told him. "That's probably what

you came to California to find out."

She was miles away from tears or the mood of tears. She put a fresh pack of cigarettes in her purse.

"It came to me tonight." She sat down across from him. "People don't just come out here to run out their string. They come out here to find out if they're right or wrong about certain things." There was awe in her voice. "To find out if they can *do* certain things. Certain *necessary* things."

"That's crazy," Richards said. He was fighting a growing sense of dread. "You can't find out for sure about anything out here!"

She tapped her fingers. "Why is that?"

He had a theory about that.

"All a bunch of bustout hustlers out here. They're all taking and they have nothing to give back."

She was an example—Grace with the odd sex and the cowlicks and the high cheekbones that made her look like a fifty-year-old adolescent. She would suck everyone around her dry.

"But you can know anyway," she insisted.

"How?"

"By just coming here. You run out of land. That forces you to be reflective. Sooner or later it comes to you, what you have to do."

She laid down her brush. Her face floated forward.

"Kiss," she said as though it were a mild rebuke.

He would be the angel who would stand between her and her sadly mistaken dream. She would kiss him.

"Kiss the virgin," she said.

Her eyes closed and he leaned forward to kiss her. She had put on perfume. It filled his lungs. The feeling in his belly came back.

"Kill the virgin," she murmured.

He was alone and over fifty. That was loneliness. As you got older, all kinds of things expanded to fill that loneliness. The only advantage he could see to getting old was that you stopped worrying about *how* you died.

"Don't the bad nigger went to sacrifice his virgin no more?"

He had put the pistol in his coat pocket. He now took it out and put it in his lap.

"Stagger Lee," she said.

She knelt before him and put her arms around his waist. She leaned forward and kissed the pistol in his lap.

"Show me your gun you cold bad-ass nigger Stagger Lee!"

"My gun is for fun," he said with difficulty.

She nuzzled at his shirt. "The other one, then."

"This one?"

He picked up the pistol. She nodded.

He popped out the cylinder. Each little bullet sat in its hole. He showed her the neatness of it.

"Get 'em," she said.

"You don't know the first thing about it."

He had always found shootings unpleasant.

"When was the last time you used it?"

"A guy tried to come through the window." He remembered. "Afterwards he was screamin and bleedin all over the place. I had to clean it all up myself and I couldn't get back to sleep. Cops took him to the hospital. I heard they let him out the next day." He pushed the memory back. "Ten years ago—more like fifteen."

"Let me see it."

"Don't fool with it."

He reached for his glass of wine. He held the pistol by

the barrel with his left. As he lifted the glass of wine to his mouth she grabbed his right wrist. She pulled it toward her as though she wanted to drink it. It spilled onto his lap.

He was tired of her games. He wanted to throw the glass of wine into her face.

"Stop it!"

The glass upended into his lap. It was a full second before he realized what had happened. He had released the pistol with his left hand and she held it pointing it at him.

"Don't you move."

He stared at the gun in her hand. Her finger was on the trigger. She hoisted her purse and moved backwards.

He was embarrassed and extremely angry. He stood up.

"Sit down," she told him.

"I can make you use that."

He had the feeling they had been through this all before.

"I know what I have to do."

"I don't," he said shrugging.

He eased toward her. He saw she would fire. He saw the trigger finger pulling and the action rotating to index the cartridge. There was a terrific explosion. He felt flesh and bone fly off his right foot, like a small door being blown off its hinges by the wind.

There were exclamations in Spanish from the apartment below.

"Stay back!" she ordered.

Using the gun had made her excited but not shaken up.

There were further exclamations from downstairs. He

saw she was aiming at the other foot and shouted in fear. She stopped and they stood frozen. They were engulfed by the slow crawling explosion of silence that occurs after a pistol shot.

"No!" he cried out.

The first lick of pain. Already the familiar but distant sensation that it couldn't be happening. For the first time in many years he was smelling gunsmoke. That was fear.

"Good-bye," she said.

Richards sat down at the kitchen table and began to cry. He did not particularly want to do this. It just happened. If she had shot him in the chest he thought he would have killed her. Somehow being shot in the foot signaled total defeat. Truly now it was time to give up, the pain was saying.

There were times like that.

"Get out," he told her.

He did not look at her. With one part of his mind he believed she was about to kill him. With another he was simply humiliated. Most of all was sadness. When she shot him he had seen confusion and even panic in her eyes but not the slightest trace of hesitancy.

He heard the door close and light running steps on the stairs. The street door of the apartment opened and harumphed shut.

"You win!" he shouted after her.

The tears welled up thick and silently. They dripped on his hands. He pushed himself back from the table and looked down. There was a small hole in his right cowboy boot. Through it bubbled thin blood. He had an image of what his foot looked like inside the boot. The hole was perfectly circular and clean as a cut made by a butcher, so radical that the flesh would fall open as if it had been made that way. The boot held the foot together.

Outside he heard the Volvo door slam shut. The motor was turned on and revved impatiently. The car pulled away in the direction of Mission Street.

The pain in his foot quickly reached the throbbing stage. The Salvadoreños downstairs would almost surely call the police, but not necessarily an ambulance. He sighed and limped to the telephone in the front room. Even without putting any weight on the wounded foot, he felt considerable pain.

Quinn sat on the bed in Deggan's room. He massaged his calf. He had pulled it slightly when he went after Deggan. The burning sensation was not entirely unpleasant. There were times when it was good to hate yourself, he thought.

So stupid—overconfidence. There was more to Deggan than met the eye. It would be very hard. It might take all night. It might take a lifetime.

He had to make Deggan come back to his room for his gun. To do that he had to scare him more. Threaten him. It wasn't just strategy. He wanted to hurt Deggan in public. Humiliate him.

Wide-open street maneuvering. Total war in public.

He had no choice—the stakes had been raised.

He tore the lining in the left pocket of the pea jacket. The gun rode easily. He was carrying two guns now. He wondered about hiding the backup thirty-two on the roof.

The bourbon was gone. He drank some of Deggan's wine, fighting the stiffness in his body. The pulled muscle

in his leg still burned and his wind was very bad. He
waited until he was breathing evenly.

"You bastard. You bastard."

He cursed not at Deggan but at himself. Deggan was
the shadow. *Putting him out like this. He was supposed to
lie down and die.*

"Fat chance," he told himself shortly.

He had tasted blood and then moved too fast. The
oldest mistake of the fighter.

He gave the messy room one last glance. There was
nothing more here for him. He kicked some hamburger
wrappers and a shirt into the corner. He decided to leave
the door closed, although with the sliding lock torn off
the wall it could no longer be locked from within.

He checked out the hall. Empty.

On his way down he noticed one of the light bulbs had
been stolen. This had required some effort, since the
lights were enclosed in chicken wire. Somebody had
pulled the chicken wire out of the ceiling with a rope or
chain.

There were fewer junkies in the lobby. Those remaining sat in decaying chairs along one side. Most of the
dealing was now being done along the street in the
deserted storefronts. The room clerk had long since fled.

On the sidewalk he stopped to check out the action.
The drag queens were fewer and were not particularly
attracting anyone's attention. He saw Shelly, the streetwalker he had talked with earlier. She was stooped over
talking intently to a john in a car. She did not see him.

The Traffic Jammer had a thick velvet curtain inside
the door. To get inside you had to walk around it. The
jukebox blared and there were purple lights in it. Quinn
kept his back to the wall and lit a cigarette.

He thought there were about fifteen people in the bar. Some of them stared at him hostilely. He spotted Deggan immediately.

Good. That meant no hunting. No tracking.

Walkin talkin! sang powerfully amplified voices from the jukebox in the blues key of E.

The customers were a loathly Tenderloin sideshow of freaks. Bikers without bike clubs. Bikers without bikes. S and M wonders. Tattoos, cutoff denim jackets biker-style, leather wristbands. Broken pockmarked faces with the starved and permanent sneer of adolescence. Lots of leather. Punk styling all the way. Also lots of military trinkets and graphics—swastikas, Iron Crosses, Luftwaffe badges. Someone playing the pinball machine had a nazi Death's Head on the back of his jacket.

He eased down the bar. There was an empty stool on Deggan's near side. Deggan had seen him.

Quinn grinned. "Don't get up."

He sat down next to him. Deggan did not move. He appeared to be lost in thought. His walleyes stared down at the bar.

"So you know who I am, do you?" Quinn said.

Deggan's shirt and flannel jacket sat bunched up on the bar. He wore a sweat-patched T-shirt that said AIR-BORNE—DEATH FROM ABOVE on the back. It had gaily-colored graphics of floating parachutists blazing away with automatic weapons. How they loved the military stuff, these kids who could never make it in any military organization in the world.

"Yeah I know," Deggan said sullenly.

He wore jeans and smoked with quick furtive motions; his short knobby forearms flashed blue tattoos. His face was the color of processed flour and there was a bright red scar at the edge of one eye. He was quite small—his feet did not quite reach the bottom rung of the barstool. The short elfin legs made him childish.

"Aw man," Deggan said in a bored way.

He had seen all this before.

"Shut your mouth."

The walleyes were fascinating. In addition to the vague look of dope, they seemed strangely wise. Sometimes wall-eyed people appeared to be seeing more than they were.

"Come on."

"You shut your mouth," Quinn repeated.

The bartender appeared. Quinn hadn't seen him before. He was an old short Chinese. He seemed excited but moved quietly.

He walked past them. He turned at the end of the bar.

"Double bourbon," Quinn said.

Quinn smiled but did not take his eyes from the bartender. The old Chinese whispered to himself as he meted out the bourbon with a jigger.

When the bartender served him, Quinn pointed at Deggan's head.

"He a friend of yours?"

The Chinese stared at him in amazement. He had dark sparkling eyes. Quinn took out ten dollars for the drink.

A leather punk on the other side of Deggan guffawed. "He wouldn't give him a glass of water if he was on fire!"

The bartender looked at the ten dollars. He shook his head *no*.

"Then hand me that."

Quinn pointed to a baseball bat that leaned against the wall behind the bar. The Chinese picked up the bat but did not hand it to anyone. He stood waiting.

"Why you want it?" he screamed finally. In the

Cantonese manner he put even heavy stress on each syllable.

Quinn pointed again at Deggan. "To break his back."

He made no move toward Deggan. He had attracted considerable attention from the other patrons. There was a sudden outpouring of noise as a new record came on the jukebox.

"No." The bartender grinned but shook his head.

Quinn leaned over the bar to shout at him. "Is he a bad man?"

The Chinese giggled. "They all bad man."

"Then why can't I beat him up? Hit him?"

Deggan started to get off his stool. Quinn grabbed his arm.

"Huh," the Chinese laughed uncertainly.

Deggan was trying to break free. The bartender set down the bat behind the bar. He picked up Quinn's ten dollars.

"I know what this is," Deggan was saying importantly. Quinn continued to hold him by the arm.

Quinn kicked over his stool. "Why don't you pick it up?"

They both looked at the bartender. He had his back to them. He was ringing up Quinn's drink. Deggan clung to the bar. The punk on the other side moved off.

Deggan stared at him with awe. "Can I borry your bat he says. To break your back he says."

"No—to crawl your fucking sorry ass out of here." Quinn pointed down at the fallen stool. "Lean down and pick it up." He shook Deggan like a rat. "Sweetheart."

"You'll hit on me."

"I'll *piss* on you."

There was a crash of silence as the record on the

jukebox ended. Everybody in the bar watched. Still the bartender did nothing.

"I got friends," Deggan said.

His voice was loud in the silence. People laughed.

"Bigtime friends?"

Deggan nodded. "Gospel."

The impression Deggan gave was of nothing particularly wrong. It made his threats seem unimportant. Quinn grasped him by the opposite shoulder and pushed him down toward the floor.

"Real bigtime friends?"

"Big enough to kick your ass!"

"Sure?"

"Fucking A, I'm sure!"

Deggan fell on his knees. Several punks cheered.

"Then crawl back to them!"

He grabbed his hair and shoved his face at the floor. Deggan cried out. There was more laughter from the bar patrons.

"Come on. Crawl!"

Deggan crawled toward the back. Quinn flipped him over by his T-shirt, like a crayfish. Deggan shrieked. There was a small snapping sound from his head hitting the floor.

"The other way!" Quinn staggered with rage. "Right out the door. Down the gutter where you belong."

He saw red. A moment later he regained control.

Deggan crawled. When Quinn kicked him he mewed with pain. "I got them friends! It ain't no lie!"

Quinn walked him to the door like a dog. Deggan looked up at him. Quinn saw the snarl that until now he had only heard. At last the kid was getting mad. About time, he thought.

"Listen," Quinn said. "This is just the beginning. I'm following you. Everywhere you go I fuck with you. Each time it'll get worse."

Quinn went back to the bar. He sipped his drink. Deggan stood against the velvet curtain just inside the door. His palms were black with dirt. People were laughing at him.

"You better leave me ALONE or you'll be SORRY!"

Quinn laughed. Deggan turned and exited.

Two blocks away from the Traffic Jammer was an alley where the buildings rose so sharply that at night the darkness was especially deep. In this spot sat an old Chrysler. About ten minutes after Quinn's encounter with Deggan, the three men in the car were joined by a younger man named Thomasson.

They were all narcotics officers.

The two men in the back seat were unshaven and dressed shabbily. The man in the driver's seat was also unshaven and wore a checkered hunting jacket and prescription sunglasses with thick plastic rims. In addition he wore scuffed boots and soiled dress pants. The car was full of cigar and cigarette smoke.

Thomasson sat in the front seat.

"Did you hear what I said?" Thomasson was demanding in a manner that stopped just short of hysteria.

The two men in the back seat were laughing. Thomasson decided to interpret this as nerves. One of the men wore a hunting cap. The flaps were tied on the top of his head with a small bow. They were drinking from flask.

"Shut *up* you guys," said the man in the driver's seat.

This man smoked a cigar in a studied way. Although he had dressed himself as a south-of-Market bum, his manner set him apart as a man intent upon observing those around him. His name was Raffo. He was Thomasson's boss.

"Ter*ri*fic," said one of the men in the back seat.

Thomasson heard the metallic rustle of the flask being passed. He wished the hell he knew Raffo better. He could talk to him about those two.

"Well there it is, goddamnit," Thomasson said. He spread his hands angrily at Raffo. "What do we do?"

Raffo stroked his stubbled cheeks thoughtfully. He watched the two men in the back seat through the rearview mirror. At length he turned. He was pointing a lightweight thirty-eight-caliber revolver with a short barrel in the face of the man wearing the hunting cap.

"*Look.* I'm gonna take this gun and shove it down your throat, you don't shut *up*, Morrissey." The two men suppressed their giggles. Raffo turned back to Thomasson. "You let me handle it."

"Will you talk to him?"

Raffo put up his hand and looked away.

"No. Of course not."

Thomasson shrugged in a way that indicated he only wanted to learn. "I mean—"

"That's important. I don't know anything about this." He paused to make a point. "I don't *want* to know anything. We're supposed to bust dope, not get ourselves in trouble."

Raffo's tone was direct and somewhat contemptuous. It irritated Thomasson. Unlike many narcs, Raffo had not forgotten the difference between a lie and the truth.

It was just that his entire style was set up to prevent you from ever being his equal.

"The less you know, the better off you are. Always."

In the military, Thomasson had been appalled by the institution of idiocy. He still was. The endless possibility of fuckups was something he could not accept. But maybe not knowing anything was the way, he thought.

"You could spend your whole *life* answering questions."

Situation normal—all fucked up. But if that was normal, what was the point of it all?

"*Listen* to me," Raffo rasped softly.

Thomasson lit a cigarette. He rolled down the window to let out smoke. His beard stank of tobacco.

"I'm listening," he said in an even voice. "I got no argument with that. But there it is anyway."

He allowed himself to smile across the darkness at Raffo.

"Now how good is the buy?" Raffo wanted to know.

"The *buy* is good." Thomasson became businesslike. He was determined to breeze through this. "Always was."

"But we are up late at night." Raffo liked to use the vague meandering sentences of criminals.

Thomasson caught himself. He was not going to sound defensive. "The buy is also a big one," he said.

"It was. The damn thing keeps getting smaller."

It was getting chilly with the window down. Raffo switched the motor on and ran the heater for a moment. The criminal who had owned the Chrysler before the City got it had let the car go. The engine jerked as though it had been designed to move back and forth rather than forward. The idle was set too low.

"I really ought to mercy-kill this sonofabitch," Raffo said.

There was a silence. They were thinking of something.

"Like that Mauldin cartoon—" began one of the men in the back seat.

"*Stars and Stripes*," said the man with the hunting cap. He leaned forward to address Thomasson. "Did they have *Stars and Stripes* in your time?"

"All they had in his time was junkies. He was probably a user himself. Right?"

Thomasson said nothing. They all laughed. Thomasson felt loathing. There was a pause as they waited for Raffo to start in again.

Raffo put his hand on Thomasson's arm. "*Where* is the buy?" He smiled ingratiatingly. "As of now?"

"I'm *trying* to get—" he emphasized this— "*trying* to get the room at the Southern Home." There were groans from the back seat. "There's room there. In fact you should come up the stairs at the Regina and wait on the roof."

"It'd be easier to wire you."

"Yes it would."

"You want the fucking brothers for the roof," the man in the hunting cap interjected.

"You been there before," Raffo said without turning. "You *walk* across, meatball—one roof to the other." Now he turned. "You think you can swing across on a vine?"

There was an undertone of resentment in the laughter from the back seat this time.

"You'll never play for the majors yourself, Raffo."

The point was you got well paid for this, Thomasson thought. There was excitement. That and the fact that every so often something turned out right.

"Where else?" Raffo was asking him quietly.

Combat, hunting, and sport, all rolled into one. When things went right. But even then he hated it. It was having to depend on people who went around in circles.

"They might want to use the restroom at Jax. Or Deggan's room."

He had worked fairly hard on this. By this time they were all oppressively aware that the size of the buy was not going to be worth the work that had gone into it. At this point Thomasson simply wanted to make a bust. If he didn't, it would look very bad.

"I don't think these guys down here are exactly sophisticated enough to ask for a mutual search," Raffo was saying. "But look, it could happen. If it does, the next step is up to you. Jack off. Stall until we get there. Or just turn around and beat the guy up. Use that stuff they taught you in the service. You know how quickly they respond to strong-arm stuff down here. They eat it up."

A salvage operation. At fault was the snitch. Yet you had to have faith. You ended up believing him. It was a good thing he'd had the lucky bust in North Beach. Without that his short career would be in sorry shape.

At length Raffo stretched. "Well, what do you think of it so far?"

"If I never work undercover again it'll be too soon. I'd like to blow my cover on network TV."

Raffo remained benign and unruffled behind his dark glasses. He enjoyed Thomasson's problems.

"What an attitude!"

"You can't face the neighbors, coming home every evening looking like something that crawled out from under a rock."

"Well—" Raffo said. "It ain't for everybody. I think it's harder on the married guys."

Raffo couldn't know the half of it. Thomasson's wife was an ex-sorority girl who did her housework in alpaca sweaters. They were buying a house in a quiet suburb down the Peninsula. All the neighbors knew was that she was a nice girl married to an animal.

"The pits," Thomasson said with bitterness.

Raffo turned off the engine and put out his cigar. He sat staring into the night, rubbing his whiskers.

"Detail won't last forever."

There was a silence. Thomasson guessed Raffo was thinking about what he would say to Dunaway. He said nothing. He was afraid of what the night was turning into.

"No," Raffo said, opening his door with sudden force, "it won't last forever. It just seems like it. Am I right?"

As soon as he walked in Quinn spotted him. He crept in like a cat and stood off to one side looking down the bar. He was middle-aged and dressed like a drifter on the outs, complete with rumpled suit pants. He walked with a rolling slouch and talked quietly to himself. His gray crewcut was clipped too neatly and his eyes were too clear and unafraid.

The eyes stopped on Quinn, who smiled and leaned over his drink with his forearms on the bar. He welcomed all confrontations.

The unshaven stranger cocked his head slightly. A bum would never do that. At least not while staring at someone. It was a cop move. He was not what the clothes said he was.

"Lee!" he shouted over the rock music.

Everyone looked at him. The stranger walked over to the jukebox and shook it slowly to and fro. He appeared to be in a controlled but dangerous fury. The easy strength with which he shook the jukebox revealed a man of good coordination who was probably in excellent shape for his age.

Quinn guessed he was probably a few years older than himself.

"Lee. LEE!"

The Chinese bartender was all smiles. He was almost skipping down the bar. It was embarrassing to watch — as he rounded the far end of the bar he nearly fell. He stared at the stranger with awe.

"Turn this damn thing down!"

The Chinese fumbled with the switch. The jukebox went suddenly and darkly silent. The patrons laughed.

"Not that low."

The bartender hastened to turn the music on again. It crooned softly. The middle-aged man put on dark glasses. He walked slowly but without hesitation over to Quinn.

"Somebody said they left some property down here."

Deggan's shirt and flannel jacket sat on a barstool where Quinn had put them. The cop picked them up. A flat black sap fell out of the pocket of the jacket.

The cop shrugged and looked at Quinn. "Now why do people carry these things around if they're not gonna use 'em in self-defense?"

"They want to make sure they don't get four elbows."

The cop nodded. It was no more than the truth. If you tried to use a blackjack and someone got it away from you, they were entitled to break your arm. At least one.

"I guess he knew you used to wear the gloves."

He wagged his finger at belt level. The thick forefinger cut back and forth like a tongue.

"Dunaway?" A moment passed. "Get outta Dodge. If you don't, I'll put the hurt on your ass. Like you wouldn't believe."

Quinn placed a stool between them. Dark glasses with unfashionably thick rims. Unshaven. The loose ratty boots for carrying weapons. Thomasson's boss or partner. Maybe both.

"You got no clout like that down here." Quinn was smiling steadily. "The criminals run the show down here. You're just a cop. That's okay. Sit down."

"*Just* a cop? I didn't always work narcotics. Get out of here. Now. Move it."

"Make me move."

The other man didn't turn away. With the dark glasses there was no eye contact. Quinn kept both hands on the bar. Finally the man shrugged.

"Now what the hell was that?" the stranger asked himself.

He made a sour expression with his mouth and beckoned at the bartender, who waited at the end of the bar.

"Lee." The stranger sat down beside Quinn. "That's the bartender's name. You can call me George." He pronounced the name carefully."

"I think you know who I am."

The Chinese trotted over. "Scosh and wah ta!" he said happily. He waited to be complimented.

"That's very good," Raffo said.

The bartender brought the drink. He stood watching intently as Raffo drank. No one made any attempt to pay. Raffo smiled and nodded.

"Oh yeah—he knows me." Raffo pointed at the Chinese. "You wouldn't think an old man like that'd be any good in a holdup, would you? He's got an army-issue forty-five back there'd knock your eyes out." He held his drink out stiffly with both hands and sighted along it. "Holds it like this."

"Hong Kong?"

Raffo nodded. He would be in a position to know the arrangement. "Daughter's been here twenty-five years. Signed him up for seven years at this fucking corner."

Rich Chinese-Americans brought people over and put them to work paying off their passages. People in Hong Kong entered into the arrangement willingly, to get to San Francisco.

"Is he picking up the language okay?"

Raffo shrugged. "Would you want to talk to these creeps?"

People in Hong Kong couldn't know how dangerous certain jobs in San Francisco would be.

"I have a message from your pal Monahan," Raffo said casually. "Remember Monahan?"

Quinn remembered. Monahan was the ugly cop with whom he had first spoken about the rape.

"I know who the man is."

Without his intending it, Quinn's voice had become harsh. Raffo gave him a quick approving glance.

"The man is moonlighting," Raffo said.

Raffo's face told him nothing. Quinn cleared his throat. They waited while a new record came on the jukebox.

"Who for?"

Raffo took a good ten seconds answering. "A guy in this area who's had the same trouble you had. He's looking for somebody you're looking for. To get even. He hired Monahan. He's rich."

He would have to give Raffo an A for effort.

"Why does he want to find this guy?"

"You know why."

"Why?"

"Probably to put a hole in his head."

Not bad—particularly for something cooked up on the spur of the moment. There might even be some truth to it.

"Money can buy," Raffo continued in an authoritative manner. "Why should you get in trouble?"

Quinn decided to play along.

"That conniving, cutthroat sonofabitch Monahan! That fucking bogtrotter! He wants to make a deal!"

Raffo maintained a discreet silence.

"And they talk about the Jews," Quinn said disgustedly.

Raffo sighed in commiseration.

"No," Quinn said.

Raffo's face darkened almost at once. He stared past him.

"Thanks for the message. I'm sorry. Are you sure some people aren't turning you out on this one?"

Raffo smiled, but at the corners of his dark glasses the eye muscles narrowed in small rhythmic contractions. He was taking aim.

"Maybe I could personally make sure you get busted for first-degree murder."

Quinn gestured down the bar. A skinny leather type had dropped a vial of pills and was stooping to pick it up. To great whoops of laughter another youth pretended to enter him from behind. Quinn gestured again.

"Want to know the difference between me and these bastards? I'm ready to do time. Furthermore I won't squawk about it. Put me in jail. I'll *do* the time. On my head if necessary."

Raffo was looking at him oddly. He shook his head.

"Seriously. I'll plead guilty. And I'll tell the world what I did was wrong. Necessary, but wrong."

"No. I don't believe that."

"You'd be surprised the freedom it gives me."

Freedom. All you had to do was take the consequences, and you could do anything. Why did people have trouble with that?

Raffo was so impressed he seemed hypnotized. He shook his head slowly. At length he laughed angrily.

"Fuckers were right about you." He waited. Quinn said nothing. "Better thank your lucky stars you got a reputation around this town. If you didn't know so many people, I'd kill you."

Quinn laughed. He decided he liked him. "Go on. What'd they tell you about me?"

"That you are crazy. That you were a Communist."

People in law enforcement were invariably fascinated with the Communism thing. You couldn't explain it to them.

"*Were* you a Communist?"

"I was possessed by evil spirits."

Raffo was angry. "Don't talk down to me. I don't like that shit. I don't like people making small with me."

Quinn turned on him. "You think I'm patronizing you? All right. Look what you do to me. Did I ask you to come in here with your stories? You don't know a damn thing about me."

Lee the bartender was watching them. Raffo raised two fingers. Two drinks were made. The two men remained silent until the bartender retreated to the far end of the bar.

"Okay?" Raffo asked. He raised his glass. "There are hard feelings all around? Am I right? I really don't give a flying fuck."

They drank in silence while the jukebox changed records.

"People misunderstand things because they want to."

"Tell me about it," Raffo said with feeling.

They laughed. Quinn felt comfortable now that limits had been set. Also he felt suddenly close to the other man. It wasn't necessary that the other man understand.

Raffo lit a cigar. "About the other thing."

Negotiating. They had to find a way to stay out of each other's way. At least try. But it couldn't be discussed openly.

"Back off from it. Just back off."

It had never been necessary to explain everything. All that was necessary was to be himself. To fight and to negotiate.

"No," Quinn said.

"I'm telling you."

"If you have to stop me, shut up and do it."

Raffo was infuriated. At the same time he seemed impressed. "Watch your step with me. This is no boxing match."

Quinn nodded vigorously. "Yeah it is. Who set something up? Certain brother officers. Now let's give each other a break. I don't know you. You don't know me. Somebody said something to you, but it is no longer any big deal."

Raffo got up abruptly as if to go. Turning around, he leaned back against the bar, his elbows resting on the top. He lit a cigar. He seemed to be looking at a point near the door. He cursed softly and was clearly infuriated. At the same time, he appeared to be acknowledging a form of defeat.

"Insanity!" he barked softly. He turned to Quinn. "Could it be the sauce doing it, Dunaway? What the fuck's wrong with you?"

Quinn lit a cigarette. "You know damn well."

The steering on the Volvo was loose, but the amphetamine gave her the whip hand she needed. Grace sang along with the radio. Her window was down, and she gloried in the lush river of cold air hitting her face. The dryness of her mouth felt good—she had always liked the dehydration part of speed. Depleting the juices to get to the bone.

Really the blues. The old Mezz Mezzrow escape.

The radio played adenoidal imitations of Mick Jagger. Another cop-out. Why did they all want to sound Black?

"Whip it out, Chonga," she told the wind.

Lenny Bruce. A hero of losers.

The perfume of gunsmoke clung to her purse. She kept a weather eye out for patrol cars—if she was stopped they would smell it and find Richards's pistol. Driving south of Market she sang an old Annie Ross song in counterpoint to the radio's Creedence Clearwater. Speed enabled her to hear two melodies at once.

My analyst told me
I was outta my head
The way he described it
I'd be better dead

than alive . . .

"Once more the KID—" she shouted to the wind.

The power she had was dreamlike. She could feel so many different things at once. Pity for poor Don Richards. Also a blinding joy at her ruthlessness. It was odd about that. Pity fed the hatred and made it purer. Also more enjoyable.

"Who *knows* what evil—" The 1940s radio mystery of her childhood. Freewheeling and free-associating. *The Shadow do.* Then the Shadow laugh. It came out with an unexpected hoarseness that startled and pleased her.

She could do any damn thing she wanted to. With this magic hate she could address the wrongs of a lifetime. Of a world.

In the Tenderloin the night stalkers were out for Saturday night. She braked to let two streetwalkers cross a corner. An aging drag queen with painted silver eyes crouched on a curb to stare at her. He grimaced with loathing. Grace laughed.

"Fuck you," she told him.

Ahead were the Regina and Southern Home hotels. Shadows moved in the storefronts. A tall figure walked down one side of the street, holding something in from of him. It appeared to be a Bible.

She turned the corner with the mom-and-pop grocery.

Yea though I walk through the valley of the shadow of death. Thy rod and they staff. They comfort me.

She turned into the alley. The darkness flickered with neon shadows. They reminded her so much of the colors of peyote that as she approached the rear of the Regina she neglected to brake. When she did, it was too late. She skidded on the gravelly asphalt and crunched gently into the hotel and sloughed away, a headlight tinkling out.

The car stopped dead. This caused her to laugh. She turned off the remaining light and scrambled out, tossing the keys in her purse.

She threaded a no-man's-land of refuse between two buildings to the street. There were junkies talking in low heroin monotones. Inside the lobby of the Regina they sat in old chairs dreaming and scratching. She went directly to the stairwell. Strangely, no one followed her. That displeased her. She had looked forward to shooting a complete stranger. That would prepare her for what came later; practice makes perfect.

She stopped on the landing of the sixth floor. She stood catching her breath. She sensed Deggan was gone. She went to the door of the room. No sound. She waited a moment longer—still nothing.

When she pushed, the door floated open. Empty.

She went in and sat down on the bed. The door was closed behind her, but not locked. There was plaster on the floor from when Richards had torn the lock off the wall.

It occurred to her that people in her present state of mind were the most dangerous people in the world. She wondered if that had been the secret of Himmler and Stalin and the others. How had they gotten hate-driven people to work together? By what private signals had they recognized each other?

At length she got up and knelt in the doorway of the closet. She pulled up the floorboard. There was nothing in the dark rectangular hole but the fine yellow dust and a fleeing roach. She was momentarily confused. Of course Quinn had kept Deggan's stolen piece. What was she looking for? An answer? To what?

She patted Richards's Saturday night special in her purse.

"I have you," she said to it.

It had turned out to be his greatest gift to her.

"Thank you," she murmured.

There were two things Thomasson feared above all. One was getting hurt so badly as to be unable to support his family. The other was the miasma of depression that came from working in irredeemably sleazy surroundings. Now, as he sat talking to Deggan at the bar and discotheque called Jax, he felt depression snaking up on all sides, like swamp fog. This set was just too low.

Also he felt fear. He was not in control.

Jax was long and filled with smoke. It had a huge and complicated sound system from which rock music pounded. Down one side stretched a bar. There was a dance floor at the back. About half the drag queens were Black. There were a surprising number of butch men dancing with them and hanging out at the bar.

Thomasson was particularly outraged that one drag queen had dressed in a wedding gown but left his beard on.

"*Love* to be turned out," Deggan was saying. He had been bragging about putting women on the street. "All them bitches love it. They love it real good."

It wasn't clear to Thomasson whether he referred to real women or drag queens. He wasn't anxious to find out.

"All of them?" Thomasson asked politely.

"Gospel truth."

They sat at the bar near the door. Here the music wasn't so loud. "Ever make any money? Off the—ah—bitches?"

"Got to whip their asses. Looky here." Deggan's walleyes sparkled as he recited. "Got to *school* that bitch, got to *rule* that bitch, ride her like a mule! Got to *stomp* that bitch, got to *tromp* that bitch, whip her like a fool! Learnt that at Q." He looked at Thomasson for approval. His left eye was so far out of orbit he seemed to be beseeching the whole room. "Ain't *no bitch alive*," he said slowly like a preacher, "don't like a righteous ass-kicking now and then!"

Thomasson watched two men down the bar, a pimp called Sonny Mac and a dealer from LA called Red Top. They were drinking together and laughing up a storm. The man called Red Top was a well-known criminal from whom Thomasson had already made two buys, which had been sealed and labeled and were now in the San Francisco Police Department property room. Thomasson was going to arrest him after making a third and much larger buy.

Deggan also watched Red Top. He was bald-headed with a bright red pate. He wore flashy ex-con clothes. "Be a pleasure and a blessing, getting that asshole off the streets."

Thomasson cleared his throat. "I won't forget the help." He drank his bourbon. He cleared his throat again. "I got someone to do something with what's-his-name. Dunaway."

"How'd it go down?"

"Don't know."

There was a pause. Thomasson decided to concentrate on the bust. He had concluded long ago that Deggan's viciousness made him just as vulnerable to manipulation as fear. Now, with real danger in the wings, it was time to push the power angle.

"Won't be long now," he said with relish.

Comrades. Partners. Sharing the power.

"Look for that fucking Red Top to crawl," Thomasson continued.

He looked at Deggan out of the corner of his eye. It was working. Deggan began to giggle. His eyes were bright and muttered like a kid at Christmas.

"Fucker looked like a girl in the big yard. Looked like something that'd sit on your cock whether you wanted him to or not. Here he is, big as life an a fuckin gorilla, don't he think *he's* bigtime—"

Thomasson tuned him out. He had heard it all before. There was something he had to tell Deggan. He waited until his fulminations had more or less stopped.

"Ah," Thomasson said, "the actual bust itself."

Deggan cackled. "*He'll* go through some changes!"

"I don't want you there when I bust him. I'll tell you to go out and watch for heat. I want you to take off and not come back."

Surprisingly, Deggan accepted it without any objection whatever. He gnawed on a toothpick.

"You understand?" Thomasson's suspicions were aroused.

"You send me out before you make the bust. Whatever you say. We is running partners—ain't we?" Deggan reflected a few seconds. "What happens to you after the bust, partner?"

"Never mind."

The script called for Thomasson to get busted too. Once in jail, a phony warrant would be produced and Thomasson would be taken to an office on another floor where he and the other narcotics people could weigh the dope they had gotten. The routine was a familiar one.

Actually Thomasson hoped his cover would get blown. That way he could get out of narcotics. But first he needed this bust.

"I was talking to Red Top whilst you was gone," Deggan began innocently after a pause.

Thomasson felt alarm. He sensed he was about to be raised.

"Hell you talking about?"

"Red wants two buys." Deggan held up two fingers. "First time on the roof of the Southern Home. Next one in the room like you said. Second one is the big one."

Thomasson folded his arms on the bar. "Who is the first buy for? For what purpose?"

"Me."

So that was the trade-off. He wouldn't get to see Red Top go through his changes (or perhaps get blown away) when he was busted; in return he wanted a buy for personal use. Thomasson was surprised he hadn't proposed that already.

"That's nice. Partner. But I'm on the roof listening to it all."

Deggan was shocked. "Why is that, partner?"

"So I can pop you down with the others if you get clever. You understand? He makes a small sale to you on the roof. You go with him down to the room and wait for me. I get my backup people into the hall. When I come, you leave and I pop him."

Deggan sulked. Thomasson wished he had time to work him over a little. A few hours earlier they had been running partners, cutting partners, and general asshole buddies. Why was he suddenly harder to handle? It had to be Dunaway and his threats.

"We clean up the streets together," Thomasson warned.

He had been flexing his biceps. Now he grabbed Deggan's arm. He did this well. His arms had what the street punks called firepower.

"Because you do time if I say so." He breathed heavily with anger. He spoke directly into Deggan's ear. "If you take a third fall, you spend the rest of your life in prison. You do *all* of it."

"Turn me aloose!"

"I'll turn you every way *but* loose if you get smart on me."

Thomasson let go. He went back to his beer. Down the bar Red Top and Sonny Mac were talking to a tall drag queen with a high red wig. Thomasson stared so intently that the drag queen murmured something to her companions. They looked at him and laughed.

In a moment the pimp called Sonny over to them.

"My man!" he said to Deggan.

"Righteous," Deggan said.

Sonny Mac turned to Thomasson. "Where's your bike, man?"

"Grounded. I blew it up."

Thomasson continued to stare at the red-wigged drag queen down the bar. He was wearing a full-length dress that showed a considerable amount of cleavage. How did they do that? For a fleeting second he felt sexual desire. With great haste he repressed the feeling. He cursed to himself.

"I seen bigger buys than this in Nam," Deggan was telling Sonny Mac. "If it weren't dope, it were guns."

Thomasson groaned. Why had narcotics insisted on this cover? He was supposed to be a crazed Nammie with friends and money looking to deal. Naturally Deggan told people they had been service budies. He liked to talk about their fictitious exploits in Vietnam.

"Eighty percent of the guys in my unit were asking AK-47s when I left," Deggan was saying. He turned to Thomasson. "Remember?"

Thomasson had decided it would be several years before he understood what Vietnam had done to him. Until then he wished to avoid the subject. It made him sick.

"Excuse me," he said.

He got up slowly. He caught a glimpse of himself in the mirror behind the bar. The scraggly bearded face never failed to disgust him. Self-hatred—it really was the strongest kind.

Deggan shrugged. "What's his problem?"

Lord only knew what it would find in the restroom.

"Look like he want to throw up," said the pimp named Sonny.

Halfway to the back, Thomasson saw the street door open in the mirror behind the bar. Some intuition told him it was danger. He turned to face it. In the door came Quinn Dunaway.

Don Richards lay on a metal gurney in a large hospital run by the city and county of San Francisco. He was dressed only in his underwear and a starched white gown that came to his thighs. His other clothing had been stashed on a thin shelf at the bottom of the gurney by the nurses in the emergency room. The gurney was parked in the hall outside the X-ray room. The hallway was full of people lying on gurneys, waiting to be X-rayed.

They were mostly male and mainly Blacks and Chicanos. There were knife wounds, gunshot wounds, and every kind of broken bone.

It was a hospital for the poor and it was Saturday night.

They chatted with each other in friendly fashion. People seemed to handle their pain well, except for one slumbering bluish old Black man who breathed out long rasping sobs in his sleep.

"Bitta traffic here tonight, ain ter?" asked a cheerful oldtimer on a gurney in front of Richards.

He had a broken arm and a gash in his grizzled red cheek which had already been sewed by an intern. He listened to a cheap portable radio and wore a sunshine smile.

"Knife and gun club," Richards said bitterly.

The oldtimer pointed a trembling blue-nailed finger at Richards's bandaged foor.

"Drilled you," he observed happily.

A wino. Food and a flop.

"No—I fell on a bullet."

A nurse with a clipboard passed among them. When she reached the sleeping Black who was breathing loudly she looked at him with alarm and wheeled him away.

"What'd they give you?" Richards asked the oldtimer.

"Darvon N."

"Darvon N," Richards sighed.

The old man's tiny radio played KABL. Its lush gaga strings and nowhere arrangements sounded tinny and unearthly on the cheap portable. Music of supermarkets and elevators. Heroin of the middle class. But Richards found it strangely relaxing.

"Darvon N," Richards repeated bitterly.

He rolled over and reached below to get his pipe and tobacco pouch out of his shirt pocket. As he did, he noticed that his pants were lying on the tiled floor thirty feet down the hall. Apparently they had fallen off the gurney as he was being wheeled to his present station.

"Damn," Richards said.

First he lit the pipe and inhaled deeply. It tasted good, as he knew it would. For some reason tobacco went well with pain.

"Smokes," the old man said vaguely. "Lost em is what I done." He looked around as though he expected them to reappear.

Richards slid gingerly off the gurney onto his good foot and hopped down the hall to retrieve his pants. The wallet was still in the back pocket. Hopping back, he was conscious of how ridiculous he must look. When a man was hurt he was a baby.

"Fell outten my pocket in the emergency room," the old man continued as though Richards had never left.

He lay stiffly for a moment to let the throbbing go all through him. It was faster now. The Darvon was worthless. When he had gotten control of the pain somewhat, he laboriously pulled on his pants. They tugged at the metal bandage stays and made him wince.

He hit on his pipe. To hell with it.

Next came the shirt. He put one cowboy boot halfway on his good foot and stomped it firmly all the way on. The old man was smiling and watching him.

"Know where the pharmacy is?"

There was a good chance the old man had been here before and knew the setup. He squinted at the ceiling.

"Cain't remember," the oldtimer said finally. "Sorra partner." He winked. "There's a bar across the street."

No help for it. It had to be done. He would not be missed here, since it would be at least two hours before his turn came.

"Save my place in line," he told the old man, "and I'll

bring you back some smokes."

The old man beamed. His radio played a bizarre drugged Muzak version of Ellington's "Satin Doll."

The hall had handrails. He got all the way to a street door without putting pressure on the wounded foot. After that it was a matter of toughing it.

The night was black and chilly and there was a misting breeze. He wished he had brought his coat. Every time he stepped on his right foot, the pain knifed redhot straight up to his stomach. It felt like the foot was a cloven hoof and a chisel was being driven between the cleft parts, splitting apart the leg from the distal extremity upwards.

The bar was neighborhood and vaguely Irish. Muscular working-class types, country music on the jukebox, old women with blue hair, a smattering of Blacks from the Muni maintenance barn. A flabby bartender was swamping out the flats behind the bar with a steaming mop. Closing time would not be far off.

He tapped lightly on the bar with his ring finger. The bartender looked up sharply like he was trouble, then dropped his mop and nodded noncommittally. "Waiting for your medicine?" he asked, leaning over the bar to look at Richards's foot.

"Painkiller." Richards sat down. "And if it don't knock me dead away, I want to know the reason why!"

Two of the patrons wore blue hospital robes. They nodded solemnly in his direction.

The bartender reached for Canadian whiskey. Richards experimented with putting pressure on his foot. One way to slow down the throbbing was to stand on it — but if you stood too long, the pain was intolerable. There was a trick to it.

The bartender served up a double shot. "What the

doctor ordered—"

Richards drank deeply.

"What happened?" the bartender asked.

"A woman."

The bartender nodded.

"I asked her to marry me and she shot me in the foot."

It came out sounding funny. They laughed. Richards put pressure on the foot to stop the throbbing. Tears as thick as sea water jumped into his eyes. "Oh Lord . . ."

"Some woman," the bartender said. "Where is she now? In jail?"

"On the bridge."

He drew a blank. "The bridge?"

"The one they jump off."

"Oh *that* bridge." The bartender picked up his mop.

Again they laughed. Again it seemed the natural thing to do. Richards could feel her powerful spell lifting. Laughing while she died was a turning point—he was embracing it.

"How do you know she'll jump?" the bartender asked.

"She tried it once before. Tonight's her night. She'll either kill somebody else or kill herself."

She had made him feel so alive—so alive.

The bartender was shaking his head. "Ain't they a bitch? Women?"

"I'm out of it."

The tears were thicker. One rolled down his face. "I loved her too—best damn fool way I knew how." He downed the whiskey and stood. The bartender looked up in surprise.

"Cap? Where you going?"

What was it about a woman? *She gave you life*.

"The bridge—"

And all along she was already dead.

The bartender turned down the corners of his mouth and shook his head strongly once. "You're out of it—remember?"

Gracie—sweet sleep.

"Almost." Richards nodded. "Almost—"

As soon as Quinn entered Jax he took two steps sideways. His back was to the wall. He saw dancers in the back. The music was loud, and from one corner of the dance floor emanated revolving lights. Reds and twilight blues and heavy saturated oranges crept across the floor and ceiling. Almost immediately he saw Deggan—he sat at the bar near the door, talking to a Black man dressed pimp-style.

The bar stool on his left was empty.

Thomasson poised, watching, near the dance floor. Quinn recognized him from their brief encounter near the Embarcadero.

Deggan saw him. His sneering expression did not change.

Quinn sat down next to him. Thomasson was now strolling toward them.

Deggan seemed almost happy. "Speak a the devil," he said.

The Black pimp guffawed. "What devil? He ain got blue eyes."

"Ain't your bro," Deggan said archly. "This here's my bro." He did not seem scared or upset. It was as though the intimidation at the Traffic Jammer had never happened. "*Air*-yan bro."

He referred to a prison gang called Aryan Brother-
hood.

The pimp snorted and moved off. "Dude. Don't be
signifyin that Q shit." He gave Deggan a parting put-
down glance. "Later bro."

Quinn nodded in Thomasson's direction. "You think
he's going to protect you—you believe that."

Down the bar the bartender threatened a drunken
male patron and a tiny Oriental drag queen with a
rubber penis. There were demure screams of delight from
the drag queen. The bartender was a big freckled woman
with wide unblinking eyes. When she turned in his
direction, Quinn tapped the bar lightly.

"You never learn," Deggan said leaning toward him.

Quinn stared into the vacant walleyes. Brown? No,
more like dark blue or purplish black. Muddy sloe. Fruit
of the blackthorn. But you didn't see color really, nor
luminosity, shape, or size. You saw the space where the
lines of vision did not converge.

"No." Quinn grinned. "I never learn."

The bartender ambled toward them. A few feet away
she tossed the dildo into a pail beneath the bar without
stooping. In the revolving light her wide-set eyes shone
like polished turquoise. She stared at Quinn without fear
or curiosity.

"Bourbon," Quinn said over the music.

She closed her eyes and slowly shrugged her broad
shoulders.

"Bar bourbon is fine."

Thomasson stood behind Quinn and Deggan. He put
his hands on their shoulders. He looked tired and
potentially dangerous.

"A friend of yours," he said pointedly to Deggan.

Deggan chewed his toothpick. Thomasson stroked his beard.

"Shur nough," Deggan said finally.

"Intro*duce* us you idiot!"

Anger flickered in Thomasson's eyes. He was forgetting to slouch like a biker. Finally he settled for nodding in a long-suffering way.

"Uh huh, thought we were running partners," he said thickly.

Deggan started to get up. Thomasson grabbed his arm above the elbow. Deggan snickered. There was a moment of confusion; the sound system momentarily went silent and the lights stopped circling. Thomasson was having difficulty controlling his temper.

"You know who I am," Quinn said. He made a slight accommodating sideward nod of the head. "Stop insulting my intelligence. Relax. Have a beer."

Deggan used the moment to jerk his arm free. "Fucking lord and master? Okay if I take a piss?"

Thomasson got his cool back. He spread his arms junkie-style.

"Well?" He managed a weak smile. "Am I stopping you?"

Deggan swaggered off. Quinn noticed that his DEATH FROM ABOVE T-shirt was torn. He had probably done that at the Traffic Jammer.

Thomasson sat down. "Well," he said wearily.

Quinn folded a dollar like a tent and set it on the bar. When the bartender brought him his bourbon he pushed it toward her with his index finger.

"That's a dollar and a quarter."

Quinn produced another dollar. "For the entertainment."

The bartender harumphed. She did not turn to look at the dancers.

"I guess you'd call it entertainment."

She left. Quinn turned to Thomasson and smiled.

"You are asking me something. You are not telling me something."

Just then the sound system played again. With the new song the lights crept once more. The music was loud; they were just able to talk.

Thomasson made a flat violent gesture. "No way am I making myself an accessory to you."

"Just do what your boss tells you to do."

Thomasson gave him a look he could not read.

"How the hell do you know what my boss is telling me to do?"

"I know."

"What?"

"Telling you not to think too much." Quinn was not probing or kidding. "It's a form of conceit when people want to know too much. Can be, anyway."

Quinn leaned into his drink like a sailor on watch leaning against the wind. With as much as he'd had already, he still wanted more of the firewater. He was amazed at how much he could drink. It made him oddly proud of himself.

"I don't see how you can get away with this."

Quinn looked in the mirror behind the bar. What he saw on Thomasson's face was fatigue and disgust. He had a way of flexing his biceps while he thought. It wasn't a bad move. Quinn had him figured as a strong natural street fighter.

"Maybe I won't."

Thomasson's eyes dropped to the bar counter. "Just

stay away until I make my bust," he said.

Quinn put his arm around his shoulders. Thomasson's hairy face was eclipsed by darkness. Quinn grasped him roughly by the hand and tried to arm-wrestle him. Thomasson's arm was stiff and muscular, but he did not respond to the challenge.

"You'll make a damn good cop." Quinn felt a surge of generosity. "Seriously."

Thomasson did a small double take. He looked around. No one was close enough to have heard. "That's cute. That's cute."

Quinn shook his head. "Thinking too much again."

"Let go of me."

Quinn dropped his fists to the bar. He engaged Thomasson's eyes in the mirror. "Seriously. Better to line up your shots one at a time. Don't try to play the whole table at once." He broke eye contact to light a cigarette. "Don't rush yourself—the boy wonders always burn out first. This is good advice."

The alcohol brought not stupor but clarity. It was a rare privilege for a man to see things as clearly as he was.

Thomasson shrugged. "I don't want your advice. You're crazy and you don't even know it." He gestured at the drag queens dancing at the back. "What do you think of them?"

Quinn looked. Only a few of the drag queens were dressed well. One wore a flounced and ruffled pink tulle prom dress.

"Dead."

The word came out by itself. Thomasson looked at his watch. The word apparently reminded him of Deggan, who was late getting back.

"Take the guy in the wedding outfit. The beard isn't

consistent. If you can't do a good job of dressing up like a woman, you shouldn't do it."

"And the others?"

Quinn shook his head. He wanted to say something about ghosts. "I don't like them. Not that they dress up like women, but that they cater to scumbags like Deggan."

Thomasson lit a cigarette. "Sure!" He exhaled smoke violently. "Only ones'll have 'em."

"Then let them dress up like women in private."

"Nobody made you come down here."

Quinn gave him thumbs-up for scoring. At that moment Deggan appeared, ambling back their way. They were silent until he sat down. Thomasson was in the middle.

"Took you so long?" Thomasson wanted to know.

"Had to fist fuck your friend's old lady."

He neither looked nor gestured in Quinn's direction.

"I told you not to—" Thomasson began. He sat looking at Deggan in wonderment. Finally he shook his head. "You can't remember." He sighed and addressed himself in the mirror. "These people have no attention span. None at all." He got up slowly. He flexed his biceps and gave the bar a last quick once-over. He turned back to Deggan. He seemed to have aged.

"Remember what I told you before? Just remember that. You'd *better* remember that. If you don't so help me I'll take it out in hide, if you have any left. Understand?"

Deggan shrugged. Finally he nodded. "Partner."

"Take care," Thomasson said, and left.

It was not clear to whom he had directed this last remark.

Deggan sat two bar stools down. Quinn moved over to sit beside him.

There was a long period of no words. When Deggan tried to look at him in the mirror, Quinn would not engage his eyes. Instead he looked at himself. What he saw in the lurid crawling light was a strong face made soft with alcohol and something else. What was it? The excessive thinking he had warned Thomasson about? Hate?

Only the eyes remained hard. The forehead was now reddish brown or bay, the dark russet of leather. The puffy chin was ruby. The bulbous nose was blood red, a comic prop from W. C. Fields. The face was deteriorating daily. Hourly, he thought.

Deggan was doing it. At least partly—that was only common sense. He would have to take care of Deggan before he could deal with other problems.

"Scrub hills we was," Deggan began. "Indian Nation."

The Life Story. It would make no more sense to him that it had to Deggan or his victims. But they always wanted to tell it.

"Hunt like a Indian. Ride like a Indian. Rode my pony with the best of em! *Run* like a Indian too." He stopped to remember. "Like a deer. Like that pitchur *Bambi* when the forst far come down."

Down the bar there was the slamming of liars' dice. Appropriate. Yet it was surprising how much their fantasies told about them.

"Mama lived in Blackwell, Oklahoma . . ."

Quinn looked at him in the mirror. "This is all a lie."

He sought not respect but knowledge. Respect was impossible.

"Gospel truth!" Deggan cried. He held up the Boy Scout sign. "Blackwell. She and the old man fought like a house afire."

The condemned man got a final speech. Quinn knew

he would listen. The more you knew about the prey, the more satisfying the kill could be. He remembered that from prizefighting.

"Your old man beat you up."

"Broken his braincase with a shovel," Deggan said. He paused to invent or remember. "He weren't my real dad anyway. No indeedy. No siree."

"Reform school?"

"Training school. Industrial arts. The boys tried to put the boots to me, but I weren't broke to ride. No siree."

"Really kicked some ass, did you?"

Their fantasies were as close as they got to reality.

"Set a few fires, too," Deggan confided enthusiastically. His sloe walleyes sought out Quinn's eyes hungrily in the mirror. "Set more fires than a month a Sundays. Got so's the firemen in that neck a the woods started sleepin in their clothes."

Down the bar Thomasson was drinking with the criminal named Red Top. He was putting a lot of energy into being jovial. The two of them now talked alone. Both the pimp called Sonny Mac and the red-wigged drag queen had disappeared.

"Mistreated you pretty badly," Quinn said.

"Mama was all right. Made me build her a mud fence behind the house onct for punishment. She was oney jes crazy, was her oney problem. Now the others. The others, most of em I'd as lief kill em as look at em. Know what I mean?"

"But you didn't. You waited and took it out on innocent people."

It was as though the statement had not registered at all.

"Anything wrong with that?" Quinn asked sarcastically. "Hurting people who never hurt you?"

Deggan was losing interest in the conversation. "People jes can't stop me," he allowed finally. "I don't know why."

The punch happened like a moment from a dream, so quick Quinn almost didn't see it himself. One moment his fists rested on either side of his drink. The next moment *smack* as the right fist hit the upper lip level with the two front knuckles and the head whipped back. Deggan fell softly. He wasn't out. He looked up from the floor.

"Does that hurt?"

Deggan's two front teeth were bent backwards. Quinn laughed. Deggan was incensed.

"Kick the CRACK A YOUR ASS!" he screamed from the floor.

He got up. Quinn punched him again. Deggan fell against the bar. He was bleeding from the mouth.

"I'm following you," Quinn said. "Everywhere you go, I follow. Next time it's worse."

Down the bar Thomasson cursed and shook his head. The disbelieving look had come back into his face. The bartender stared at Quinn. He was very wary of her. Bartenders in the Tenderloin liked to use their guns.

"I'm going!" he shouted to her.

He nodded obeisance and threw her a sharp wave good-bye. He backpedaled toward the door. "I'm going!" he repeated.

This bartender would do nothing but stare. Several dancers had stopped dancing and also stood watching. A drag queen squealed. This was followed by laughter.

"*That's* it! *That's* it!" Deggan was screaming. "That's all she fucking WROTE!"

"Good," Quinn said.

He eased out the door. The bartender still had not moved.

"Honestly," Raffo said, "I can think of worse things. I always have hated that creep."

He rolled down his window before lighting a fresh cigar. Both men in the back seat of the ancient Chrysler were smoking. He could see the red dots of their cigarettes glowing in the rearview mirror.

"Wouldn't you laugh if that little lying bastard got blown up?"

The two cigarette dots glowed in unison in the mirror.

"Laugh, yeah," said the cop called Morrissey.

"I'd like to *see* it," said the one with the hunting cap. "In Technicolor. In what-you-call living color."

"Might have a nice effect on certain people."

"They *all* turned up dead."

There was a short silence.

"You can't tell young guys about snitches," said Morrissey. "No reflection on Thomasson. You know what I mean."

"Course not." Raffo shrugged. "Would you *want* to tell them?"

"Hell no."

"If Thomasson knew what we know . . . " He shrugged again. "He couldn't operate on the street."

There was another silence.

"When you're young, all you think about is the bust. You think everything is bigtime. You want it. You can't see anything else. You're a Popeye Doyle and the whole world is a French Connection."

"Another thing," said Morrisey. "Lookit the crap the senior citizens go through around here. The mayor even makes a speech about it. What can we do really? It's war, but they won't let us fight."

"We bust dope."

Raffo watched in the rearview mirror for the reaction.

"Yeah, we really bust dope," Morrissey said.

They laughed.

"I don't know," Raffo said after a pause. "They all fall in love with the snitch when they start out. It never fails. He'll learn like we did, he survives this shit."

Raffo shifted in his seat. His butt was getting numb.

"I hear some guy make claims in a bar. I can't go by that shit. Now suppose some guy goes out and does something against the law. Maybe he gets caught. Maybe not. It has nothing to do with me." Raffo leaned forward. He put his cigar out carefully. "Me? I got a job to do."

He checked his watch. It was about time.

"I don't want to know about that shit anyway," he said.

Raffo opened the glove compartment and took out a thermos. He handed it to the men in the back seat.

"Coffee. Drink it. Both of you."

"I don't know," the cop with the hunting cap said.

"Do what I tell you."

Raffo checked his watch. It was the luminous wideband waterproof variety used by military men.

"Synchronize," he said.

The men in the back seat also looked at their watches. They wore the same kind as Raffo. They held the tips of their cigarettes directly above them; they made just enough light to read the time.

"One forty-five exactly," Raffo said.

Quinn sat cross-legged on the tarpaper-covered roof of the Regina Hotel. He smoked a cigarette. His cramped legs and a knuckle on his right hand were shooting pain.

He felt ready.

When he finished resting and smoking his cigarette, he would go down to Deggan's room and wait for him.

Sounds of the night drifted by. Fragments of arguments, whoops from a car, squealing tires. Glass tinkling. Faint screams. The soft hum of neon lights from the streets below, amplified by the black wet mist. Foghorns. The dull electric murmur of indecipherable City sounds at night.

Like . . . like what?

Like night rain heard through deep sleep, he decided.

Above, the low clouds forked slow pink-edged tongues of fog. The pink neonglow it reflected was just strong enough that shapes could be seen. It was not strong enough to cast shadows.

Dreamlight. The roof was bathed in its pink softness.

Quinn inhaled deeply and rubbed the knuckles on his right hand. Cracked or broken. That was good. Strange, but a familiar wound helped you concentrate your energy. And anger. It didn't even hurt that much.

On the other roof was an outhouse-sized doorway where the stairs opened onto the roof. It was the same size as the one on the Regina, a few feet behind where he sat. There was considerable refuse on both roofs. On the Regina were wooden cartons and some rusted beds, and on the Southern Home lay stacks of what appeared to be mattresses. Around both roofs ran a little concrete wall about a foot and a half high, except along the narrow space between the two buildings.

The total area of both was about the size of a football field.

Along the wall near him was briefly silhouetted the small running figure of a rat against the pink sky. It ran

like a tiny coyote—head down and tail back. It made no
sound.

Quinn had a last drag on his cigarette, scraped it out
roughly on the tarpaper, and stood up. The pain from his
pulled leg muscle flashed. He tensed his legs, then shook
them. The pain faded.

Concentration.

For the first time that night he felt like he had drunk
enough. Yet there was wine in Deggan's room. He could
have more if he wanted it. It was really amazing how
much he could drink.

He put on the thin rubber gloves. Now both were torn
at the wrists. He laughed. Of course. Nothing went the
way it was intended. Murphy's law—not that he really
cared anymore about the little things.

He checked Deggan's pistol. Okay—beautiful. If it
didn't work, he would use the other one. That too was
easy. Things worked when you weren't half-assed about
them and didn't push your luck.

The roof door had a loose hinge at the top and slanted
slightly. He opened it slowly. It dragged on the tarpaper
surface. There was no one on the stairs or in the hall. He
took it slow and easy, listening for action. There were no
sounds except the creaking of the wooden stairs.

Deggan's room was occupied. The door was invitingly
ajar.

He stopped dead at the bottom of the stairs. It was
strangely quiet. No sound of feet, no conversation here.
He moved on tiptoe toward the door. He stood next to it
with his back to the wall and took out Deggan's pistol.
Something was telling him it wasn't Deggan, but that
made him anxious because he should be prepared for
him. Who else could it be?

Concentrate. Move like pain was driving you.

He pushed the door slowly with the back of his forearm. It caught, then swung slowly open. Grace sat on the bed. Pillows were propped up behind her. Her hand was in her purse.

He was turning to hide the pistol. He put it back in his pocket. He tried not to look too surprised.

"Grace—"

She looked different. He was sure she had seen him pocket the pistol. They were both embarrassed.

"Terrific," she said.

"Where's Richards?"

She gave him a sour but friendly grimace. "Probably in a hospital."

Her hair was no longer mussed and her clothes looked clean. She was smiling, but her eyes followed him carefully. There was faint perfume in the air. He had an overwhelming intuition that she was armed.

He sat down on the chair by the washbasin. "What did you do?"

It came out as more of a demand than he had intended.

She continued to smile, but made a small pushing movement with her left hand. "Look, he's alive." She stared intently and raised her eyebrows. "You got that?"

He shook his head. He still didn't understand.

"Why?"

She said nothing. The steadiness of her gray eyes reminded him of their father, the way he had stared when angered. The steel nerves were a side of her he had never seen. Negotiate, he thought. Use the negotiator's trick of setting aside the pork chops and dealing with the side issues first.

"Listen to me." She continued to smile but seemed genuinely concerned to make her point. "I'm sorry about Richards."

"You're *sorry.*"

Her strange unyielding smile of triumph did not waver. "Yeah. Sorry."

"But I'm responsible."

"Not for me anymore."

It was true. It occurred to him that at exactly that moment he was passing the point beyond which he could no longer feel even nominal responsibility for Grace. Her survival was no longer worth any risk to anyone else, including himself.

"I feel responsible for Richards because he tries to live decently."

"And crazy Grace doesn't." Her right hand had not left her purse. "You both took me a little too much for granted."

"We did that." He nodded bitterly. He murmured: "Poor bastard. Poor *bas*tard."

"Stop that." She sat up and put her feet flat on the floor. "I want neither sentiment nor threats. Do you understand me? They won't change anything. Bu-*lieve* me."

He almost smiled. *Sentiment or threats.* Such a smart cookie. What a waste—that intelligence with the toughness she showed now was a formidable combination.

"Why Deggan?" he asked after a pause.

Quite unexpectedly she smiled. Brilliantly.

"He was the last of a long line. Really."

"Why did you get in so deep with him?"

She thought. "I wanted to inoculate myself. Aversion therapy."

"Is that true?"

She looked at him a long time. "I think so."

"Then it's probably true."

The brilliant smile had faded slightly. Now it returned.

"I knew I had to change. There was a kind of mistake going on." For the first time she blinked. "I'd say there was a kind of mistake, wouldn't you?"

She asked as though they spoke of someone else.

"You weren't directly responsible for what happened to Dawn. Indirectly, yes."

"That's enough."

He gave her a thumbs-up. "Very nice! If you're strong enough to face that, you're strong enough to learn from it."

"No. It's been going on too long."

Bar signs were going out. The room seemed darker now. What would he do with her? He was worried about Deggan coming in on them. Get her out of the room.

"I don't want to talk to you," he said finally. "I don't like you. What you stand for. Never have."

Surprisingly, she nodded. Her smile remained firm.

"You're supposed to love the sinner and hate the sin. I had it all turned around, didn't I?"

"You can't punish one without punishing the other."

She nodded strongly once, twice, and continued to smile.

"I know that now."

The chilly breeze had turned cold. He stood to close the window, stopping to drink from one of the wine bottles on the dresser. The cheap red sloshed weakly in his gut. Worthless.

"You're the kind of loser who hurts people. You're dangerous."

She leaned forward to hit the bed with a bony fist.

"So are you. You're going to hurt innocent people, the people you love most. Can't you see that?"

He wished he had bought some whiskey before everything closed.

"I got a deal."

"Good old Quinn." She stood up. "What if it doesn't work?"

"It will."

"You can't do it."

He shrugged in a reasonable manner. "Why not?"

"I have a reason."

"It's not up to you."

She stepped forward. She did so smoothly, without appearing to push. She wanted to say something important. He waited.

"Quinn. Listen to me. You're making Deggan into a scapegoat for everything bad that ever happened to you."

Crazy—but very clever. She wanted to stop him.

"Listen to *me*." He would lay it out for her. "The fundamental point is that you draw a fucking *line*. Somebody steps over it, you have to do something. Whatever the sacrifice. Without that you got no family, no friends, no politics, no nothing. Nobody cares about nobody." He spat out the words. "You wouldn't know. You care about nothing but Grace."

"It's insanity."

"Have you tried analyzing your behavior lately?"

"Yes. That's how I know what you feel."

She moved past him to the door. He was temporarily unable to respond. When the anger came, she was already opening the door. Her timing was spectacular.

She leaned toward him. "Dawn will hate you for this."

The gray eyes were so hard they reminded him of his own.

"She'll never know."

"She'll know. I can tell her."

Tomorrow he would have her committed. For sure. She would hate him for the rest of her life. Maybe she would end up moving away from San Francisco. That would be a blessing.

"You do and I'll kill you too."

She did Cagney. Bending backward, both forefingers stiffened for added firepower: "Ya dhirty rhat!"

She fled. Anger blinded him. Her footsteps stopped at the stairway to the roof. He heard the stairs creak.

Grace was on the roof for what seemed a long time.

She knew Deggan would be coming. He was going to buy some heroin on the roof. He had bragged about it to her.

She hid behind a row of garbage cans. She could see as much here as anywhere. She did not flinch when the rats scampered by. The amphetamine pulsed too fiercely to allow fear.

The pink light from the low-moving clouds had weakened. It was even more the stuff of dreams. Shapes were now a deep and sensual dark blue, completely visible only when they or the clouds above moved quickly. But she felt she had been here before. That reassured her.

How long had she waited for this light and this moment?

A foghorn sounded twice, then at regular intervals.

The fog was coming in on the Bay. Here some wisps were almost at roof level.

The foghorn made her happy. Atmosphere. Mood. You wanted mood and atmosphere and that was good. When you were this high, some of the scenes were better than any movie or scene from the stage. You were watching it and controlling it at the same time.

A dream with the dreamer in perfect control.

She leaned forward on her knees. She thought she heard noises. Echoed shouts and footfalls. They came from the general direction of the other roof.

Suddenly the roof door on the Southern Home flew open. A vague human form emerged. It pirouetted and fell in a heap.

"Whoa Nellie!" came a male voice floating across the rooftops.

Two forms followed the first. They began to methodically beat up on the reclining one. She could hear muffled blows landing and fierce squeaks of protest or fear.

"No!" came the faint voice of the victim.

She crawled forward. Ignoring the discomfort was easy; she wanted to see. She dragged her purse along with her.

"Jesus God," she heard the victim complain.

Deggan. She kept crawling until she could see the faces of his attackers. They were desperadoes Deggan knew. One was a Black pimp called Sonny Mac. The other was a solidly built drug addict and dealer called Red Top. He was rumored to be from out of town.

There were grunts of disgust or pain from Deggan.

"Shut up!" the one called Red Top ordered.

Red Top walked suddenly to the two-foot drop between the two buildings. He stood only twenty feet from where she lay.

"Whaddaya think?" He stared straight down. "Throw this guy down this narrow little crack, his head'll bounce back and forth like a goddamn Ping-Pong ball?"

"I wonder," the one called Sonny said warmly. "I seen it happen once between two buildings in the projects. Just like you gon dribble a mothafuckin basketball."

Both men looked down at Deggan. He offered no opinion. He lay quietly at their feet.

They crouched over him. They spoke in low snarling voices.

"No," Deggan said.

She heard the words *buy money.*

"Don't got it!"

They fell on him again. He did not try to crawl away. This time they were kicking. When one of the kicks caught him good Deggan wheezed like an accordion. They kicked a long time. Now it was not for information but for pleasure.

The one called Sonny whistled in an authoritative way. When he had gotten the other man's attention, he pointed at the door to the roof and downward.

"The biker's got the money, man."

Red Top looked down sadly at Deggan. "Of course he does. But do you think this scaly little dickhead would tell us that?"

"I forgot about him," Deggan said miserably.

"What's his name?"

"Thomasson."

"His other name."

"What other name?"

Grace expected the beating to be resumed. Instead

there was a pause as Red Top thought to rephrase the question.

"His *real* name."

"Oh," Deggan said.

The two interlocutors waited with amazing patience.

"He calls himself Rocky sometimes," Deggan said.

They began beating up on him again.

"Okay!" Deggan yelled. "Ferguson!"

"What?" the two men yelled in unison.

"Williamson!"

"What's his first name?"

"George! George Williamson!"

Both men kicked him at the same time.

"That's the phoniest-sounding name I ever heard in my life," said the one called Red Top.

It was time. Grace stood up slowly. The two men stopped their kicking almost at the same time. The pimp called Sonny Mac took a step forward.

"Fuck is that?" he wanted to know.

Grace walked to the edge of the two-foot crack between the buildings. They were not ten feet away. She withdrew the pistol. The two standing men both stepped backwards as though they had seen a ghost.

"Ah Grace," Deggan wheezed.

She had the impression he was glad to see her. Pleasure hit her like a heroin rush. To arrive as a savior before killing.

"Hi there," she said.

The voice was cheerful and seductive. She had not so intended it, but it sounded right.

"Hi baby," she said even more cheerfully.

The pleasure continued to build. It had begun when the two standing men had stepped backwards. It was now necessary to find out how powerful she was, how excessive were her dominions.

"Can everyone see what's in my hand?" she asked.

No one said anything.

She was enjoying the weight of the pistol. She pointed it downward into the crack between the two buildings. There were no windows. She squeezed the trigger. The piercing hand-held power exploded. It had very little kick. The bullet ricocheted off to one side in a red-orange streak like a spark of phosphorus off a struck match. It flew straight up the crack and into the sky at a forty-five degree angle to them. They could hear it humming.

"Did you see that?" she asked.

It was different when you fired outside. The sound and smell were not so intense. But the power was the same.

Red Top and Sonny Mac put up their hands.

"Pick him up," she ordered them.

There was a silence. Deggan sat up.

"Who?" asked the pimp called Sonny Mac.

"Deggan," she said patiently. "Who do you think?"

The one called Red Top tried to say something, but nothing came out. He cleared his throat.

"Why?" he asked finally.

Her impulse or fantasy was to make them throw Deggan off the roof and then shoot them. She decided that was too much. Only Deggan's death was required. Besides she had another idea.

"Wait," she said.

In fact they had not moved an inch. They stood gaping at her.

"Take off your clothes!" she hissed at Deggan.

It was not hysteria. It was her life. She was one person who had to become another to survive. She had not only a staggering moral ascendancy but the obligation to punish transgressions.

"Did you hear me?" she asked softly.

Suddenly she was screaming. "Take off your clothes! Now! Take them off! All of them!"

Red Top and Sonny Mac no longer had their hands up. They edged backwards.

"Wait!" she ordered them. "I need you for something."

Deggan still didn't move. Anger peaked. She took aim at him. He whipped off his T-shirt with the speed of light. She was amazed. She had almost shot him.

"Take off the pants."

"Ahhhhh . . . " said Sonny Mac.

He lifted one hand higher for permission to speak.

"You'll get your chance," she promised.

Deggan shed his shoes. His shorts were blue with grime, and flared out stiffly from his body. It interested her that in the world she had inhabited before this would have seemed merely pathetic. Here it seemed an insult. Everything was arranged to heighten her fury.

"Take it off!" she screamed.

He meekly complied.

"Lay down on your stomach."

Her vision was to make him kneel or lie across the crack between the buildings while forcing the other two to rape him. Then she would kill him.

"Crawl."

He was ten feet away from her and eight from the drop. He stared at her numbly. He looked down at the drop.

"*Crawl*, you fucker!" She added, "This way."

He began. He stopped and looked up at the two men behind him. They were laughing. A foot or two away from the long drop he stopped again. She cheered him on.

"You can do it!"

He stared up at her. His face was bloody from the beating.

"Attaboy," she encouraged.

Fear of the long drop was hitting him. As he neared the edge he moaned and his face began to twitch.

"Up on your knees," she ordered.

The front of his pale naked body was covered with dirt and pebbles and small pieces of glass. He tried to brush them off.

"Lay across it," she said.

She jerked the pistol at the two-foot divide.

"Uhhhh . . . " he said looking down.

The other two were edging away again.

"*Across* it," she told Deggan.

She moved back slightly to give him room. She took aim at the pimp called Sonny Mac. He and Red Top stopped dead in their tracks and once again raised their hands.

"Hurry up," she told Deggan.

She took aim at him again. He fell face-forward across the chasm, landing on his elbows. He gave a sharp bark of pain and began to groan without stopping. His head and upper torso were on her side, his legs on the other. He appeared too weak to raise himself up on his knees.

"Very good," she said.

Besides groaning he panted. His shrunken genitals swung free between the buildings. He dug at the tarpaper with his fingers.

"Don't fall," she advised him.

The hoodlums called Red Top and Sonny Mac were edging away again. Once more she took aim. They stopped. She was about to order them forward to begin Deggan's destruction when she saw a vague and threatening human shape moving behind them.

From his hiding place behind a row of decaying springs and mattresses, Thomasson watched the action with growing wonder. These were amazing people. Fuckups — but amazing.

And himself: a pigeon's pigeon. Another mark.

No chance for the big bust. No way. Maybe there never had been. Sonny Mac had long known he was heat. Red Top was out to rip off the buy money; probably there was heroin, but damn little.

All along a fantasy. And now this.

He had to act now to save the bust. However small.

He withdrew his lightweight revolver from an ankle holster. He stood up. For a moment he was sorry he had the weapon. *Don't be so quick to get your gun out. You might have to use it.*

But his objections to shooting people had diminished greatly.

"Everybody *stop,*" he shouted.

Red Top and Sonny Mac already had their hands up. They turned to stare at him. When they saw who it was they guffawed.

"I wouldn't laugh if I were you," he told them.

They saw he held a gun. They stopped laughing.

He was moving steadily forward. *Glide. Off to one side where everyone can be seen.* When he was almost abreast of Red Top and Sonny Mac, he concentrated on the bluish-pink figure of Grace Dunaway on the other roof.

She seemed to waver. About to kill Deggan. Now she would kill. He could see her take aim.

"Don't do that," he said loudly.

He saw the hesitation. He knelt and aimed at her two-handed.

"Why not?" she asked.

He had met her only once or twice with Deggan. He knew little about her. He didn't care. She was just another crazy person.

"Because I'll put a hole in your head," he told her.

"He'll be dead."

"Not if you miss. He'll be alive and you'll be dead."

She was moving back. Okay—he would accept a strategic withdrawal. But he should have ordered her to drop the gun.

"Drop the gun!"

But she had already taken cover behind some cartons. Deggan jerked like a piece of bacon between two skillets. He was trying to pull himself across to the other roof with his hands and elbows.

"Stay right where you are," Grace Dunaway said with surprising strength. "Andy? I'm aiming at you!"

Deggan immediately stopped crawling forward. He remained suspended over the two-foot-wide drop. Thomasson turned to Red Top and Sonny Mae.

"You people have business with me. Remember?"

They grinned and nodded energetically.

"So go down to your room and wait for me."

"Sure," Red Top said.

"Both of you."

"Damn straight," Sonny Mac said.

"I'll be down soon."

They exited. The roof door slammed. Steps pounded

and faded. No complaints. No caps. No bullshit. They just wanted to get off the roof. That was good, Thomasson thought.

"I'm falling," Deggan complained.

Thomasson lay down flat. He kept his weapon out. He could not see her. Somewhere behind the short row of cartons.

"Be careful," Grace warned. "You might get hurt."

It was not clear to whom she was talking. The voice was very strong. Powered by the high voltage of drugs and who could say what else. For the first time since Vietnam, Thomasson wished he was high.

"Hey!" Thomasson called over to her. "Let's talk!"

"Talk about what?"

"Andy Deggan."

"What do you want with Andy Deggan?"

She was right. He had served his purpose. More or less. Thomasson's stomach turned slowly. There was no good answer.

"Listen to me." She was ordering him. "This is something between him and me. Get off the roof."

The fog was hovering. One tongue of it had reached roof level. They were figures in a dark movie with dry fog. The weight of it drained them and made them weak— bloodless.

Of course he wanted to leave. Let her kill him.

"Get off the roof," she repeated.

He feared the aftershocks of abandoning Deggan. Nagging guilt. After all, the guy had helped him. In Nam he had abandoned a shithead, and now dreamed about it regularly. The subconscious mind was a great Monday morning quarterback.

Guilt operated independent of what you wanted.

"Get off the *roof*."

She didn't want a witness. Street smarts told him other things. Alone, she could pronounce Deggan guilty before she executed him. A tongue-lashing ending in hysteria and homicide.

One last effort for the record. Kamikaze.

"You're under arrest!" Thomasson shouted.

Grace laughed. It was harsh and carried well on the breeze.

"Get fucked."

The door on the other roof opened suddenly and a figure burst out running. It took cover behind a row of garbage cans that was almost parallel to the wooden cartons behind which Grace hid. The door made a sharp scraping noise like a file. It stood open.

Thomasson laughed. Don't tell me, he thought.

"Thomasson!"

Quinn Dunaway's voice all right. Thomasson was delighted.

He took his time answering. "Yo. Thomasson."

Another pause while a long pink-edged cloud trundled by like a slow train above them. The pink light brightened. Still, they were too far away to see each other's faces. The misting breeze was getting just strong enough to carry away some of the words.

"What's it look like?" Quinn Dunaway wanted to know.

It was like talking long distance with a bad connection.

"Ask your sister." Anger peaked. "Go on—have a family reunion. Crawl all over each other."

Primly Grace commanded. "Andrew—"

Deggan had succeeded in pulling himself across the divide. He lay on the roof panting, a few feet in front of her.

"Andy?" she asked gently.

She stood up slowly. He looked up at her.

"Still here if I ain't gone someplace." Pouting and resentful.

"Gwan and kill me you fuckhead! That's what you wanna do ain't it?"

The world was new. In the wind that blew across this rooftop were the smell and taste of the sea. Bodies and kisses. Also childhood. Grass both green and warm sun-brown. The wheat running in ripples under the wind as gently and smoothly as glass shadows. The piercing massed echo of birds. Burning leaves. October air smoking yellow and blue in the twilight sliding dream-bound into night.

Was it not this magic shock she sought? Once childhood did it. Then sex. After its failures came drugs. After that, when the heart had forgotten how to pump and the skin died but did not shed itself?

To kill. To strike down in rage your own ghost.

It stood between mind and feeling. The feelings were lost. What were you without your feelings? Another ghost.

She raised the pistol. Deggan was staring at it.

To get life you had to take it. Exactly the opposite of what she had been taught. The symmetry of the inversion was complete. The Quaker in her wanted resurrection too.

The panting figure of Deggan twitched.

Now. But another ghost or shadow barred her way.

Quinn moved rapidly. He stood between Deggan and Grace. He had never hated Grace more.

"Grace. Grace."

On her face was an expression of fear and loathing. She tried to speak but the words stuck. She cleared her throat.

"Get out of the way!"

She put so much emotion in this she sounded like a child trying to scare herself.

"Please," she begged.

How had she come so quickly to beg? There had to be enormous emotional stakes at contest. But she was deranged. Her emotions were either not of her own choosing or fundamentally wrong.

"Please. This is something I have to do."

He had never heard a voice so desperate. It was as if she were dying of thirst and begging for water.

"Why?"

Strange, that he had not seen his coming. But of course. She had been meaning to kill Deggan all along. She had just found that out tonight.

"I have to do it," she said. "I can't live if I don't kill him. Please believe me."

He took a step toward her. She jumped in alarm. His boot made a light popping sound dragging on the tarpaper.

"It's my decision. It's for me."

Instant bravado. The influence of drugs. He was not at all sure she wouldn't shoot him. But she wouldn't kill him —he wouldn't let her. At her best she would never have the control he had.

" . . . for me, Quinn, for *me*, why won't you let me make a decision for myself for once?"

He had never seen her eyes so big.

He took another step toward her. "Grace."

"I'm willing to go to jail. I *want* to go to jail."

He nodded. She was willing to pay the price. He respected that. But he was unwilling to let her pay it.

"Quinn. I'll shoot you if you don't get out of the way."

He took a half-step toward her. Experience had taught him to press at the moment an opponent threatened, no matter how small the move was. Between threats you negotiated.

"I'm warning you."

Her voice was deep but had the rising inflection of hysteria.

"I don't think you want to shoot me."

"Then stop bluffing me."

He shrugged. Quinn saw Thomasson shaking his head on the other roof. Thomasson would do nothing.

He took another step.

"Stop!"

He shrugged again. It was important to maintain the rhythms of nonchalance. "Okay. I'm saying you're crazy enough to shoot someone."

She stared goggle-eyed. "You're saying that."

"Sure."

"And you think that's enough for me."

In another moment she would direct her rage at him.

"Thomasson!" he shouted.

When she looked over at the other roof he rushed her. There were four long running strides. In the middle of the second she turned back to see him rushing her. The middle of the third step she aimed two-handed. In the middle of the fourth she fired. He saw the cylinder revolve and the hammer go back in a single action. The explosion did not cause him to hesitate.

With his left he parried away the pistol. With his right he hit her in the solar plexus. He felt the thick breastbone bending. Once was enough. She doubled in pain. He held her tightly by the wrist.

The pistol lay at his feet. She stared at him in horror.

"I missed," she said a moment later.

"You had to miss that one."

Only then did she cry out. He wished he had not said that. It was not necessary. He picked up the pistol.

Deggan was still on the deck. He looked up at them.

Quinn turned toward Thomasson. "Come here!"

"Are you hit?"

"Nothing like that."

There was a pause. Finally Thomasson jumped over. He approached Quinn cautiously. Quinn held Grace's wrist with his left hand.

"Take her."

Thomasson stared at him. "What do I do with her?"

"You'll think of something. You put her under arrest Didn't you?"

"You heard that?" Thomasson shook his head. "All right. Wise ass. You're under arrest too."

Quinn pointed the pistol he had just taken from Grace at Thomasson's head. "I didn't hear that."

"Crazy. You people are crazy."

"Just take her. Then why don't you rejoin your playmates?"

Quinn took the pistol away from Thomasson's head.

"Those guys just want to rip off my buy money."

Quinn nodded. "Good. Get your backup people to hurry up. Maybe you can get them for something besides dealing. Maybe you can shoot somebody. Up here your life is in danger. That's a fact."

Quinn was threatening him, but also sounding like the sweet voice of reason. Quinn thought: *he's buying it.*

Thomasson looked a long time at Deggan. Deggan sat up. Thomasson grunted. "If I'm ever called to testify . . . "

"Just tell the truth."

His brother officers would help him determine the truth and how far the truth would go.

Thomasson turned to Grace and took her arm.

"Looks like you're taking off," Deggan said.

"Looks like I'm taking off."

Thomasson left without further conversation. To Quinn he appeared relieved the decision had been made. It gave him one more shot at busting dope. Then, if there was no heroin and someone got physical over the buy money, a little deadly force to make up for the hard time he had been shown.

Grace allowed herself to be led away. She seemed in shock.

The roof door scraped closed. Quinn was alone on the roof with Deggan, who sat squatting on his haunches. His face was covered with blood and he swayed slightly. His nakedness was pathetic. It made Quinn angry.

From the Bay came the sharp double *whuuck* of fog-horns.

Quinn lit a cigarette. He inhaled twice in rapid succession. Gradually his breath became shallower. He squatted beside Deggan and handed him the cigarette. He watched while Deggan sucked at it.

Not much time. But enough.

"Haw," Deggan said in a satisfied voice.

Quinn took out the rubber gloves and put them on.

"Yo," Deggan said curiously. "What're we got there?"

"Surgical gloves."

Deggan snuffled disgustedly. "*I* ain't sick."

It was a ritual. Good. Rituals were essential to exorcisms. The familiar stations of the hands and the things they touched were given a new formula and were born again.

"I don't know. You don't look so hot to me."

Truly, he felt as if he were about to operate on Deggan. To cure him of his nakedness.

"My sister wanted to kill you."

Deggan was contemptuous. "*Waited* long enough."

Quinn laughed. He smoothed the thin rubber glove where it had torn at the wrist. "Too long. Like everything else she did."

The backup gun he had stashed in a garbage can. He put his hands on Deggan's pistol in his pocket. Hard. He curled his fingers around its chassis. The solidity of it was almost sweet. Bittersweet, like the taste of green apples.

"We're all set."

Let it build a little. It was reasonable to enjoy it after waiting so long. A quick bourbon would be good, too. But he really didn't need it. He had already had a lot and the gun was like bourbon anyway.

"You're all crazy," Deggan was snickering.

Take out the pistol. Slowly—let him see it.

Deggan started. Quinn gave him a quick shake of the head.

"You know what it is."

Deggan's bloody face went blank. Fear hit it. The eyes crossed momentarily as one eye fixed itself worshipfully on the gun. After a moment the other rolled sadly toward the Bay. His legs turned rubbery on him and he slid slowly forward to his knees. He rubbed the muscles in his thigh.

"Give you a dime bag," Deggan said in the small weightless voice of a child.

Again Quinn shook his head. Deggan made vague questioning shapes with his hands in the manner of charades.

"All right *what* then?"

"You."

Deggan shook his head energetically. What came out of his mouth came with a sigh like wind in a dream.

He was trying to say some one-syllable word like *stop* or *no*.

Quinn looked up at the long pink clouds above them. One looked like a finger lowering toward them at the tip. But there was no Adam here. There was not even a Cain. There was a fighter and there was an animal who talked like a man. He was dangerous, and he was most dangerous to the weak and innocent.

He looked back at Deggan. Two feet away. So close.

"I wonder what you would do to stay alive," he murmured.

Deggan's eyes neither begged nor accused. The one fixed on the pistol shone like black oil on glass or water; its pupil seemed to have shrunk to a pinhole. The other eye searched vainly for a way out.

Quinn cleared his throat.

"I said I wonder what you would do to stay alive."

Deggan tried to giggle. "Hoo," he said suggestively.

An unwanted image of men embracing flashed through Quinn's mind.

"Not that." Quinn laughed. "but I guess you would."

Deggan responded by starting to cry. He wept exactly like a little boy. "'Cause I'm scared," he said finally.

"Because you're scared."

The Deggans of the world could not postpone anger. So also were they unable to know fear until the moment you began to kill them.

"Scared!" Deggan repeated as though the word alone would save him.

Quinn hoped he would turn mean at the end. To struggle. To turn surly. That would give him the symmetry he wanted. What if he didn't? Okay, you could kill someone with a bad taste in your mouth as well as not.

"Talk—" Deggan exclaimed desperately through his tears.

Quinn laughed again. "You or me?"

"I could talk!"

The mist ate at Quinn's eyes. He blinked twice to clear them. He grasped Deggan's shoulder and gently shook him back and forth.

"Now old Andy wants to talk."

Quinn did not like to talk about things as he did them. It was too much like seeing the world twice. Intellectuals did. So did criminals. Because of that and the sin of pride, they thought the world began in their heads.

"To explain!" Deggan cried.

"Explain what?"

"Why I do . . . those things."

"You already explained that. People can't stop you."

He had to laugh. It was so simple and correct, what he had said about himself. Yet Quinn suspected there was more. It was like something in the corner of the eye. You almost saw it before it slipped away.

"Cherokee—!" Deggan whooped without warning.

He laboriously pulled himself back onto his haunches. He duck-walked a tentative foot forward. "Taken me from the orphanage home. See. I weren't mama's blood child at all!"

At the words *orphanage home* Quinn felt anger. A fresh pleasure joined it. He experimented with pulling back the hammer on the pistol a fraction of an inch. Deggan's teary eyes widened.

"You're Cherokee."

He nodded wildly. His face was white around the cuts and drying patches of blood. "Gospel—!"

"Is that why you hurt people?"

Deggan leaned closer. He was about to impart something big. Quinn felt he was losing time but wanted to hear the secrets. That was power too. To take the last words away and own them.

"Double-Y chromosomes!"

Deggan nodded with abandon. He would have strutted had he been able. A profound and wonderful chord had been touched. All would be forgiven.

"Told me about em in Q," he continued. "Can't *help* the things I do."

Pride not only in telling but in knowing. Science had triumphed.

"That's why I'm killing you."

He stood up and pulled back on the hammer. The gun was jammed. Possibly when he had checked the action earlier, some of the cartridges had slid out slightly. They were keeping the chamber from rotating. Deggan saw him struggling to cock the hammer and began the baby-talk of panic.

"Hey hey hey man no c'mon hey be *serious* man—"

The helplessness of his fear gave Quinn a solid feeling of control, despite his difficulties with the pistol. He laughed.

"Nothing personal—"

He had always been aware of the special cruelty of the phrase. Here he took pleasure in it. Deggan wobbled on his haunches and continued to babble.

"Nothing personal," Quinn repeated softly.

To his surprise Deggan shut up and nodded knowingly.

"Because you're not responsible for your actions."

He opened the chamber and pushed the cartridges flat with his thumbnail. He closed it and pulled back on the hammer again. It had a double action and the trigger would pull it back anyway. But if he couldn't cock it with his thumb, the trigger couldn't cock it either.

This time the hammer came almost all the way back.

"Not responsible?" Deggan raced on greedily. "Then I don't have to be punished! You don't have to—"

He stared at the pistol as though it would finish the sentence for him.

"No." Quinn shook his head. "That's why you have to go." From Deggan tottering below came a sound like wet paper being torn. "It's a mystery. You have to take it on faith."

White fire in his stomach. Mystery. That was the word. A religious fire. Like the gun its effects were not unlike bourbon.

"You got no choice in the matter," Quinn added.

"You fucking TRICK SLAVE!" Deggan screamed. At last came the rage. "Ask me a fucking QUESTION and tell me a fucking LIE!"

He cocked the pistol. It was aimed downward and to

the left of Deggan. His finger brushed the trigger and it fired. Quinn cursed. It was a hair trigger. They were both amazed. All Quinn could see was the yellow-and-orange flash where the explosion had been. He could not believe he was handling the pistol so clumsily.

Quinn turned and threw the pistol away. It had been ruined. No way could he use it now. He stood over Deggan. His bare hands; or probably the roof. Whatever it was supposed to be—

Deggan opened his mouth to speak. Last word or words.

"Orphan—"

It stung. Somehow Deggan was hurting him. Magic. He had never been hurt by a word before.

"Cherokee—" Deggan murmured huskily, looking up at him.

The tear-stained broken eyes glistened with messianic fervor and sincerity. Somehow the religious fire had reached him too. But necessarily a snare and a delusion. Perfectly counterfeit, this proselytism. A highly detailed shadow with everything reversed—like the negative of a photo.

"Cherok*eee*—"

He struck Deggan on the temple hard enough to give him a concussion. His eyes showed white. He collapsed into semiconsciousness.

Quinn dragged him a few feet. Oddly, he proved able to walk for himself. He force-walked him toward the street side. It took a long time to arrive at the edge. Or seemed to.

Don't let him speak. Don't let him speak.

He stopped three feet from the little brick wall that ran around the roof. He let go of Deggan. He wobbled but stayed on his feet. A glimmer of consciousness flickered in the walleyes, the white interspersed with flashes of the brackish sloe—

Do it. Please. Now. One believer to another.

Quinn scooped Deggan up like a bride. The little-boy body was light in his arms. He took several steps and turned toward the edge. Deggan whinnied like a child imitating a horse as they ran. As Quinn threw him over the edge his arms and legs opened like wings, and to Quinn it seemed at that moment Deggan wished nothing more than to fly in just that way.

They reached the corner half a block away from the Regina. Thomasson was moving her along briskly. The prostitutes and drag queens were mainly Black now. White males in late-model cars cruised the block.

She stumbled and went down. Thomasson pulled her upright.

"Come *on*."

He was holding her arm far too tightly. He cursed. He had said nothing about where they were going, or why. Grace assumed that was because he didn't know himself.

"Where are you taking me?" she demanded.

Thomasson looked put-upon. "You're in trouble!"

Resist, a voice told her. Stop walking.

She stopped short. "Let go."

He dragged her down the street in rough jerks. Brute force. She made herself go limp like a civil rights demonstrator. The streetwalkers paid them no mind.

A cruising john in a Camaro slowed to watch. "Hot to trot, honey!" yelled a streetwalker. She ran toward him.

The car sped away.

The mood on the street was dangerous Saturday night gaiety.

Thomasson stopped to slap her. "Okay?" he wanted to know. "How does that feel?"

She could not tell him now. There were no feelings left. She shrugged. And she had been so close to getting them all back.

"You bastard," she said over and over.

Thomasson got the self-satisfied put-upon look on his face again.

"Not you," she said. "My brother. Quinn Dunaway."

The reaction was immediate. "Shut up!" he screamed. "I don't want to hear that name! I don't know that name!"

"Is that what you'll tell the district attorney?"

He stared at her. "Nobody is telling anybody anything," he said mechanically.

She wanted to hurt him. Let him feel as empty as she did. He knew what she was doing. The fatigued bearded face got angry.

"Watch that. I'll burn you."

The threat came across much better than the other. Still he was unsure what to do with her. He walked to the corner and looked both ways.

"Terrific," he said disgustedly.

She guessed he was looking for a partner.

"There's somebody I want to meet," Thomasson said vaguely. He turned back angrily. "I got business."

He probably wanted to dump her on the partner. If he didn't see his friends soon, maybe he would leave her here.

"Sorry?" she shrilled at him. "Is that what you want me to say? That I'm sorry? For whatever it is?"

"I don't care what you say."

She was suddenly afraid of losing him. Someone to talk to. She was afraid of what came next.

"You're a cop. You know what's happening now."

"How do you know I'm a cop?"

"You were running around putting us all under arrest before. Remember? Anyway," she said wearily, "you know exactly what's happening now. Don't say you don't."

"Don't talk about it. Whatever it is." His hands were palms-up. He shoved them forward as though he wished to cup her breasts. "*Look.* I got work to do!"

From high above came a gunshot. There was a little metallic punching sound at the end of the report, like an icepick poking through the top of a pressurized can. She wondered in which part of the body the hole was being punched.

Thomasson looked up. She laughed.

Everything belonging to Grace Dunaway was gone. She felt as empty as a gutted fish.

Now the brain went. The lightning of amphetamine had brought on the rain. Ocean visions. The veins inside the brain had burst, and the neatly divided hemispheres were drowning in a lassitude more powerful than hashish.

Thomasson was a few feet down the block. He appeared to see something or someone in an alley. He turned back to her and opened his mouth. A scream came from behind her. Their eyes met and Thomasson sprinted toward her.

She turned slowly around. It was hard to move.

There was a *whoomp* with glass breaking. Something landed on top of a parked car in front of the Regina Hotel. It bounced straight up. It did two cartwheels and

waved broken arms and legs at her like a rag doll being
shaken in slow motion. It fell back in an arc to the middle
of the street. There was the hollow sound of the head
splitting on impact. There was the sound of brakes being
applied. The streetwalkers started running up and
screaming joyously.

"Oh shit," Thomasson said in a surprisingly sad voice.

She ran. There was no doubt where to go now.

The basement of the Southern Home was a junkyard.
Army cots, moldering mattresses, the horrible cheap
metal suitcases abandoned by transients fleeing room
rent. It seemed darker than before. Quinn tripped twice
before forcing himself to slow down. At the door to the
alley he stopped altogether for a few seconds to catch his
breath.

It was important now to get away.

In the alley he tore off the gloves. He stuck them in his
pocket. They were badly ripped. He was afraid he might
drop one.

Later he would take care of Grace.

Down the alley a car engine turned over. When the
engine was running the lights did not come on. The car
moved slowly forward. There was something familiar
about it.

A single headlight came on. It was Grace's Volvo. He
shielded his eyes from the light.

"Grace?"

She was driving. She was alone. The car continued to
move slowly forward. "Stop," he ordered.

The Volvo stopped three feet in front of him. He

322   *Lawrence Swaim*

approached the window on the driver's side.

"I could use a ride," he said through a small crack in the window.

Her eyes were closed a long time. At last she opened them.

"What did you say?"

Grace looked crazy. He walked in front of the car to get in the other side. She disengaged the clutch. He skipped backwards into the two-foot passageway between the hotels.

Damn her. He should have smashed the glass.

The Volvo pulled away at high speed. It fishtailed and cleared the alley. He ran after it. From the general direction of the street in front of the Regina came the sound of horns honking.

One more job. There was no getting around it.

He walked slowly but unhesitantly north. On Geary there would be cabs. He heard a siren working its way across Market. There was little traffic on this street and no police.

Half a block from Geary he hailed a slow cab. The driver was hip, with long hair in a bun, and a buckskin jacket.

"Where?" the driver wanted to know.

Quinn closed his eyes. He didn't particularly want to hear the words. But they were necessary.

"Golden Gate Bridge."

He wanted to be alone. To rest. To let the victory seep through to him. Yes, he would go to Grace this one last time; but it really was the last time.

The young driver used the mirror to look him over. "Ending it all? I can give you a few reasons not to."

Quinn lit a cigarette. His breath was slowly getting more even.

"Just drive."

His shirt was wet with sweat. On the back of his neck it was starting to dry. He rolled up the window. He didn't want to catch cold.

"Seriously." The driver was leaning against the door as he drove so he could talk to Quinn. "They counsel us about this. They tell us what to say. 'Keep them talking.'"

"Save your breath. I'm not jumping. I'm just a spectator."

"Uh huh." The driver was not convinced. "First we're supposed to tell them whatever they're feeling is only temporary . . . . "

It was a nice drive to the bridge. Traffic was light. Grace was numb and deferred to other drivers. At a red light on Van Ness, a man in a customized Ranchero revved his motor behind her and tapped his horn as he passed. She gave him a saintly smile. The chesty blond bomber with him gave her the finger.

On Lombard it was green lights all the way.

She made the right turnoff on the bridge approach. This brought her to a parking lot well away from the span. She parked carefully and turned out the lights. She had been here before. Sometimes she was overcome by an almost physical need to see the bridge. It was very reassuring to know it was going to be there when you needed it.

She turned off the motor and lit a cigarette.

There were walking dead who came regularly to haunt this parking lot. She had seen them. The Highway Patrol kept an eye out for them. Sooner or later the regulars jumped.

Or made an attempt. She sighed and closed her eyes. That was the worst. To get up there ready to take the step and suddenly find you weren't ready after all; to allow yourself to be talked down by marvelously gentle men whom you never saw again. Three years before, that had happened to her. Seventy-two hours under observation at San Francisco. They had given her a kind of reprimand when they let her go. She had sensed in the eyes of the harried staff a certain impatience. *Live or die—make up your mind. How much class does it take to jump off a bridge?*

You can't even kill yourself right. The ultimate failure.

And gradually it had come to her that killing herself was the great challenge of her life. Until tonight. For a brief hour or two she had seen an alternative. Killing Deggan, she would have given herself the right to live.

Why in God's name couldn't Quinn have seen that?

She had failed Quinn as well as herself.

She pulled herself forward to look in the mirror. She wanted a kind of inventory. In the highway light she saw a thin face with luminous gray eyes. It was not a bad face. It was almost beautiful (Richards had seen that). But how disquieting the almost beautiful could be! One always tried to supply the missing element.

People had seen something subtly accusatory in the drawn uncentered face with the high cheekbones. They had not taken kindly to it.

She finished the cigarette and threw it out the window.

She did not need a note. She had nothing to explain. No gifts to bestow. She was not sorry. She wanted no pardon. Sympathy? The amphetamine allowed her to smile. That was another world; a different drummer she had left behind long ago in the pell-mell smartass race to the outer limits.

She got out and started walking. She did not lock the door. At the corner of the parking lot she shed her coat; she left it lying on a shrub. She looked back once. The Volvo was still there.

Idiot. Did you expect it to drive away by itself?

She sang "Keys to the Highway" as she walked. What was important was moving on. No impasses. Go around them.

She continued her inventory. Good riddance to the coat (she wanted to feel the freezing wind and fog). Purse no longer a problem, it was in the back seat of the Volvo. Sandals. Her favorite pair of jeans. A clean shirt (Macy's she thought). In the pocket of the jeans, cigarettes and a matchbook and a few other small odds and ends. That was it. She didn't even have a comb in her hair.

All declared and accounted for.

There was another parking lot for a restaurant. It was a circular glass bubble filled with tourists and Highway Patrol. It was late and the customers were subdued. She could hear no sounds from within. It seemed to revolve slowly as she walked past. Its fluorescent vinyl-and-stainless-steel brightness reminded her of a Hitchcock set.

Vertigo? North by Northwest?

Moisture stung against her face and sandaled feet. The wind here was stronger. It blew not mist but fog. She could not yet see the bridge clearly; fog obscured it. Where she was walking it was thin and pulled apart in the wind. Higher up she could see it roiling like surf.

She was climbing stairs. She saw the Golden Gate.

She paused to light a cigarette. She cupped her hands. To her surprise the cigarette lit up like a small explosion.

Her thin hands were red and shaking. She could not feel them. It occurred to her that neither could she taste the cigarette. Looking up she saw the bridge clearly. Its burnt orange and its arching cleanness were so good they made her dizzy. She inhaled again and the bridge allowed her to taste the cigarette. Her heart pounded.

Thank you. In front of her was the wire gate. In front of it were shrubs. Hitchhikers with backpacks passed her. She could not force herself to nod to them. *Thank you.* Once again she saw the bridge. It gave her excitement and strength.

Next the lights of San Francisco. She had to walk for those. Let's go, she thought. The first step of the long march.

Walking. Head down watching the feet. One perfect step after another. Traffic was light and there were no other walkers. The sidewalk was wide with a four-foot railing. It was all hers.

Fog poured through the bridge. It was like walking through a river. Above were red lights to warn away the airplanes. The fog whipped around her like freezing smoke. She opened her mouth—the windblown moisture pierced her tongue like needles. The diamond lights began to wheel slowly into view. Again like a set but theater rather than film. It was all on wheels. Obstructing trees rolled slowly backwards. Forward on the sparkling lights. Market Street. California Street. Hotels of Nob Hill. Telegraph Hill.

All the way to the middle of the bridge. The view there was better. She had to force herself not to run.

Take it easy. Rituals were not to be rushed.

She saw the car after it had passed. Highway Patrol. It didn't slow. She thought the driver picked up the hand mike. Most likely they had seen her. They were too far along the bridge to stop. They wouldn't want to spook her.

They would come back. Or others would come.

It would be good to talk to someone before she left. Of course they wanted to stop you. If you jumped they thought they had failed. Couldn't they see you needed the conversation just as much when you jumped as when you didn't? It gave the leave-taking a certain tidiness and courtesy. A rite of passage—ceremony, if you wished. A little dignity at the end.

She got another cigarette but it was broken. Okay. The wind was too strong here anyway. Besides, the humming of her nerves was stimulant enough now. She threw it over the railing. It fell slowly into fog.

Over her shoulders she watched the City lights. The fog made them twinkle like stars. Only the electric tinsel of neon. But also Christmas and childhood and friends and the soft ache of good times as they should have happened. Wonderful with promise even when you knew the treachery in them. The bridge gave you the magic distance. From here you enjoyed a state of grace as long as you looked at the lights. They took away fear. They took away defeat. They took away the nausea of emptiness. You were safe as long as you looked at them.

You were home free.

From below somewhere came the drifting *whuuck!* of foghorns. Watch out. She could not see the boats. So aware of each other but not touching. Sending out signals like old maids in the dark. Waiting for the reply. Touching would be disaster.

She stopped walking and turned slowly. She was about one-third of the way across the bridge. Okay. This was good. The City lay before her like a picnic of lights. Eat them. Drink them. Shoot them into the fat veins in the crook of your arm. Sleep them and dream them. Day and night forever.

Beauty always greater than the sum of the reasons offered—

Oh Daddy I have no feelings left. I spent them like money.

Home free.

Quinn I gambled them and lost. Understand.

A ship passed slowly under the other side of the bridge. Probably a tanker. It was a long black shadow in the fog. She could hear the distant pinging of the screw. Its vibration traveled up through the metal of the bridge.

She reached out shyly to touch the railing. Flat on top. So cold it burned like fire. Through it she felt the brittle metal pulse of the passing ship. Her hands were perfect white all over.

Home free. That was the promise.

San Francisco was made of glass. On the other side were her feelings. They were in cold storage until she passed over. Yet even from this first and most perfect world she sensed an anomaly. Several emotions had gotten very tangled up. They awaited her arrival to straighten them out.

She leaned over the rail. *Hello down there.* Through cracks in the rushing fog winked the huge sleeping green mass. On its wave-capped surface rippled fingers of red light from the underside of the bridge.

Home free.

A clump of cars passed with their lights on bright. Next there was the unmistakable hum of a patrol car. When she turned she saw it was not the same one as before. She waved angrily for it to stop.

The patrol car stopped short.

She pulled herself up with one leg. The stinging metal cold struck at her through the jeans. She went gently over the rail and crouched on the narrow ledge below. Once before she had knelt at this station. Three years before she had waited to jump here and had not been able.

She giggled and peered through the railing.

The patrol car was about fifty feet away. The red bubble on top was on but not revolving. The door on the passenger side stood ajar. One patrolman had gotten out and stood looking in her direction. She heard the scratchy muttering of the radio. The driver was smiling and fumbling with a spotlight, which pointed straight up into the drizzling fog. Small droplets whipped through its intense narrow beam like particles in a cloud chamber. The effect was interesting.

She sat down to wait for the right moment.

Quinn paid the cabdriver in the restaurant parking lot. He walked toward the lookout point in the adjoining lot. He spotted Don Richards standing by Grace's Volvo. He was stooped over in pain.

He walked toward him. "Richards—"

Richards turned slowly. His eyes were closed against the blowing mist.

Quinn stood next to him. "What are you doing here?"

"Grieving."

"How's that?"

Richards grasped the door handle of the Volvo so tightly it was as if he were holding onto Grace herself. "I have to know I can stand here while she does it—and not go out there and beg her not to."

"My God."

"Like saying good-bye." Richards shook his head maniacally. "But I'm not going out there and talk to her. No way. No way!"

"Relax. I didn't say you should."

"You know what else I'm not going to do?" Richards's eyes flew open. Tears mingled with the mist. "I won't identify her goddamn body. You know why? I don't want to."

Quinn laughed. Good for Richards.

"Wait here."

He trotted toward the bridge.

She had worked her way to a lower station. Here the metal ledge upon which she wobbled was slippery with grime. It had not been at all easy getting down here, and she was winded. She squatted contentedly on her haunches, aware of the rushing about above her. The dreaming green water stretched below like a net.

She was the queen. They held court for her. She was aware of the ritual. They thought she was hesitating. They couldn't know she was only waiting. Odd—how important it was to jump at your own time. It was the difference between jumping and falling.

Last chance to do something right.

Although it was literally true it made her laugh.

"Grace?" Quinn shouted suddenly from above.

She had been expecting him, but his voice was unexpectedly harsh. He was not very far above her. She wondered if he knew how much anger was in his voice. Even from Quinn that came as a surprise.

It was not unreasonable to want people to defer to her now.

"You don't have to shout at me!" she called up.

Maybe she should have shouted at him a long time ago.

"How many people—" Not how many, but whether he was alone. She was surprised how disgusted her own voice sounded. "Are you alone?"

"Just me."

He was now directly above her. She did not bother to look up. Even with the stiff breeze she would hear him coming down. The amphetamine was letting her hear and see everything.

"Quinn you bastard—"

She sensed strength in the way it waited to answer. Had he begged or started out glib, she would have taunted him.

"Make it good."

"It's not up to me to make anything good," he shot back at her.

"Then what the hell do you *want?*" she demanded crossly.

"To talk."

The second time tonight someone had used those words. Earlier it was Deggan's life to negotiate or spend as she chose. Now she was left with nothing but her own; which meant she was left with nothing, period.

It would be such a relief to step away from the talking games—

"*Talk—?*" Without intending it her voice had gone suddenly shrill. "Talk about what?"

"Two things. First, I want you to wait. Don't jump. Just wait. Second, I don't want you to come back up here until you're ready to at least try to live."

Below the whitecapped Bay sighed like a river. It was the wind. Deep channels of fog stroked the Bay. On its green surface the red bridge lights sinuated slowly lengthwise like snakes.

Peaceful. *Yes goddamn it and inviting too.*

Suddenly it came to her. "You want me to jump," she said wonderingly. "You want me to go on and do it."

"I didn't say that—"

"Either that or stick me in a state hospital." She waited. "You're tired of putting up with me. Aren't you?"

There was another pause. The wind and the powerful presence above here were taking her breath away.

"Yes. I'm tired of putting up with you."

She tried to say "thank you" but couldn't.

He would not patronize her. She was thankful for that. Yet her reaction was mixed. To the extent that Quinn was honest with her, it had always made her want to please him. But that in turn made her angry. There was arrogance in it. Quinn used honesty to control people.

But this wasn't control. Drunkenness? Insanity? Maybe both—

"My God—" At last she laughed. "I think you just fucked up. Can you imagine the guilt you'll feel when I do it?"

"Guilt," he said contemptuously. Yet she sensed hesitation for the first time.

"Don't you want to stop me?"

"Of course," he said too quickly. "Otherwise why would I be out here talking to you?"

She tried to look upward. A gray grotesque that was probably his face floated like a balloon tied to the railing above her. Looking up made her extremely dizzy. She decided not to do it again.

"Well then, use humor on me," she advised.

They shared a laugh. "See?" she said. "Like that."

"What are the advantages of humor in this situation?"

"Makes it easier for you."

He laughed. "Thanks."

"Bitte schön."

"What?"

Another violent gust of wind took the words away.

"That was 'you're welcome' in German. I *majored* in German," she continued in a neutral but officious tone. She was not quite shouting. "At Cal. The last year." She cleared her throat. "Now give me some reasons why I shouldn't jump. So you won't torture yourself with guilt later."

"Curiosity. Aren't there things you're curious about? You can't get an answer by running away from life."

"That's pretty damn good," she acknowledged.

She was curious about women like herself who were attracted to Black men. She wondered to what extent it was first of all a sin of pride—an attempt to heal in one life a sickness of millions. She wondered also about the mathematical probability of someone having the kind of bad luck she had had with men. Mathematics could be applied to music and even philosophy; why not to suicide?

"What if I'm not curious *enough?*" she asked.

Her hands were black with grime. She was glad she wouldn't have to wash them. Finished, all those house-keeping chores of the body. Not that she would have minded if she'd got more out of it. This particular body hadn't been worth the trouble.

"You can change if you want to," Quinn was saying. "Whatever your life is now—"

"You did a good job on Andy."

"Sweetie, you can't blame me for everything. Or Deggan either. You were suicidal long before."

Back to the conventional talk-her-down. Or Quinn's version of it.

"What's your point?" she asked suspiciously.

"That you can't blame anyone. Including yourself."

"What makes you think I'm interested in placing—" She searched for the right word. "In *asserting* blame?"

"You're suicidal. You must blame yourself for something."

"*You* blame people."

"I'm probably wrong," he said wearily. "Blame doesn't work with you. You need help."

"From you?"

"No. Not from me anymore. But if you make up your mind to change, there are all kinds of people who will help you."

Another long gust of wind. The bridge whistled and moaned like a freight train. Cold but free. The bridge was truly immense. Crouched inside its lowering wet steel wing, she embraced the lights of San Francisco without touching them. In her own good time she'd reach them.

"How's Don Richards?" she asked.

"Do you want to talk to him?"

"No."

Freedom was floating in perfect balance. Even drugs told you that. Family (like gravity) you broke away from. So the leavetaking and its roulette of good-byes; good-byes—

"How is he?"

To inquire about each one formally before leaving. Courtesy, or the illusion of courtesy.

"Scared as hell. Like you, I guess."

"Don't be so damn sure I'm scared—" she threatened.

"Good. We can build on that."

"You smug bastard."

"I'm doing the best I can," he complained.

". . . *build* on that."

She laughed. Now she was the one who was contemptuous.

Down the span there were blue lights to chase the whirling red ones. She wondered if maintenance men had been called. Sometimes they were sent to retrieve jumpers who had changed their minds but had crawled too far out to get back alone. They could tell her nothing. The bridge had made her immune to fear, and she was on the offensive.

Her thigh muscles hurt. Her haunches would no longer support her.

"Jesus. Do me a favor and leave off with the psychiatric bullshit." She stood up unsteadily. "You know you hate that crap anyway."

"Just *wait*." For the first time Quinn's voice was urgent. "You can help me understand. Try to wait. Sweetie, I got to know more. You have to tell me—"

"Tell Don Richards I'm sorry," she said.

"—just try, honey. Talk to me. Talk."

There was one more person to bid farewell. That was her son Martin. Since bringing him into the world, she had used this tiny human being almost exclusively as a scapegoat. The knowledge of her inability to be a mother had simply made her sicker. There was nothing she could do or say that would wipe away this wrong. There was in fact only one way she could help him. She had to go where she could never hurt him, never under any circumstance.

"Quinn?" she demanded.

He knew what was coming. He refused to answer.

"Take care of Martin. Promise me."

"We'll do it together."

"Promise me! Hurry."

The bridge was actually swaying. That and the wind made it hard to stand. She went back down on her haunches. It was almost time—

"*Promise* me," she wailed up to him.

She could feel the desperation building above her.

"Grace. Tell me why. Tell me *why* you want to kill yourself."

"Why? Just why?"

"Why."

Anything to keep her talking.

"Because you wouldn't let me kill Andy Deggan."

"Don't let the deputy hear you say that." He was trying to joke about it. "Anyway—" She felt him searching for words. The pause went on too long. "What's done is done," he said finally.

The words struck her with amazing force. Truly they were beautiful. They summed it all up. Irony, that he should provide her with the consummate explanation of her life. A delicious shiver traveled up her spine. He was challenging her to go ahead.

"What's done is *done*," she whispered experimentally.

To leave behind finally the prefabricated sequences of a lifetime of mediocrity. The last years hadn't even been cause and effect. It had only been effect upon effect; the jerking of an insect—

"What's done is done!" she screamed up joyfully.

"I did what I thought was right," Quinn said.

"Well, you were wrong," she said without bitterness.

"It was something I was supposed to do. If you'd let me kill him—" She paused to think. "I could have changed my life. I would have been able to live. Paying my debt in the penitentiary—"

"Prison," Quinn corrected gently.

They had once argued about these words. *Penitentiary* had come from the Quakers and the other early prison reformers. It meant a place to do penance, or experience penitence. Quinn had said the word no longer applied. Not necessarily so, Grace had argued.

"Penitence," she whispered up to him.

"Can't you forgive me for that one mistake?" he cried.

Living, she would never forgive him.

"Sure," she said.

There was nothing now but anticipation.

An excited conference was being held down the span. She smiled. This time around she was way ahead of them; success was in her grasp. She shut out all the worlds except two. She stood up once again.

"Wait—"

"Good-bye—"

So she was done with it. Quinn dropped out of her mind as though he had never existed. She trembled forward bravely. The water was so vast she no longer had to look at it. Instead she looked at the lights of the City hanging before her like worlds in perfect balance—

Hello . . .

Hello. She was empowered by the word.

Anticipation became pure excitement. Her chest swelled with gratitude. Miraculous new words exploded—

How lucky they were,
in the end
travelers to the West,
to have the power to set things right—.

She took a deep breath and stepped forward toward
home and the promised land.

PART FOUR

The Golden Gate

8

It was a stucco church with a large basement partitioned for teaching Sunday school. At one end were wooden folding chairs around a worktable. Near it was a wobbly green clothboard upon which a pair of cardboard zebras lockstepped into Noah's ark. Above them burst a storm cloud, complete with two sinister-looking lightning bolts.

Quinn was ten minutes early. He sat down to wait.

The lightning bolts that threatened the zebras intrigued him. They were shaped disturbingly like the nazi SS symbol. Could that be intentional? Almost certainly not, he decided. It was not the function of Sunday school to deal with things like that.

Preschoolers would meet here on Sundays, Quinn thought. Wednesday night it would be Adult Bible Class.

Today was Saturday and it was Alcoholics Anonymous.

At four people began to arrive. They settled in chairs around the table. To Quinn there were murmured hellos. People who knew each other nodded without speaking.

A tall man with a briefcase set out AA literature on the table. "Most of it's free," he explained. "All except the hardbound books."

Quinn started. It was Telford Frahm—the Quaker with whom he had talked about Deggan one week before.

Frahm put his briefcase under the table. "The Big Book is seven dollars. There are a couple of other things here which are three and four dollars respectively." He pointed them out. "The pamphlets are all free, I think."

There was a slight anticipatory pause. He turned to a young man sitting beside him.

"Would you say the Serenity Prayer tonight?"

A short prayer was recited from memory. Quinn kept his eyes open. There were more men than women. They had in common a plainness of feature and a tendency to redness of face.

Frahm saw him and blinked. "Amen!" he said.

To the group at large he said, "Tonight the subject is self-deception. Who has something to say about self-deception?"

"Who doesn't?" someone said.

There was laughter.

They were good storytellers and liked talking about themselves. Quinn was pleasantly surprised. Several of the stories were quite funny. They reminded him of people he had met in bars.

When it was his turn he shook his head. "I'll pass."

"Your first meeting?" someone asked.

"None of your business."

It got a laugh.

After the meeting Frahm picked up the AA material and put it back into his briefcase. Quinn sat drinking coffee. They were alone in the basement. "What did you think of it?" Frahm asked him.

"I liked the spirit of it." He lit a cigarette. "How did you get to be a drunk?"

"How did you?"

"Pressure."

"Pressure. So you drink."

"How do you know if you're an alcoholic?" Quinn asked.

"Was alcohol interfering with your life?"

"Yes."

"Did you ever lie about how much you drank to anyone else?"

"Yes." He had lied to the adoption people. Others who had been through it told him to say he didn't drink at all. "At the time I didn't know how much I was lying."

"Do you think you're an alcoholic?"

"I don't know. Probably."

"Don't worry about it. Just keep going to the meetings."

Frahm sat down beside him. His handsome face was tense. "Is that all that's bothering you?"

Quinn was angry. "You know damn well it isn't."

"Grace?"

"Yeah—Grace."

"We always blame ourselves."

"I was just tired of her. I didn't care if she killed herself or not. You were right about that."

They were silent a long time.

"I heard about Andy Deggan," Frahm said.

There was another silence.

"Do you expect me to be sorry about that?" Quinn put out his cigarette in an ashtray on the worktable. "To blame myself?"

"It was wrong."

"It was necessary." He stood up. It was time to go. "You don't know the half of it. Forget about it."

"Aren't you afraid I'll tell what I know?"

"No—I'm not." Quinn put his hand on his shoulder.

"You're crazy but you're consistent. If you wouldn't put Deggan in a cage, you wouldn't put me in one either." He laughed. "How does it feel to see a criminal go unpunished?"

"Damn your arrogance!" Frahm was furious. He pushed his hand away. "How can you be so sure?"

"I'm sure."

On the road it was noodling. Easy driving. There was surprisingly little traffic. All he had to do was keep on his side of the divided highway.

They had reserved a cabin in the Sacramento Delta. Dawn was napping in the back seat. He kept his hands busy with cigarettes and driving.

"Smoking too much," Rozalyn said.

Quinn hadn't had a drink in the six days since Grace's death. He was smoking close to three packs a day. That was more than Rozalyn.

"Some people were born to smoke."

"Some people smoke too much. It's nothing but slow suicide—" She gasped. "I shouldn't have said that!"

Quinn was amused. "Maybe they'd be doing something worse if they weren't smoking."

"You guys!" Dawn said from the back seat.

They had woken her up. "Sorry," Quinn said.

For the last six days he had fought off the shakes with ten-hour days and No-Doz and workouts and cigarettes. It was hell without bourbon.

"How was the meeting?" Roz asked softly.

"Okay."

She put her arm around him like a teenager.

In fact the meeting had left him with a lingering warmth. It reminded him of the Hicksite Quaker meeting at home. His father had been the clerk of the meeting. Frequently he would begin a meeting with a query: *Do we keep to moderation and simplicity in our standards of living? Do our vocations provide constructive and beneficial service? Do we observe integrity in our business transactions?*

"Love ya," Rozalyn said.

His father had been right about the Inner Light. But it was not enough to know the right. You had to act on it.

"I love you too."

There were highway lights. They came on mysteriously.

"Hallelujah!" he said.

Their fluorescence was safety against the twilight. He switched on the car lights too. The west was dark red along the horizon.

Another moment and night had come.

They shared a cigarette. "I want to move away from San Francisco," he told her. "I can take a month off next spring to look for a place."

She was surprised. "Where?"

"The Sacramento Delta. Grass Valley. Someplace like that. It's something we have to talk about—I'm not going to shanghai you someplace where you're miserable. Do you have any particular objection to talking about it?"

"No."

"San Francisco is a door to other places. It's a dream. People like us work hard keeping the dream alive. But other people get the benefits. The hippies come out here and ruin a perfectly good integrated neighborhood, and what does the press say? 'A Summer of Love.'"

"We we move on?"

"Right."

"*Poor* San Francisco." She yawned and put out the cigarette. "Can you really commute that far?"

"It'd be worth it."

"Well—we can talk about it."

But she was already dozing.

He turned off the freeway at Fairchild. He stopped at a small park to take a No-Doz. It was deserted except for a Peterbilt rig with a darkened cab. He sat down at a picnic table and took off his sandals. The infrequent whizz of cars and the slow accompanying march of headlights along the ditches relaxed him.

It was warmer here than in San Francisco.

He saw the car door open and a small shape hop out. It was Dawn. She sat down across the picnic table.

"Thought you were asleep."

She was still sleepy-eyed. "I was."

"We'll swing back on the road in a minute."

She was wearing the stitched jeans and Fisherman's Wharf sweatshirt she favored for weekends. She leaned back on her elbow and beheld him solemnly through sleepy slit eyes. "Why are you smoking so much?"

"I'm nervous."

She giggled. "You're not drinking anymore."

He didn't like having to talk about that. "That's just the way it is with me."

She seemed to understand.

"I liked Grace a lot," she said.

He paused. "There are people who have studied suicide all their lives and still don't know why people do it," he told her.

He understood well enough. But it was hard for a kid

"You tried to stop her."

"I tried."

He tried to imagine what she was thinking.

Odd how close they all were now. There were the tensions of any family, yet underneath a new peace. It had begun almost exactly the day after Grace's death. Their parenthood of Dawn had been—consummated? But he couldn't think of a more accurate word.

"You did your best," she said.

It was finally a question.

"Sometimes you don't know what your best is."

"Like me in school."

He remembered their talk about her grades.

"Something like that."

She nodded. She was jiggling one leg across her knee so hard her shoe fell off. She looked down at it disapprovingly.

"Did you get in trouble?"

He knew what she was asking. All his instincts as a father told him she did not want an answer. So many walls between them were coming down—that made more critical the walls that had to remain.

"That's my business."

She smiled.

"Okay."

He got up and started back to the car. She skipped along behind him on the stone path. It occurred to him she would be beautiful in a few years. Even when skipping, she moved with dignity.

"Wait for me!"

That and the dark demanding brown eyes would attract good men.

"Okay," he said.

The bruises on her face were gone.

He got on the road to Rio Vista. A full moon was rising in the north. It gave off just enough moonlight to make the hills beautiful. Crickets in the ditches chirped its arrival; their silken wail rose and fell precipitously as he sped by.

The sounded like freight trains. His mind wandered.

Odd how little he felt about Deggan. He could remember the pleasure in doing it. Weird how guns had been floating around that night. Very American in its own way. They had been copping them off each other like they were going out of style.

Adult toys.

Rozalyn stirred suddenly beside him. "Honey—"

Her eyes came halfway open. She was still drifting. He could feel her next question coming. She liked bringing up dangerous subjects when half asleep—later she could say she didn't remember.

"What are we going to do about Grace's child?" she whispered. "About Martin?"

She was awake now. He could tell because her eye were closed too tightly. He checked to make sure Dawn was asleep.

"That's the most important decision we'll ever make." He sighed. "Or one of the most important, anyway. We have to think about it and talk about it from every possible angle."

"You think we might adopt him?" There was wonder in her voice.

"Maybe so. Maybe not."

"Damn right!" she said with surprising spunk.

He lit a cigarette and handed it to her. "The important thing is to make a decision based on some kind of logic and not fear or guilt."

"Can we?"

"Yes. Before, we probably couldn't. Now we can." The closeness he felt to her was exciting. Without alcohol that would become more important. "We won't let anyone rush us. We have to take as much time as we need to think about it. Are you in agreement with that?"

"Completely."

"If we give Martin to an adoption agency, it'll have to be with our eyes open. No second thoughts. The same if we adopt him ourselves."

This was their big chance. They could win back the control of their lives they had lost with the double tragedy of their first two children.

"This is the big one—" he murmured.

Yet he had not the slightest doubt they would do the right thing.

"We'll make it."

She was already going back to sleep. It had been a long time since they had had this kind of confidence in themselves.

Again his mind wandered back to Saturday a week before.

He had practically pushed Grace off the bridge.

Okay. You can live with that.

And he could too. Grace—forgive me if you can. I know damn well what I did. I'm as sorry as it's possible for me to be.

Grace had been right that night. She had seen how crazy he was. But of course killing Deggan had been necessary. It had given him the one thing every human being needed most—hope.

He wondered how many killers there were out there. Clearly they tended to come to California. Killers of selves and killers of others (they used every weapon including love). It was as though California had crept by stealth into everybody's sensibilities and taken over. People who had never been there knew it intimately—and how to use it.

Here you found your myth. You tried it on for size. But California went one step further. *You already were what you dreamed to be—all you had to do was go there!* Elsewhere the dream came first, and only afterward if you could make it public did it become a myth. In California your fondest hopes were already in the public domain, recorded faithfully on indelible records and tapes. In public restrooms and on the street and in the middle of wars you heard them. Its movies were the enchanted mirror in which you saw the impossible dream beyond a shadow of doubt. How could you help but recognize yourself?

Going to California was a basic impulse of all advanced industrial civilizations—like sex or collective bargaining.

Years before, Grace had told him of her favorite fantasy about California. One day everybody began making plans for the big move. People sold their houses and hard-won income property and their RVs and Chris-Crafts—everything but their cars. No one could say why. They had all planned to go to California someday. Now everyone planned to leave the same day. Government leaders and various conspiracy theorists thought it a plot.

The CIA speculated that Soviet research in mind control was finally paying off.

On a certain Sunday everyone in America took to the road. There was a big traffic jam. Nothing moved. People got out of their cars and started walking. They did not speak to each other.

People nearest California were actually running.

And so they began to arrive in California by the millions and tens of millions. They were sick and starving. Some of them died immediately upon arriving. The others settled in teeming Hoovervilles around the urban centers. They refused to go back. The squatters' shantytown around San Francisco stretched up to the Mother Lode country. The squalor was unimaginable. The inevitable epidemics set in. Millions died.

They died happy because they had reached California.

They would make a movie out of it called *The Day Everyone Went to California*.

California or bust!

But it was in the magic heart of San Francisco that the shocking denouement occurred. One day everyone in the cool gray city of love awoke feeling suicidal. Hitherto normal people made out wills and put their papers in order. People listened to endless recordings of cool jazz and the songs of Jacques Brel. On the last day of the week the fog came in as it never had before. People filed off in neat lines toward the Golden Gate Bridge . . . .

When they had jumped new people moved into San Francisco to take their places.

It was understood there would be a complete turnover every ten years.

In the warm wind that blew through the open window of his Chevy, he heard Grace laughing. Ah Grace! He was

glad she would lie under the earth of a Kansas graveyard.
But even as he left her he was moving toward her. After
he penetrated the mystery of her death, she would be with
him for a long time. They shared a difficult secret.

He aimed not to understand but to live it.

"I'm coming—" he shouted to her.

They were both afraid of death yet attracted to it.
They supplied each other with details. Gradually they
worked it out. You could kill someone to save your own
life.

Then she had killed herself.

Okay. What did that make him? In California you
found your story and your place in it. He already had a
good idea what he was.

He laughed.

*I am a bullet. I am a tracer arching and burning white.
I am spending softly toward you through the night. My
trajectory is long and pretty. In the end I stop and fall
where everything else here stops and falls—in
California—*